HORN DOGS

PRAISE FOR DAN SHAMBLE, ZOMBIE P.I

"If mainstream urban fantasy is Star Wars, Dan Shamble is Spaceballs—quick, lighthearted, humorous stories that poke gentle fun at a genre that often takes itself overly seriously."

—JIM BUTCHER

"Sharp and funny; this zombie detective rocks!"

—PATRICIA BRIGGS

"A dead detective, a wimpy vampire, and other interesting characters from the supernatural side of the street make Death Warmed Over *an unpredictable walk on the weird side. Prepare to be entertained."*

—CHARLAINE HARRIS

"Master storyteller Kevin J. Anderson's Death Warmed Over *is wickedly funny, deviously twisted and enormously satisfying. This is a big juicy bite of zombie goodness. Two decaying thumbs up!"*

—JONATHAN MABERRY

"A darkly funny, wonderfully original detective tale."

—KELLEY ARMSTRONG

"The Dan Shamble books are great fun."

—SIMON R. GREEN

"Anderson's world-building skills shine through in his latest series, Dan Shamble, P.I. Readers looking for a mix of humor, romance, and good old-fashioned detective work will be delighted by this offering."

—RT BOOK REVIEWS (4 STARS)

THE UNNATURAL QUARTER BECOMES A GRIM FAIRY TALE IN DAN SHAMBLE'S MOST POINTED CASE.

When the Big Uneasy returned all monsters and mythical beasties to the world, something was missing. After his vampire half-daughter Alvina flunks a school report on unicorns, Dan is embroiled in a deeper mystery: With unnatural creatures on every street corner, why has no one ever seen a real unicorn?

But other weird clients demand the attention of a zombie P.I.—a lovestruck frog demon just wants her handsome, befuddled prince back after an evil spell wears off.

A fairy godmother entrepreneur and her Pegasus partner launch a line of glass footwear, but they find that it's a fragile market.

Hardworking lagoon creatures struggle with trespassers, vandals, and civic ordinances as they launch a new swampy resort and spa.

A gambling-addict dragon needs a special support animal, and the local Bigfeet just want to be seen for who they are.

These cases lead Dan Shamble and his companions to a secret society of Horn Brothers, where unicorns are murdered, where an evil wizard is just trying to make amends, where fairy godmothers are not what they seem, and where the unicorns' magical pets—their beloved horn dogs— are being dognapped by a mysterious force.

And the unnaturals just want a Happily Ever After, like everyone else.

HORN DOGS

THE CASES OF DAN SHAMBLE, ZOMBIE P.I.

KEVIN J. ANDERSON

Chapter 1

ometimes, you can smell a new client even before you hear their footsteps coming down the hall. And that smell isn't always pleasant.

In the front office of Chambeaux & Deyer Investigations, I was chatting with Sheyenne, our beautiful poltergeist receptionist, who also happens to be my ghost girlfriend. I wrinkled my nose when I caught a moist fishy stench that reminded me of one of the Unnatural Quarter's slime emporiums.

Being one of the undead myself, I'm not one to talk about odd smells. My skin might have a pallid gray tone, and the bullet hole in my forehead tells prospective clients that I'd had a very bad day at some point in my past. But I'm a well-preserved zombie, and I take care of my decrepit body. I do regular workouts at the All-Day/All-Nite Fitness Center, and I get a monthly top-off at Bruno & Heinrich's Embalming Parlor. So, I don't tend to smell bad, contrary to the frequent snide comments of Officer Toby McGoohan, my best human friend.

I sniffed again, then heard soggy, squelchy footsteps approaching the office, accompanied by wet sniffles mixed with the blubbering sobs of a woman ... but not a human woman.

It was going to be one of those clients.

With a bright smile, Sheyenne turned toward the door.

She's always welcoming, never judgmental. Besides, as a ghost, she has no sense of smell. Shadows appeared on the other side of the stippled glass as a figure approached.

A dashing young man swung open the door. He wore an embroidered jerkin over a shirt with poofy medieval sleeves and a purple cape over his shoulders. A gold circlet held down his straight blond hair, and his square jaw and fine features came straight out of a Disney fairy-tale cartoon. Instead of pants he wore embarrassingly tight hose that emphasized his royal package.

He swept a hand in front of him with a dramatic flourish. "After you, my lady RRita."

Following him on squishy amphibious feet came a female frog demon. She had a spotted green head like a large watermelon, and her yellow eyes were as big as decorative yard lights. Wide plump lips made me think of a large-mouthed bass. Her slick skin glistened with a coating of slime, covered with blotches of green like a camouflage garment.

The frog demon pressed her splayed fingers against her face, and she sobbed miserably. As snot dribbled from her nose slits, she cupped it in her palms, then wiped it over the top of her head to remoisten the amphibious skin there.

"Oh, I hope they can help us!" she wailed. "I just want things back to normal."

With an adoring look, the prince gallantly ushered her inside and then closed the door. "Don't you worry, my lady. I love you, and that will never change."

Sheyenne wafted through the receptionist's desk and approached them with a sparkling smile. "Welcome to Chambeaux and Deyer Investigations. We can help with all sorts of problems, natural or unnatural."

The prince said in a bright, vapid voice, "You see, my lady RRita! Our problems are solved."

"Not quite yet." I stepped forward, always professional, knowing how to greet new clients. "I'm Dan Chambeaux, zombie private investigator. If I can't help you, then my lawyer partner, Robin Deyer, certainly can." It was an easy and comforting promise to make, although here in the Unnatural Quarter, one could never imagine the bizarre cases that monsters—and even some humans—came up with.

I extended my hand, but after looking at the murky moistness on the frog demon's hands as she wiped her nose slits again, I turned instead to clasp the prince's. "Now, what seems to be the problem?"

RRita's enormous lips quivered as she blubbered again. She licked out a long, dark tongue to dab at a fresh set of tears coming out of her eyes. "How can you ask what's wrong? Just look at him!" She flapped her fingers in the prince's direction.

The handsome man adjusted his purple cape and stood embarrassed.

Sheyenne took charge, all business. "Let's start with your name, shall we?" She had already pulled out a new client form.

The frog demon's throat bulged out like a stretched water balloon as she panted hard. "I'm RRita."

The prince gave another bow with a flourish, and even Sheyenne giggled at the dramatic gesture. "And I am Prince Dirk, rightful heir of the royal kingdom."

"Which royal kingdom?" I asked.

The question flustered Dirk, and he looked in confusion toward RRita. Despite his handsome features and regal demeanor, he did not seem overly bright. "Why … the local one, of course."

Using a pen from her desk, Sheyenne began filling in the blanks on the new client form.

Behind us, Robin Deyer emerged from her office. The firebrand human lawyer had been my partner since just after the Big Uneasy, the cosmic event that had returned all mythical creatures and strange beasties to the world.

Robin is a smart and attractive African American woman in her mid-thirties, but she hasn't lost her youthful idealism, even after years of defending bizarre cases and working to get unfair laws changed. Today she wore a charcoal-gray business suit, though she was mainly doing desk work rather than appearing in court.

Her expression didn't falter at all when she saw the miserable frog demon and the fairy-tale prince. "I was just wrapping up an important case, but you have my full attention now." Her rich, reassuring voice was like honey for our clients and razors for her courtroom opponents.

We glanced at the two prospective clients and waited for one of them to explain.

Though Dirk looked brave and regal, he didn't pick up on social cues. Finally, RRita said, "My Prince Dirk is a role model in the Quarter. Even before I met him, he stood up for good versus evil, and he fought to maintain his princely brand."

She nudged Dirk in the ribs, and he finally took the hint, speaking up. "Oh that! Why, yes! I challenged the evil wizard Oorgak, whose dark magic was a blight on all the land. After his depredations caused great harm and extreme discomfort to numerous peasants and other lowly people, I challenged him to undo his nefarious spells. I urged him to turn his back on unkind ways and find the good person that I knew was inside of him."

RRita looked adoringly at her prince. "Dirk always thinks

the best of people." She sniffled again. "Often to his detriment."

Dirk continued, "I confronted him in the royal neighborhood with my righteous sword Pointy Thing, but Oorgak was not swayed by my appeals to his better nature. He created waves of black sorcery, like oily smoke." His eyebrows raised. "Like a car with a bad head gasket."

"Then what happened?" Sheyenne asked.

Prince Dirk lowered his chin in deep disappointment. "Although my heart was true, Oorgak's magic was greater, and he concocted a curse." He squeezed his eyes shut. "He turned me into a frog."

Robin held a yellow legal pad, and her magic pencil was taking notes. She frowned. "That's patently illegal. We can sue Oorgak for that."

RRita began sniffling and sobbing again. "But that's when we fell in love!"

Dirk wrapped his arm around the frog demon's quivering shoulders, not caring about the slime stain he got on his poofy sleeve. "I still love you, my fair lady, no matter what tribulations our relationship faces."

RRita picked up the story. "We were happy. We were made for each other. It was a true storybook romance. When I found dear Dirk, he was so miserable. He had lost his crown, which was too big for his frog-sized head, and even his local royal kingdom was in question. But that didn't matter to us!"

Dirk leaned down to kiss the top of RRita's moist, spotted head. "It didn't matter to me at all. We were so happy."

RRita continued, "We were a royal couple. Dirk was an ensorcelled prince, and I was the only daughter of the rich and powerful Bubo and Lubo." She blinked her yellow eyes, looking at us for recognition.

The names meant nothing to me, but Sheyenne perked up. "Oh, the pool-supply specialists!"

RRita nodded. "Chlorine or no chlorine, indoor pools, hot tubs, or outdoor ponds." She placed her squishy fingers on Dirk's embroidered vest. "Even my parents liked him, a little. I had found my perfect soulmate."

"And then what happened?" Robin asked.

The frog demon flailed her hands. "Just look at him!"

"The spell wore off?" I asked. "Isn't that usually a good thing?"

Dirk hung his head, as if bearing a heavy weight on his shoulders.

"It didn't *wear off!*" RRita cried. "That evil wizard reversed it! He turned my prince back into a prince. Oorgak is truly, unspeakably evil."

Dirk's cheeks flushed pink. "To be fair, he thought he was doing a good thing. Most of his victims genuinely wanted to be restored."

"But he ruined our lives!" RRita said. "Our romance is devastated, and I want my frog prince back."

"I did rather like my life as a frog," Prince Dirk admitted. "Fewer responsibilities, and no confusing political matters."

Robin's hard expression showed that she had already sunk her teeth into the problem. "So, the wizard's first spell attack was an aggressive act, but you found you liked being a frog. Then later, when Oorgak thought he was making amends, he actually harmed you further." She tapped her magic pencil on the legal pad, frowning at the bullet points the writing implement had scribed. "Either way, you have a strong legal case. Regardless of the motive, involuntary bodily transformation is against the law. I can cite numerous precedents."

Sheyenne finished filling out details in the intake form. "You definitely need our services."

"But what exactly would you be hiring us for?" I pressed.

Prince Dirk lifted his square jaw. "We need you to find the wizard Oorgak and force him to reverse his cruel reversal of his evil spell."

"Make my prince a frog again!" RRita's throat belled in and out as she fought back sobs.

"You can count on us," I vowed.

Some days are just magic.

Chapter 2

When my vampire half-daughter came home from Nosferatu Academy that afternoon, I could tell she was upset.

As a zombie P.I., I've faced hordes of angry monsters, end-of-days traumatic events, and spectacularly ridiculous evil plots, but nothing gets me angrier than seeing little Alvina in tears of frustration.

The kid strode into the office and slammed the door behind her. She wore a fuzzy pink sweater and a pleated plaid skirt, and she shouldered a pink backpack stuffed with a hunchback's worth of textbooks. The backpack was her favorite, sporting a smiling cartoon figure of a magical unicorn. Alvina's pointed white fangs poked out of her mouth, but her lips were turned down in a frown. She's normally strong and stoic, a bright ray of sunshine (not always a good thing, as far as vampires were concerned), but now she was deeply troubled.

I tried to cheer her up. "Hey, kid. How was school?"

Sheyenne picked up on the girl's sour mood right away. "What is it, honey? Is something wrong?"

"Everything's fine." Alvina uttered her words as if they were stabbing implements. She shrugged out of her shoulder straps and dropped the unicorn backpack with a thud onto the table. The movement made her two blond pigtails bounce. "I've got homework to do—but what's the point?"

Sheyenne drifted closer. "You need to do your homework so you can grow up to be a really smart vampire."

Alvina glared at her. "I'm not going to grow up! I'm always going to look like a ten-year-old vampire girl, and I'm always going to have to go to stupid school." With a huff, she unzipped her pack and rummaged among her folders and textbooks. "And I'm already a really smart vampire."

"No argument from me about that, kid," I said. Alvina gets her brains from me, definitive proof that she is my daughter rather than McGoo's.

About thirteen years ago, both McGoo and I had a fling with his ex-wife, Rhonda. When Rhonda got pregnant, she didn't tell either of us until ten years later when the little girl got into a skateboarding accident, and a botched transfusion contaminated with vampire blood had turned her into a fanged little sweetheart. Never the best mother even on her good days, Rhonda couldn't handle having an unnatural daughter, so she dumped the kid with me and McGoo. Since paternity tests don't work on vampires, we decided to each claim her as our half-daughter. Alvina was in a far better situation than being doomed to a life with her real mother.

The kid was now thirteen, but as a vampire, she would always look like a ten-year-old. Fortunately, she was cute as a button.

"I don't like that school anymore," Alvina said.

That surprised me. Nosferatu Academy, a special school for gifted unnaturals, had seemed a perfect fit for her.

Robin emerged from her office, concerned. "Is someone bullying you?"

"No, the kids are fine," Alvina pouted. "But my teacher, Miss Nifflesmoth, just doesn't understand." She pulled out a school report, looking at it as if she'd been betrayed. "She's so mean!"

I had met stern and intimidating Miss Nifflesmoth during a recent parent-creature conference. A spelling demon with completely inflexible lesson plans, she probably went to sleep with dreams of ruler-whacking knuckles.

Alvina dropped the paper on the desk so we could all see. She had worked on the report for more than a week, excited by the subject and proud of her work. She had been effusive around the office, gushing about all the new things she had discovered.

Now all I saw was the glaring red "F" on the top, with additional comments that appeared to be scrawled in blood. "Poor effort. Choose a more worthy subject."

Alvina dropped into the chair and burst into tears, pulling the unicorn backpack onto her lap.

I picked up the paper in disbelief. "Why would you get a failing grade, kid? I know how hard you worked."

Alvina had researched myths, folklore, and even historical sightings of unicorns. The kid adored unicorns. She drew pictures of them and added rainbows around them with colored markers. She loved a unicorn-blood frappé at the Talbot & Knowles blood bars.

"Miss Nifflesmoth says unicorns don't exist, so I can't write a paper on them."

"That's ridiculous," Robin said.

I tapped my forehead, as if trying to jar loose some ideas from the bullet hole there. In all my years in the Unnatural Quarter, I'd had countless encounters with strange beasts and legendary monsters of all kinds, but I realized I hadn't seen a single unicorn. Sure, I'd had encounters with minotaurs and dragons, even an unpleasant drinking game with a satyr once. I'd been to the stables at the nightmare races, and I'd seen GrueTube videos of a flying Pegasus.

But never a unicorn.

Puzzled, I turned to Robin. "Have you ever seen a unicorn?"

She contemplated, but shook her head. "That's odd, because during the Big Uneasy, the magic unleashed every sort of legendary creature, even Santa Claus."

Sheyenne added, "Maybe we haven't seen one, but that doesn't mean they don't exist."

"I haven't seen the Taj Mahal either," I said.

"She gave me a failing grade!" Alvina said. "I did my research, and I found a lot more folklore about unicorns than I found about mean, spelling-demon teachers."

Sheyenne sniffed, indignant. "We should talk to the principal, maybe even the school board!"

"Or possibly talk to the teacher first," I suggested.

Alvina zipped up her backpack and ran a finger over the cartoon unicorn. "I know unicorns exist. I know they do!"

I picked up her school paper. "Let me read this, so I can do research of my own." This would be more enjoyable reading than the case files that littered my desktop.

"Whatever …" Alvina said. "This sucks."

"It'll be okay, honey," Sheyenne said. "Can I help with your other homework?"

"I'll do it later." Alvina grabbed a blood box from the refrigerator. "It's only math, so it'll be easy. Right now, I just want to watch TV. My favorite show is on anyway." Each day after school, the kid enjoyed watching *Escape from the Valley of the Game Show Hosts*.

Meanwhile, I had important cases to work on, such as tracking down the last known address of the evil wizard Oorgak. And now, I had another curious mystery to investigate.

Why hadn't I ever seen a unicorn in the Unnatural Quarter?

Chapter 3

The poster at the gate said *Bilge Bay Aquatic Resort. Everyone Welcome!* Next to it stood an ominous "No Trespassing" sign.

As we walked to the entrance, Robin tucked her briefcase against her navy blazer, impeccably professional even in the humid air. I wore my brown sport jacket decorated with clumsily stitched bullet holes. It was my signature look, though it felt rather warm in the miasmic swamp environment.

I tilted my fedora to shade my pallid skin from the sun. Mosquitoes swarmed around us, and though they found nothing of interest in my embalming fluid, they were still annoying as hell. When they harassed Robin, I waved my fedora in the air to shoo the bugs away. In this circumstance, her warm blood was a disadvantage.

The Bilge Bay resort was silent, like a ghost town in a swamp. "This is a grand opening?" I asked.

"They aren't ready to open just yet," Robin said. "Gil and Finn are well aware of the complexities of launching a new amphibious resort."

She had been working with the two lagoon creatures for months. Dealing with the sheer number of permits and sewer easements, water board approvals, concession licenses, and exclusive product lines (not to mention logo design and trademark registration) had been a monumental task. The extensive legal work had paid the Chambeaux & Deyer bills for a while.

"Let's have a look and see what we're about to unleash on the Quarter." I opened the gate and gestured Robin inside. "Next time, we should bring flip-flops and our bathing suits."

Robin stepped ahead of me on the ornamental gravel path. "I'll be fine like this." She waved more mosquitoes away.

Bilge Bay was a large, tropical place filled with palm trees and bent mangroves. Spanish moss dangled down like green, hairy beards above rustic, open-air cabanas and refreshment stands scattered around scum-covered pools. A murky, lazy river rolled through the property, and in one of the nearby pools, the floating duckweed stirred to reveal dark water where large leeches frolicked. A water slide plunged into a bubbling sulfur mudpit. Crickets, cicadas, and other pesky insects tried to make beautiful music together.

Otherwise the place was empty.

"Where are all the customers?" I asked.

"Gil and Finn aren't really open yet," Robin said, looking around in concern. "We're finalizing the permits."

Two lanky green creatures waddled toward us on feet as wide as a scuba diver's flippers. They had scaly bodies, slitted eyes, and fishlike mouths; gill slits flapped in their necks. Serrated fins adorned their cheeks and heads and ran like frills down their arms. They came from a towel shack next to a sign pointing to sulfurous mud baths.

One of the lagoon creatures held an armful of white towels. The other raised a webbed hand to show long, hooked claws in greeting. "Miss Deyer, thank you for coming! Finn and I are proud to show off our spectacular resort. A sneak preview."

The other creature spread his thick fish lips to show rows

of needle-sharp teeth. "We appreciate all your help navigating the red-tape swamp."

I tipped my fedora and nodded, rather than attempting a handshake, because those claws could cause a lot of mangling.

Finn dropped the stack of towels on an empty massage table under a palm-frond awning. "We've had to delay our opening yet again. Sometimes it feels as if the whole unnatural world is against us."

Gil clapped a clawed hand on his partner's shoulder, and both of them turned their milky fish eyes to us. "We've got our personal finances wrapped up in this venture," Gil explained in a burbly voice. "Our investors are impatient. We have to open Bilge Bay very soon, but … it's a disaster."

"How can we help?" I asked. "Is it a security issue?" I had my trusty .38 in my jacket pocket, but I saw no menacing evildoers who needed to be shot.

"Come, we'll show you." Gil led us deeper into the empty park. "We're plagued with vandals and trespassers—and there's a constant flow of junk from the drainage canal."

Concerned, Robin clutched her briefcase, ready to whip out signed copies of documents that she carried with her. "The drainage canal? Bilge Bay has a special easement and very intricate irrigation and plumbing systems, exactly according to code. Do you have unwanted effluent pouring into your resort?"

Finn blinked his eyes. "No, we *want* the effluent! We pay extra for the high-quality stuff."

"But not the other junk," Gil said. "People think our swamp is a dumping ground."

Ahead, I caught a glimpse of a tall, hairy creature carrying a mop and rolling a large trash can to a line of restrooms with various doors marked for male, female, hermaphroditic, non-gender-specific, and non-species-specific. A sack of spare rolls of toilet paper hung at the side of the trash can.

"Is that a Bayou Bigfoot?" I asked.

Gil and Finn both glanced toward the restrooms, but the hairy janitor had ducked inside. Gil shrugged. "I never noticed before."

"Didn't pay much attention," Finn added. "The janitorial crew is pretty much invisible."

I brushed aside what I had seen as we walked past a pair of shaded spawning pools marked "For Adults Only." A plank wall around a service shack blocked unsightly maintenance machinery, recirculating pumps, and chemical tanks. The fence was covered with spray-painted letters that made no sense, scrawled and dripping phrases that might have been curses, but were just incomprehensible.

Finn gestured to it. "There! See what we have to deal with?"

"Is that gang graffiti?" Robin asked.

I had seen similar markings before. "No, just teenage zombie hooligans. Their spelling is bad and their words are slurred."

"Those punks came in through a hole in the fence," Finn said. "Gil and I ran them off, and then put up more 'No Trespassing' signs. But I fear they'll be back."

"Could you maybe get the Bigfoot to repaint the fence?" I asked.

"What Bigfoot?" Finn asked.

"I didn't see any Bigfoot," Gil said.

"They often go unnoticed," Robin said.

I let the matter drop as the lagoon creatures hurried us along. "That isn't the important part," Gil said. "Come look at the confluence of the Lazy River and the drainage canal. It should be our most popular area in the resort."

Robin gasped when we saw the sluggish, lumpy water that flowed along a decorative bed of colorful Venus flytraps.

The drainage canal was clogged with floating milk cartons, discarded tires, a rusted shopping cart, rumpled Monster Mash packages, as well as magical paraphernalia, including candlesticks, bent amulets, gaudy sacrificial daggers, and one large and soggy spellbook. The book's stained leather cover had an oval with a dot in the center, a design that looked like the eye of a startled cyclops.

"This garbage all washes up on our property," Finn said.

"We scoop it out every morning, and by now we've got quite a pile of discarded junk," Gil said. "Or treasures. Some of it might be valuable."

I was amazed by the huge pile of refuse the two lagoon creatures had scooped out of the confluence. Robin made a scolding cluck with her tongue. "This is disappointing, considering all of the Quarter's no-dumping ordinances. Why can't people just take care of their world?"

"It's a dump! How can we open under these conditions?" Finn groaned. "We want to offer only the finest, cleanest swamp experience."

"I'll file complaints on your behalf," Robin said, propping a hand on her hip. "The drainage canal officials should be enforcing the no-dumping rules."

With an annoyed sigh through his gill slits, Finn picked up a long skimming net that lay next to the Venus flytraps. He scooped up the spellbook and an old good-luck amulet, dragging them to shore. "It'll take an hour to clean this up— and that's only for today!"

Gil blinked his fishy eyes at us. "Ms. Deyer, would it be legal for us to have a yard sale to get rid of this junk? I mean, these objects don't belong to us, but they washed up here."

Robin sniffed. "If someone dumped it on your property,

then you can claim salvage. Anything here is yours. Finders keepers. Please, have a public sale to liquidate the garbage. It might also raise awareness about Bilge Bay."

That sounded like a good idea to me. "Sure. It would bring people here to see what a marvelous resort this place will be."

"It already is," Finn said.

The mosquitoes swarmed around us, and I again waved my fedora to drive them away. "Truly paradise," I said.

Chapter 4

Though I was upset with Alvina's spelling-demon teacher, our paying prince and frog demon clients took priority over looking for nonexistent unicorns. Since the cases don't solve themselves, I devoted the following day to hunting for the evil wizard Oorgak.

Sheyenne had searched through the UQ Chamber of Commerce directory, but the evil wizard was not a registered business. That afternoon, once Alvina came home from school, I could turn to the kid's interweb skills to investigate sorcerous attacks and amphibious transformation spells.

For now, I had to do old-school P.I. footwork.

I went out to wander the streets of the Quarter, bumping into people, encountering witnesses, spotting suspicious activity—that's all part of being a detective. Dumb luck is an important part of private investigator work, and I have a great deal of experience in dumb luck. (Sheyenne had looked into how we might increase our instances of *smart* luck, but so far we hadn't come up with any good ideas.)

As I emerged from our office building, I encountered Renfeld, the building's superintendent. He's a slow, draggy ghoul with a slurred voice, droopy features, and leaky orifices. He would often dribble greenish snot or other bodily fluids onto the hall carpets, which left stains, but he also liked to push the rug shampooer up and down the halls.

Renfeld was hauling an overstuffed black garbage bag to the curb, where he dumped it among the piles of bagged trash already there. Garbage day was always a big event for him.

"Hello, Renfeld," I said.

His rubbery lips curved up in a smile, and his breathy voice came through gaps in his teeth. "Hello, Mr. Chambeaux. It's a beautiful day for rubbish." He poked and prodded at the overstuffed black bag. The contents stirred, and I heard a faint squeak. "Just cleaning out one of the old tenants."

"Looks like a mess. What's in there?"

"Maybe the tenant," the ghoul said with a chuckle. He shifted the black sack into a stable position among the other swollen bags he had brought to the curb. "I never ask questions. Privacy and garbage, you know. It's my strict policy."

Directly contradicting his comment, he shuffled over to the trash bags in the neighbor's driveway and worked with clumsy fingers to undo the twist tie. He thrust his arm up to his elbow into the stranger's garbage and rummaged around like a plumber trying to manually remove a drain clog.

I asked, "What about the right to trash privacy?"

"Other people's garbage is a different matter. You won't believe the good stuff some guys throw out." To demonstrate what he meant, he yanked out the remnants of a pizza crust with a few strands of cheese dangling from the end. "Hmm, looks like a veggie combo."

On the other end of the slice hung a brown rat, which bit down and tugged back, trying to wrestle the pizza crust from his competitor. "That's mine," Renfeld said.

The rat squeaked. With a rustling sound, several more rats emerged from the opened garbage bag and bared their teeth at him. The sluggish ghoul was smart enough to surrender the pizza crust and withdraw. With happy optimism, he turned to the next garbage bag. "Let's see what's in here."

I strolled off, not wanting to get further involved in any ghoul-rodent conflicts. "Have a nice day, Renfeld."

The warm day had enough haze and murk that even vampires could go out and enjoy the fresh air. The sounds of clunky piano music wafted from the open door of the Hope & Salvation Mission. Jerry, the piano player and assistant, plinked out a jazz version of a classic hymn accompanied by the grunting, growling, and moaning sounds of the congregation as they sang along. I heard the bright voice of Mrs. Saldana, the mission's kindly proprietor. She always brought out lemonade and coffee, along with windmill cookies and blood roll-ups. She never gave up on the lost souls in the Unnatural Quarter.

Officer Toby McGoohan stood on the corner in his blue patrolman's uniform. He munched on a donut and kept his other hand near the holster of his police special revolver, but his freckled face held a grin. He seemed relaxed. "Hey, Shamble."

"Hey, McGoo." I decided to use him as a source of information. "Have you seen any evil wizards lately?"

He gave the question serious consideration. "You mean with long beards and pointy hats with stars and crescent moons?"

"Any wardrobe will do," I said. "It's part of a case. Frogs, princes, curses."

"If I hear anything, I'll let you know," he said, not the least bit bothered by the possibilities. "Hey Shamble, what's a zombie's favorite way to travel?"

I braced myself. "What?"

"Traaaaiiiinnnns!"

Fortunately, my cell phone rang, and the marimba tones got me out of any need to force a laugh. "Sorry, McGoo, it's Sheyenne. Important business." I spoke to her as I walked away, heaving a sigh of relief. "You saved me, Spooky."

"As I always do," she said. "I found a last known address for Oorgak. His evil lair was registered in a city directory. He was a publicly traded company at some point."

"Wow," I said. "Angel investors will put money into anything."

"Demon investors in this case, but they withdrew their support. Oorgak is out of business now." She gave me the address.

"Let's hope he still does freelance work," I said. "If he truly is an evil wizard, he shouldn't have any trouble reimposing his frog curse."

The Unnatural Quarter isn't geographically large, and I know most of the back alleys and business boulevards, but I had never been to the Magic Kingdom district, presumably the neighborhood that Prince Dirk ruled when he wasn't in frog form.

Much of the Quarter is pleasantly dingy and run down, with old buildings and rusty gutters, boutique shops, cafés, tenements, and warehouses. The Magic Kingdom, though, looked decidedly quaint and medieval, with dirt streets, thatched houses, fairy princess towers, and blacksmith yards.

Since I couldn't find any street signs, I asked a jolly bearded dwarf for directions. He stroked his beard with thick fingers and drew his enormous eyebrows together. "What's the street number again?"

"It's the lair of the evil wizard Oorgak," I said, hoping that might jog his memory.

The dwarf flinched. "I hope you're delivering a court summons to him! He's a bad one—or at least he was."

"So I hear," I said.

"Doesn't take much to stink up a neighborhood." The dwarf gave me brusque instructions, then stomped off, heading to the blacksmith shop.

I found a cobbler shop adjacent to a cookie bakery, both of which were run by hardworking elves. The green-clad little folk danced up to me, jabbering. A pair of them inspected my shoes and made clucking, disappointed noises. I had better interactions with the other group of elves, who handed me free samples of their chocolate chip cookies. When I told them I was looking for Oorgak's lair, however, they also darted away.

The evil wizard's lair was distinctive enough. As soon as I turned the corner, I spotted the dark stone towers, the pointed fortifications, the iron bars at the gate. Oorgak wasn't a very welcoming fellow, although at least he hadn't put up "No Trespassing" signs, unlike Gil and Finn.

Fortunately, there isn't any general bad blood between zombies and evil wizards, and I've always gotten along with even the necromancers in the Quarter. I'm a likable guy and pleasant enough to talk to. So, I decided to start with the friendly approach and try to make Oorgak see reason. Even a dark sorcerer might be convinced to do the right thing. I remembered the sheer misery on RRita's frog face and the vapid befuddlement on Prince Dirk's. Surely I could provoke Oorgak into a temper tantrum and make him turn the prince back into a beloved frog.

But the windows of the evil lair were shuttered, and the roof shingles were falling apart. When I stepped up to the imposing door, leering stone skulls and cast-iron points poked out at me. Carved into the dark wood was a symbol I recognized—an oval with a dot in the middle, the same logo I had seen on the sodden spellbook among the junk dumped into Bilge Bay.

A disheartening handwritten sign was tacked onto the door. "Permanently closed for business. Got enlightened."

Chapter 5

Once upon a time, the world had been without real vampires, werewolves, ghosts, goblins, or other strange mythical creatures. The time before the Big Uneasy didn't seem particularly magical, but normal life was at least predictable.

Everything had changed one night at the stroke of midnight, during a rare astrological alignment, when a drop of blood from a frumpy virgin librarian had spilled onto the original *Necronomicon*, unleashing magic that changed reality forever … and gave me plenty of job security. I became a private detective in the Unnatural Quarter, where the monsters congregated to live their abnormal lives. Those were my pre-zombie days, but the job description is the same now, whether I've got a pulse or not.

As my official investigative assistant, Alvina is always eager to help me solve mysteries, catch criminal monsters, and just earn brownie points. Since I couldn't locate where Oorgak had gone to ground, and I had no idea what he meant with the sign "Got Enlightened," I turned the kid loose to do research into fairy tales.

The vampire girl started her investigations after she finished her math homework. Still stung by the failing grade on her unicorn paper, she seemed even more determined. Diving in, she read up on fairy-tale princes, especially the tragic cases when they were turned into frogs (it happened more often than you might think), but she found no prior examples of happily-ever-after endings that resulted from such frog transformation spells.

She had set up work in our conference room with her laptop open as well as a spiral notebook (with another cute cartoon unicorn on the front). When I checked in on her, Alvina was taking furious notes on the lined paper, while scrolling through websites but also referring to fancy, illustrated editions of fairy-tale collections from the UQ Public Library. The TV was on, tuned to the latest episode of *Escape from the Valley of the Game Show Hosts*, but she wasn't paying much attention to the drama.

"Any breaks in the case yet, kid? How do we make the evil wizard turn Prince Dirk back into a frog?"

Embarrassed, Alvina pushed aside a fairy-tale book and changed the channel from her corny soap opera to the Home Capitalism Network, where a blurred-out Medusa was talking about the benefits of her remarkable new skin cream. The kid pretended to watch intently.

"Just look at these results," the Medusa said in a raspy voice. "My new cream will soften the hardest stone."

Blurry wormlike snakes bobbed and weaved around her head. Because her image had been digitally obscured, we could look directly at the Medusa without becoming petrified. (Recent research had shown that even televised images of a Medusa were potent enough to turn some sensitive viewers to stone.) With all the digital manipulation, however, we couldn't actually see the positive effects of the much-vaunted skin cream, and we had to take the Medusa's word for it.

"You're not watching your regular show?" I asked.

"It's a rerun. That sucks," she said. "I was reading anyway."

Now I noticed that her fairy-tale book and her written notes were not about frog princes, but unicorns. Feeling supportive, I said, "I know you're still mad about that bad grade, but Sheyenne and I are going to see your teacher and discuss the matter."

Alvina's nostrils flared. "Make sure you use proper grammar."

"I ain't got no other way of talking."

Her laptop screen displayed garish websites with dark and edgy images of unicorns. The headlines made outrageous claims. This one said "JFK Assassination—The Unicorn Connection!"

"Are you sure that's legitimate information?" I asked.

"Of course! It's on the internet." She scrolled to a different page to show me more wild warnings about unicorns. "When you click additional links, the algorithm always takes you to conspiracy-theory websites. And boy, am I learning interesting stuff!" Her blond pigtails bounced as she nodded. "Lots of rumors about a secret society of unicorns. They keep their existence hidden from the outside world so they can manipulate governments and rig elections and promote vaccine propaganda." She clicked to a different window. "Here's one site showing absolute proof that unicorns are responsible for climate change."

"Hmmm, did you put that all in your term paper?" Maybe that was why she had gotten an F.

"No, this is new and exciting information—source material from the dark web."

I was still proud of her internet skills, even though I was unsure about this particular information. "Once you're down that rabbit hole, avoid any talking rabbits."

She giggled. "Oh, don't worry! I've got plenty of firewalls up on our account."

"See if you can find anything about prince-into-frog spells, too, or the current whereabouts of the evil wizard."

Robin poked her head into the conference room, exasperated. She doesn't usually lose her cool, even when she's arguing a very hot case, but now she was flustered. In addition to the Bilge Bay development paperwork, she also had pending litigations for a lava monster small-business owner who was challenging outdated fire codes and another case defending a skeleton charged with indecent exposure for showing off multiple boners in public.

Her current problem was something far worse, and closer to home. Robin looked at me. "The office toilet is clogged."

Thinking fast, I said, "It wasn't me. I've got a zombie digestive system. I'm pretty sure Sheyenne has an excuse, too."

Alvina said in a cheery voice, "And I've been monitoring my toilet paper use. I keep a log, and I can show you." The vampire girl reached for her backpack.

Robin wiped sweat from her brow. "No one's casting blame, but I just spent twenty minutes using the plunger to no avail. This is beyond my legal abilities or your detective abilities. I made a call to Sewer Sweeties—in their ads, they say they can take care of any sort of drainage problem."

Alvina chirped up. "Sewer Sweeties! 'Our tentacles reach longer than anyone's.' They advertise all the time on *Escape from the Valley of the Game Show Hosts.*"

Robin crossed her arms over her chest. "They claim they can't come out for a week, but I told them the situation was urgent."

From the strained look on her face, I suspected that she really had to go.

"They put us on their emergency cancellation list.

Someone will need to meet them here if they respond to the call."

"Someone usually is," I said, "unless I'm out wandering the streets solving cases."

"Or unless I'm at school," Alvina said.

"Or if I'm in court," Robin added. "We'll have to coordinate our schedules. This is really important."

I remembered my brief conversation with Renfeld. "There's a recently abandoned unit in the basement. Maybe we can use the restroom in the interim."

"Or we can use the potty in the Ghoul's Diner when we go for lunch," Alvina said.

Robin hurried off.

On the television, the Home Capitalism Network's theme music rose to introduce the next featured guest—who received a much better response than the Medusa cosmetologist. The charming old woman on the screen had a cherubic face, grandmotherly eyes, a lavender gown, and a pointed cap with a tassel. She waved a magic wand tipped with a gold star, as if she were conducting an orchestra for fairies.

"I'm Betty Bibbity, fairy godmother for the masses and unnatural event planner. Thank you for joining me on another installment for my magical footwear business." She blinked her long lashes. "We offer glass slippers for all occasions. Buy direct from me at the number below on your screen—and hurry, because it's a fragile market."

Off stage, a small studio audience began chanting, "Dava, Dava, Dava!"

The fairy godmother swirled her magic wand, and the air in the studio filled with shimmering soap bubbles the size of basketballs. Betty Bibbity worked the audience. "Who's that you're asking for?"

"Dava, Dava, Dava!" the crowd chanted.

I suspected that regular viewers were chanting the same thing at their television sets. Even Alvina giggled and called out the same name. She nudged me with her elbow. "Wait until you see this."

A stunningly beautiful winged horse, a Pegasus, strode through a veritable prom night of floating soap bubbles. Her hide was a pale and luxurious lavender. She stretched out her wings, fluffing out the long lavender feathers. Across her forehead, she wore a gaudy gold wraparound crown, like a bandanna. The Pegasus preened and tossed her head, showing off her perfectly brushed mane. Clearly, Dava was also a diva.

The crowd cheered as the Pegasus spread her wings, then lifted her foreleg to show off a beautiful glass horseshoe that covered her entire hoof. As she walked across the studio floor, the crystal-encased hooves tinkled like wind chimes.

"We make glass slippers for all sizes and styles of feet," the fairy godmother said. "As an HCN special today, if you order within the next thirty minutes, you will also receive a signed print of Dava, autographed with her own front hoof." A toll-free number flashed across the screen. "Operators are standing by now to take your order. This is a limited-time offer. Don't let eternity go by without your custom glass footwear."

As I watched the shopping channel, I had an idea. "Jot down that number, kid."

She frowned at me. "Glass slippers aren't very good for a gumshoe."

"No, but a fairy godmother might know something about frog spells and evil wizards." I pointed to her spiral notebook. "Quick, write it down before the number goes away."

"It stays up there for half an hour," Alvina said, bored. "And I can always look it up online."

Betty Bibbity waved her magic wand while Dava the Pegasus pranced across the screen, continuing to show off her glass-covered hooves.

While soap bubbles drifted behind her, Betty leaned close to the camera and added conspiratorially, "And for that special occasion, whether it's a wedding, a birthday, or a second funeral—remember, Betty Bibbity Event Planning Services can help."

Chapter 6

McGoo usually drops by the offices when he's bored while walking his beat, and other times it's just to tell another dumb joke. He does like to see his ultra-cute vampire half-daughter, though.

Alvina sounded like a chirping bird when she cried out, "Half-daddy!" She had come to have lunch with us during her midday break from school.

"Hey, Shamble," McGoo said. "Hey, Al."

I emerged from the kitchenette with a fresh mug of sludgy leftovers from the bottom of the day's brew. I nearly dropped the mug when I saw what he carried in his arms. This wasn't his usual time-killing diversion.

Alvina ran to him, entranced by the charming furry creature he cradled. "Can I pet him?"

I followed with a more incisive inquiry. "What the hell is that thing?"

McGoo held a brown, furry creature the size of a lap dog with soulful brown eyes, like a pug or a Pekingese. It rested in his arms, perfectly content, instead of being a squirmy, annoying little yap-yap dog. A pearlescent, swirled horn about the length of my forefinger stood out from the middle of its forehead.

"It's a horn dog," McGoo said. "As you can plainly see."

The animal opened its mouth and a delicate pink tongue lolled out as it panted.

The creature rivaled Alvina's cuteness. It let out a yip that sounded like music, and suddenly the office was filled with rainbows and warm fuzzies. Since I'm a hard-bitten zombie private investigator, I found that quite unnerving.

"Can I pet him?" Alvina begged again. "Pleeease?"

"Like I could ever deny you anything, Al!" McGoo crouched so the girl could reach the animal.

Sheyenne was similarly wonderstruck. "Oh, how darling!"

"It fills the entire office with such a soothing effect," Robin said.

Alvina scratched under the animal's chin, and it let out a purring noise of contentment. She said, "They're called unidogs, or sometimes canicorns. I learned about them while researching my school paper."

"I called it a horn dog in my police report," McGoo said.

Alvina continued, "Unidogs are the familiars of unicorns. They create a sensation of happiness and delight, pure contentment to everyone around them. They are manifestations of the sense of wonder in the world."

"I bet you did a great report on them, Al," McGoo said.

Robin, Sheyenne, and I all scowled at the reminder. The kid sniffed. "My teacher gave me an F."

McGoo's freckled face flushed. "That's downright unjust. I should arrest her for indecent grading."

Though Alvina was clearly interested in the suggestion, Sheyenne said, "We'll try a few other solutions first."

The unidog let out another magical bark. As Alvina continued to scratch under its chin, she found a thin gold collar buried in the curly fur. "Look, it's wearing a tag!"

The small gold plate was shaped like a dog biscuit with the word *URMIN* engraved on it. "Urmin," Alvina said. "That's its name."

McGoo said, "No contact information, though."

"Maybe it has an implanted ID chip," Robin said. "We could try to find its real owner."

I pushed the conversation back to basics. "Let's go back to the original question. What are you doing with the thing, McGoo?"

"Somebody called in to report a loose magical creature, and I was the responding officer. A werewolf spotted it running loose in the streets and called animal control."

"But you're not animal control," Sheyenne said.

McGoo shrugged. "With so many creatures running around in the Quarter, it's all animal control, to a degree. So we answer the calls." He scratched behind Urmin's ears. "This little puppy posed no trouble at all."

"Sounds like the perfect pet," Robin said.

"Can we keep him?" Alvina said. "Pleeease?"

We had been through the pet question multiple times before, so we had our answer ready. "You've already got your piranha in his fishbowl, honey," Sheyenne said.

"But he doesn't like to be petted very often," Alvina said. "I want a unidog."

"Horn dog," McGoo said.

I hated to be the bad guy, especially in front of Alvina's other half-daddy. "He doesn't belong to us. His real owner is probably very worried right now."

My ghost girlfriend came to my rescue. "Urmin is an adorable little canicorn. Someone must love him very much."

Alvina's shoulders slumped as she continued petting the unidog. McGoo stood up straight. "I'm going to take him to the UQ Animal Shelter. It's a nice no-kill and no-reanimation place, where they take good care of every kind of non-sentient and unnatural species. I just wanted to show the cute little puppy to my cute little daughter."

Urmin let out another one of his rainbow-filled yips.

"We're both pretty cute," Alvina said matter-of-factly.

Robin crossed her arms over her chest, and I could see that determined look on her face. "I'm still filing civil complaints on behalf of the lagoon creatures, as well as extending the start dates on their permits, but I can look into the UQ's licensing requirements for horned pets. Maybe we can track down if Urmin is registered."

The horn dog yipped again, showing clear appreciation.

"This little guy will be taken care of." At the door, McGoo said, "See you at the Goblin Tavern as usual, Shamble?"

It was our regular watering hole. I said, "If you don't, then you'd better file a missing persons case, 'cause something is definitely wrong."

He left, and I knew I was going to need a tall, cold beer. Probably several—after what Sheyenne and I needed to do that afternoon.

We would be meeting with Alvina's nasty spelling-demon teacher, Miss Nifflesmoth.

CHAPTER 7

Zombies aren't generally vindictive, since most shamblers don't have the brains or forethought to plot revenge, but I sure wanted to talk some sense into Miss Nifflesmoth. I was glad Sheyenne was going along with me, because she usually has more sense than I do.

After McGoo had departed with the cute horn dog, Sheyenne and I accompanied Alvina back to school. She skipped along the sidewalk, whistling her favorite dirges. Her afternoon classes were physical education and then math, both of which she enjoyed, but she seemed extra gratified because we were going to fix her unfairly graded paper.

Nosferatu Academy was a huge, imposing stone building that looked like a castle designed by a Soviet-era mad scientist. The walls were thick and intimidating, as if to keep the most dangerous education inside, with sharp spikes and lightning rods stretching to the sky in hopes of afternoon thunderstorms.

School security gargoyles hunched in the eaves, keeping watch over the monster children at play. On a fenced-in sports diamond, vampire children were engaged in a game of catch the bat, while a werewolf referee howled out controversial calls.

Kids streamed in from the lunch break, and as we reached the street crossing, a horde of furry gremlin children scuttled into the crosswalk without looking both ways. A Volkswagen

Beetle driven by a nearsighted Igor in a lab coat zoomed down the street, despite the school zone clearly marked with skull-and-crossbones signs. An orc crossing guard in a bright yellow vest lunged into the crosswalk, extending a huge hand, palm outward. The orc slammed the front grille of the Beetle and brought it to a screeching halt, dislodging the bumper. The rear of the Volkswagen lurched up into the air, and the Igor's bald head smashed into the windshield, cracking it.

"He should be wearing a seatbelt," Sheyenne observed.

"More importantly, he shouldn't be speeding in a school zone," I said.

"An interesting demonstration of Newton's laws of physics," Alvina said, as the car's engine hissed and steamed. "Conservation of energy in the orc-versus-automobile paradigm."

"I'm glad you're learning science, honey," Sheyenne said.

Alvina skipped along the crosswalk, following the gremlin children to the Academy. The loud school bell rang, and the little monsters flowed toward the doors. Alvina waved at us as she ran ahead to join her classmates. In her plaid, pleated skirt, pink sweater, and friendly unicorn backpack, she looked adorable.

In the front office, a gray-furred, frail female werewolf typed on an actual typewriter, although her black claws kept getting caught in the keys. Near the principal's office, two ghoul boys—more sullen than ghouls usually looked—sulked in chairs that were too high for them, and their feet dangled above the floor. An illuminated digital sign on the wall said, "Severe reprimand from the principal, now serving number 11." The ghoul boys each clasped slips of paper in their gray hands, waiting their turn.

Sheyenne drifted up to the counter and got the old

werewolf's attention so we could sign in. "We're the guardians of Alvina. We have an appointment."

I added important new information. "Yeah, we have to talk to her cranky old teacher."

"Cranky old teacher …" The werewolf flipped through a directory with her furred hands. "Could you be more specific?"

"Miss Nifflesmoth," Sheyenne said. "She's expecting us." It sounded like a threat.

"Ah, of course. She's in the teacher's lounge by herself for class preparation period."

"Could we also get a hall pass?" I asked. "Alvina's about to start phys ed class, and we'd like to see her in action."

The werewolf gave a sage nod. "Lots of action in physical education." She scribbled out guest badges, then handed us each a hall pass that would allow us to peek in on the gym.

As we walked down the school corridors, we heard shouting, laughter, and the tooting of a shrill referee whistle before we reached the gym entrance.

"We'll just have a quick look," Sheyenne said. "I don't want to miss our appointment with her teacher."

I grumbled, "There isn't an expiration date on the can of whoop-ass I brought for her."

"Beaux, let's try to be reasonable first. If that doesn't work, then we can be vindictive."

Peeking into the gym, we saw a group of children running around, shouting, playing. A young mummy boy in a workout shirt and gym shorts tripped on a loose bandage and sprawled on the hardwood court floor. Ghosts drifted about, taunting the opposite team, while werewolf furballs ran interference. Two young golems slapped each other on the back, leaving indentations in their soft clay.

The kids were playing some modified form of dodgeball,

taunting and laughing as they hurled hard rubber spheres at one another. A goal net had been set up on each side of the gym, but they were completely untended. The children passed the ball, then bonked it off a goblin's bald head so another vampire boy could grab it and hurl it toward the empty goal net. Unexpectedly, the ball was deflected at the last moment and flew back out into the gym.

I realized that each side had an invisible kid as a goaltender.

Alvina ran around in her gym clothes. Her pigtails bobbed as she darted along, snatched one of the balls out of the air, then hurled it right into the face of an aggressive troll girl from the other team. Her fellow players cheered, and a fresh point appeared on the scoreboard.

Alvina waved when she noticed us standing at the door. Taking advantage of the distraction, a werewolf furball smacked her on the side of the head with a hard ball. Alvina recovered herself, snatched the ball, and charged after the werewolf kid, laughing.

"She's doing fine," I said. "Now let's go talk to her teacher. I want to get this over with."

Nosferatu Academy's lounge was dank and shadowy, with battered overstuffed furniture, a small refrigerator, a black light shining down on a thorny potted plant, and ashtrays filled with disgusting cigarette and cigar butts. The rest of the school was a safe, no-smoking zone, but the teachers used this airtight sanctuary to relax with their personal vices.

Right away, I spotted Miss Nifflesmoth lurking in the gloom at a small writing desk. An intense reading light stabbed down onto the pages of student papers in front of her; she held a red grading pen in her gnarled hand, and she wasn't afraid to use it.

The spelling demon had a face that not even a lovestruck blind man could love: jagged spiny brows, pointed ears, leathery cracked skin, and slitted eyes. Her wide mouth was filled with yellow tusks, and I could tell she paid more attention to grammar and spelling than she did to oral hygiene. Her blouse was prim and lacy, buttoned all the way up to her throat. She wore thick, horn-rimmed glasses perched precariously on the slitted nub of her nose.

"Miss Nifflesmoth, we're Alvina's guardians," I said.

Sheyenne added, "We have an appointment to discuss an important matter with you."

The spelling-demon teacher looked up at us as if we were insects, and not the collectible kind. "Yes," Miss Nifflesmoth snapped. "And you're two minutes late."

"Fashionably late," I corrected. "We wanted to be sure we had your attention."

"I have a limited attention span," she said. "I rarely make exceptions to see parents directly, but Alvina is a very troublesome case. That vampire girl is too smart for her own good."

"She's smart for everyone's good." I felt an instant dislike for this teacher.

"We want to discuss her recent unicorn paper," Sheyenne said. "We feel you were very unfair to her. Alvina put a lot of research and work into writing that report."

Nifflesmoth sniffed. "She should have chosen an appropriate subject."

"Are you suggesting that unicorns have inappropriate behavior?" I had never heard anything but purity and goodness about unicorns.

The teacher's yellow tusks ground together as she worked her blocky jaw. "The assignment was to write a well-documented essay on any species of unnatural. It was not meant to be a flight of fancy, and unicorns don't exist."

"Can you prove they don't exist?" Sheyenne challenged.

Scoffing, the spelling demon pushed the dazzlingly bright reading light away from the homework she was grading. "She could have written about countless other unnaturals. No one has ever seen a unicorn."

"Why do you think that is?" I asked. I honestly wondered.

"No one has seen a unicorn because unicorns don't exist. The answer is obvious, by Occam's Razor."

"I use a twin-bladed razor myself," I said.

The teacher made a creaking noise as she levered herself out of the chair, standing eight feet tall. "Alvina received a failing grade because she wrote a poor paper. She used nothing but her imagination, and we do not encourage students to use their imaginations. We believe education is meant to be medicinal, not stimulating."

Sheyenne's poltergeist glow brightened with indignation. "We were told otherwise when we signed her up for Nosferatu Academy. The brochure emphasizes how you nurture the students to meet their great potential."

"Unfortunate wording. The brochure needs to be updated," Miss Nifflesmoth said. "I have been challenging that philosophy for years, but the fight goes on."

"Maybe you should do more to mentor your students and make them into better monsters," I suggested.

"What would you know about education, Mr. Chambeaux? I've looked into Alvina's file, and I am aware of your background. You flunked out of the police academy, and now you make do as a freelance private investigator."

"Zombie private investigator," I said. It was a matter of pride for me.

She turned her gaze to my ghost girlfriend like a sniper

choosing another target. "And you, Miss Sheyenne Carey, were nothing more than a former nightclub singer. Both of you should defer to me as to how this little girl needs to be educated. The very idea of unicorns and fanciful imaginary creatures is ludicrous, and I will not encourage such silliness in a respected educational institution like Nosferatu!"

Just listening to Miss Nifflesmoth made me angry.

Sheyenne fumed. "So you won't reconsider her grade then?"

"Not under the present circumstances." Miss Nifflesmoth closed her folder full of partially graded student papers. "Now, please excuse me. I have to prepare for class."

Sheyenne and I left, dissatisfied. Now I was even more determined to find a unicorn. We had just seen for ourselves that horn dogs existed. Where there were unidogs, could there not also be unicorns?

As we walked down the school hall, which was empty with classes in session, we passed a tall, shaggy Bigfoot who shoved a push broom along the line of lockers. He met my eyes with his mournful gaze and raised a big, furry hand, but Sheyenne and I were too engrossed in discussing rarely seen and unrecognized mythical creatures to pay the Bigfoot any attention.

CHAPTER 8

Once again, I was off to the Magic Kingdom district. After my previous visit to find the evil wizard Oorgak, I expected quaint, charming, and medieval vibes—but the fairy godmother's operations were fully corporate.

Since Betty Bibbity had been a fixture on the Home Capitalism Network for several years, Sheyenne was surprised I hadn't heard of her glass-footwear business or event-planning operations. "For our next date night, Beaux, we should watch HCN and chill."

The next morning, I went by myself to track down Betty Bibbity's headquarters, thanks to Alvina's research skills. Following the address to the fairy godmother's main shipping center, I arrived at a facility much larger than I had expected.

Betty's event center filled the front area, a spacious open hall and outdoor reception pavilion that could be decorated for any type of community gathering or celebration. The fairy godmother rented out the space, provided caterers and decorators, provided bands and even party magicians who used real magic in addition to making entertaining balloon animals.

Behind the event center was a large industrial warehouse and shipping operation, which was not open to the public. From here, all the merchandise sold on HCN was packed and distributed by hordes of minimum-wage grunt workers, as well as those who didn't grunt.

As I arrived, the event center and outdoor reception area was bustling with activity. Golems and trolls set up numerous tables. A three-piece band featuring a mummy, a mad scientist, and a skeleton fiddled with their amps and tested out their instruments. I recognized the band from an earlier reception at Howard Phillips Publishing, and I knew how bad they were.

Electricians rolled out power cords and strung lights from a gazebo-style roof. At a mobile barista kiosk from the Talbot & Knowles blood bars, vampire workers in crimson aprons were setting up birdbath-sized bowls and unboxing chilled packs of various types of blood. A team of sparkling fairies buzzed their gossamer wings as they raised a banner that said, "Happy Bat Mitzvah, Irene."

As I walked into the hubbub of activity, I spotted plump Betty Bibbity, recognizing her from TV. She wore a fancy lavender gown and used her star-tipped magic wand to direct the activity. "No, no, set up the stage over there! And use only the two-foot riser. We don't need the young vampire lady to fall off onto her keister."

The fairy godmother's feet barely touched the ground as she bobbed along. Many of the distracting soap bubbles drifted around as if they were part of her entourage.

Weaving my way through the setup activity, I approached the fairy godmother. "Excuse me, Betty Bibbity?"

She turned, startled, and then she brightened. "Oh, at last! Are you the rabbi?" She frowned. "I didn't see *zombie rabbi* on your list of credentials."

"Zombie detective," I said, and introduced myself. "I never went to rabbinical school, although I did take private investigator training, and that must be just as difficult."

The fairy godmother frowned. "Then the rabbi is late, and we still have to go through rehearsal!" She seemed kind and grandmotherly, and she exuded warm reassurance, but she was obviously flustered, dealing with a million details.

"Everything has to be perfect," she said. "Have you ever dealt with Jewish vampire parents before? This is their daughter's coming of age."

More fairies strung black paper bats among the rafters. "Bat mitzvah," I said, "emphasis on the bat."

"Indeed," Betty said. "It's the way vampires do it."

Thinking of Alvina, I raised a finger. "But how can a vampire girl come of age, if vampire girls don't age?" I lowered my voice. "I have one of my own."

"Some special exemption in Talmudic law," the fairy godmother said. "I'm not Jewish, and that goes beyond the scope of my event-planning services. I just have a checklist." She pulled a list from a pocket in her sparkly lavender gown. Only half of the items had been checked off. "This will be a marvelous event, unless it fails spectacularly."

"I won't keep you long, ma'am, but I'm working on a case that involves an evil wizard and a prince turned into a frog, then turned into a prince again. A real tragedy."

Startled, the fairy godmother floated back into a clot of drifting soap bubbles that reminded me of white blood cells under a microscope. "Oh, you must mean dear Prince Dirk! He was a client of mine, until the disaster befell him. I did my best."

That was unexpected, but serendipitous. "Could you tell me more, ma'am? I've been trying to locate Oorgak, but his evil lair has been shut down."

"Yes, he's out of business." Betty waved her wand dismissively. "A life-changing experience. I'm still sorry I couldn't save the sweet prince, but the situation was beyond my fairy godmother abilities."

"How did you know him?" I asked.

"I took the fairy-tale prince under my wing, and under contract. I was his mentor, his guardian angel."

"You mean his fairy godmother?"

"Precisely, but we did it remotely—like a telepsychic, but I was his tele-fairy godmother. That boy was so optimistic and naive; he wanted to live in a magical world and find his princess and true love, but life isn't always like a storybook. He truly needed my help."

"He did indeed find his princess and his true love," I said, and I saw Betty brighten. "But it didn't turn out well. I'm trying to fix that."

"Then you have my full support, Mr. Chambeaux."

The band attempted to play again, and the amps screeched so loudly that several stunned fairies dropped out of the air, letting the "Happy Bat Mitzvah, Irene" banner dangle in the wrong place.

"I helped dear Prince Dirk, just as I would help any unnatural. We all deserve a little magic in our lives." With a swish of her wand, she created more soap bubbles.

I raised my eyebrows enough to wrinkle the skin around the bullet hole. "Why would a fairy-tale prince be considered an unnatural?"

Betty scoffed. "Think about it. A perfect, kind, considerate, and handsome man is as much a mythical creature as any werewolf or zombie." She looked wistful as bubbles drifted around her head. "Those were gloomy times in the Magic Kingdom district. Oorgak was dark and sinister, and decidedly unlikable. He went on a magical rampage, casting horrific spells and making life quite unpleasant. Dirk tried to stand up to him, but the wizard cast a terrible spell and turned the prince into a frog."

I shook my head. "I've been here in the Unnatural Quarter since the beginning, and I've never heard of such devastating black magic and evil sorcery. Are you sure it was really that disastrous?"

Betty clucked her tongue. "Zombies don't really move in fairy-tale circles."

"Very rarely," I admitted. "Maybe I should expand my horizons."

She bobbed in the air again. "During Oorgak's most horrific rampage, I tried to stand up to him, too. After Prince Dirk was turned into a frog, leaving the Magic Kingdom without its rightful ruler, I faced Oorgak with my magic wand, using all the charms and spells I could summon. Fairy godmothers have quite a bit of magic, you know, but it's usually used for frippery and lighthearted things."

"Well, you must have found strong enough magic, since the wizard was defeated," I said. "He's out of business."

"Oh, that wasn't me." She waggled her wand. "I was about to be utterly crushed." She drew a shuddering breath. "Oorgak almost turned me into a frog, too! But as I was driven to my knees, weak, broken, and unable to stand against him … a miracle happened. A beautiful, majestic white unicorn walked by!"

Now she had my attention. "A unicorn?"

"A magnificent creature, purest white, with a single, knurled horn. With every step, he emanated rainbows and glitter and the sound of harp strings … or maybe it was a dulcimer."

"But … a unicorn?" I asked again, even more interested than before.

"The unicorn's very presence showered peace and

contentment everywhere. When the evil wizard saw the unicorn and felt the magical rainbows in the air, it was a life-changing experience for him. Oorgak realized the error of his ways, and his heart of black ice melted. He ceased his magical rampage and left the battlefield a broken man, vowing to make amends."

"So, then what happened to him?" I asked. "Where did he go? And more importantly, what about the unicorn?"

"Oh, I don't know." Betty Bibbity looked up, caught her breath, then waved furiously. I turned to see a thin, elderly werewolf looking around in confusion. He wore a yarmulke on his head and a black suit jacket that hung loosely on his frame.

"Oh, there's the rabbi at last! I'm sorry, Mr. Chambeaux, but I can't talk anymore. I have a bat mitzvah to arrange and a million loose ends to tie up." The fairy godmother scurried away, followed by a flurry of soap bubbles.

CHAPTER 9

Robin and I returned to the Bilge Bay Aquatic Resort to support our lagoon-creature clients at their big rummage sale.

Alvina insisted on coming along. "A lazy river? Swimming pools? Bog ponds? It sounds great!"

"They're not really open for business yet, kid," I said.

"I can still run around out of control!" Alvina said.

I patted her on the head. "Yes, you can."

She put on a unicorn T-shirt, because the swampy resort was too warm and humid for her usual fuzzy pink sweater, and a floppy straw hat to protect her sensitive vampire skin from the sun. Even Robin wore only a casual blouse that allowed more airflow. I wore my usual fedora.

This time there were crowds at the Bilge Bay entrance, which was a good sign, but they had not come for the aquatic activities. A hand-scrawled poster said "Garbage sale today. All debris must go."

"I can't wait to look at all the junk," Alvina said. "Can we buy some, please?"

"You haven't even seen it yet," Robin said. She had doused herself with so much mosquito repellent that even I could smell it with my dead nostrils.

"I'm sure it'll be the best junk." She ran ahead through the gates and down the ornamental gravel path. "This is a great place!"

Signs directed, or lured, potential customers deeper into the resort. Beyond the palm-frond massage cabanas and the empty shaved-ice stands, Gil and Finn had set up long tables strewn with paraphernalia that looked as if it had washed up from a shipwreck.

The lagoon creatures stood behind the sale tables, chatting with intrigued customers who poked among the old cans, bicycle tires, torn shreds of clothes, and a rusty screwdriver and monkey wrench, sold as a set. A female mummy picked up the rags of a blue T-shirt and held it up against her own discolored bandages, then looked around for a mirror.

A golem picked up a soggy, frayed left tennis shoe, looked at the price on the bottom, then set it back down. A rock creature was haggling with Finn, trying to reduce the already-discounted price on a pile of smashed aluminum cans. Clumps of mulch, dead weeds, plastic containers, package wrappers, and a broken comb stood in a mound marked with "Make an Offer."

Robin and I walked up to our clients, who both appeared harried. "Looks like the rummage sale is going well," I said.

Gil shrugged. "Mostly looky-loos. I wish more people would buy this fine merchandise."

Finn raised his voice to the milling crowd, "Fine merchandise!"

Alvina picked up the screwdriver and wrench set, considering it.

"Put that down, honey," Robin said.

"But there's good junk here. I want to find something to buy."

"The girl has a discerning eye," said Gil.

"I want to go swimming," Alvina said. "Are you going to have kiddie pools?"

"Some areas are family friendly," said Gil. "We feature wading pools, both with leeches and without."

"I like leeches," Alvina said. "They suck blood, too. We have a lot in common."

The golem came back to the table for a second look at the soggy left tennis shoe. He made an offer much lower than the asking price, and Finn gave an exasperated, burbling sigh through his gill slits. "All right, go ahead and take it."

Robin scanned up and down the tables. "I'm glad you two are making the best of a bad situation, but we'll get this clutter stopped. I've filed papers with the Effluent Board and the Drainage Canal Preservation Society. We've already installed several new warning signs and even recruited two gator guys from the sewers to do night watch patrol. The garbage dumping will definitely stop now."

"Thank you so much, Miss Deyer," Finn said. "We put in all this time and effort, and people just trash the place. No one respects our private property—and we've had enough of it!"

Gil let out a commiserating sound through his gill slits.

Alvina had found a pile of water-damaged, discarded books on another table. "Oh, look! Books! I like to read! Can I buy these?"

Robin poked through a stained, swollen spellbook, a half-unrolled magical scroll from which most of the letters written in blood had washed away. "Not a good idea. These are magical items, but we don't know their provenance, and they come with no warranties. Could be dangerous."

"And not age-appropriate," I added.

"Pleeease?" Alvina said. "I'll test out the spells in my own room."

"We already bought you some spellbooks at the flea market. Have you used all those up yet?" I asked.

"Not yet," she pouted. "Those are hard."

"You keep practicing," I said. "Maybe you can test them out on your teacher."

Alvina considered. "Maybe."

"We won't be buying these books today." Robin pushed the spellbook aside. "Leave them for other customers. I'm sure they're in great demand."

"This sucks," Alvina said.

"I can get you a unicorn-blood frappé at one of the Talbot & Knowles bloodstands on our way back home," I offered, knowing Alvina loved the fanciful concoction. Under the current circumstances, though, I had learned that the drink was artificially flavored, so that didn't help.

"That'll make up for it," she said.

An ogre picked up the bicycle tire, flexed the rim, bent it one way, then another, and held it over his head. "I think I can use this," he said.

Finn had finished haggling with the rock creature over the pile of crushed cans. I was glad to see that some of the discarded rubbish was going to good homes.

We said our goodbyes to the lagoon creatures, and Robin promised to follow up on the permits and the complaints.

"We're really hoping to open within a week," Gil said. I heard the pleading tone in his burbling voice.

"Our test runs went smoothly," Finn added. "But it's a little hard to tell, since no customers showed up."

"It's all about exposure," Gil said. "We're mailing out coupons and even advertising on the Home Capitalism Network. I'm sure it'll work."

"I'm sure it will." I always tried to encourage our clients.

On the way out, Alvina ran down to the lazy river and threw leaves onto the water to watch them drift along. We stood together to look at the scum-covered relaxing ponds.

When Alvina dipped her hands through the duckweed and sloshed the warm water, black, wormlike figures flurried around her fingers. Leeches popped their heads above the surface.

"Oh, you're so cute!" Alvina let them crawl up onto her hand, petting the slick, black skins.

"Leave the leeches in peace, honey," Robin said. "They're wild animals, and they need to learn how to forage for their own food."

Mosquitoes buzzed around my face and Robin's, but they were frustrated by my zombie embalming fluid and by Robin's mosquito repellent.

Alvina wiped her hands on her short pants, then skipped along beside us, already forgetting about the rummage sale and looking forward to her high-blood-sugar frappé at the coffee-and-blood bar.

Chapter 10

n my years as a zombie private investigator, I had learned a lot of eclectic information, esoteric details, and useless facts. I absorbed details like a piece of toast falling buttered-side down and collecting lint.

As I wandered the mean streets—as well as the kinder, gentler streets—I filed away facts and quirks until they began to leak out of the hole in my forehead. It made me particularly good during trivia night at the Goblin Tavern, and it also gave me the raw materials to make odd connections in solving cases.

One of those odd items was knowing where to go if you were looking for true enlightenment—the Wham-Bam Ashram, managed by the ogre Guru Grbth. Since the fairy godmother had told me about her ultimate sorcerous confrontation with Oorgak, along with more background on Prince Dirk and his unfortunate amphibious circumstances, I had an idea where I might find out more about the wizard's change of heart.

Maybe he hadn't ascended into a celestial nirvana. Oorgak might simply have taken a few self-improvement classes.

The ashram sat on a stately hill above the city's miasma, which made it easy to find, because the rest of the Quarter was flat and sunken, prone to bayous and swamps, with commercial developments on the fringes. Beautifully trimmed hedges lined a zigzagging path up to the apex of the ashram hill. The winding trail was meant to signify the convoluted journey of life, but it also added a lot of extra steps for someone who was just trying to get to the front door.

The unusual and graceful structure had several stories of open Asian architecture adorned with stacked curved roofs. It reminded me of something that Godzilla would have knocked down in one of the early movies. The Wham-Bam Ashram had originally been a Japanese tea house, then an all-you-can-eat Chinese dim sum restaurant, before being remodeled and reopened as a center of unnatural enlightenment.

As I reached the top of the painstaking path, bamboo and metal wind chimes clacked and jingled from the tiled eaves. The gentle, calming tones inspired meditation, but the breezes were likely caused by impure thoughts.

On the front lawn, two groups of novices gathered for their studies—an assortment of unnatural species and a few brave humans who had chosen this as a difficult path to enlightenment. Wearing clean white robes, the students struggled to get into lotus positions. A skeleton sat among them, motionless, and I had no idea how long he'd been there.

A mummy monk stood with his head bowed on a sticklike neck, his fingers pressed together in a meditative position as he wheezed out a calming noise (or perhaps it was a snore—I couldn't tell because his eyes were bandaged). The devout acolytes joined the mummy in making the soft wheezing sound as they also tried to meditate.

I wanted to ask where to find the ogre guru, but I decided not to disturb their sense of emptiness.

More students stood around a decorative koi pond where creatures swam about. The acolytes tossed in coins, making wishes and increasing their karmic luck. A zombie girl plunked a nickel into the water, and a large piranha koi lunged up. It gulped the coin and jumped high enough to nip off the end of the zombie girl's finger. She giggled and leaned back.

"I'm looking for Guru Grbth," I said to the group. "Is he around?"

A spray-tanned vampire gestured toward the interior of the ashram building. I ducked under the ornamental eaves and entered the shade of the open communal area. I remembered the ashram and its karmic graduation ceremony when we had helped out another client, Sal the salamander, a creature with painfully low self-esteem. Now, the ashram was quiet, with classes taking place outside since it was a nice gloomy day, but the enormous guru remained inside. He sat cross-legged on the raised platform at the center of the room.

Grbth was a huge shaggy brute with a gentle demeanor, his head the size of a normal person's torso. His hair hung down in dreadlocks like thick hawser ropes used to anchor oil tankers. His beard reminded me of a grizzly pelt.

Grbth had reached his state of enlightenment by studying philosophical texts, meditating and chanting, undergoing rigorous self-improvement exercises, and just spending a lot of time thinking about stuff. He had reached such a high mental plane of existence that he no longer needed to use vowels in his name.

As a mark of his exalted status, the contented ogre wore a tentlike robe tie-dyed in pastel colors to show the sunny possibilities of inner peace. His hubcap-sized eyes were closed, deep in thought. He held an enormous spiked club in his left hand, raising and dropping it in a loud rhythm as he moaned out "BOOM!" He looked utterly calm.

I shattered that calm. "Excuse me, Mr. Grbth?" The ogre

sat up straight. His huge eyes flew open, and he smashed the club down on the platform, rattling the lanterns from the rafters. "Sorry to harsh your mellow. You might remember me—Dan Chambeaux, private investigator."

Grbth inhaled a huge breath and let it out like a blacksmith squeezing the bellows on a foundry furnace. "Chambeaux ..." He used the club as a crutch to lever himself up from the ungainly lotus position. He stood in front of me, a titanic figure. "I remember that you have a very discordant life."

"It comes with solving crimes among monsters all the time," I said.

"You could use some of our meditation and ascension courses."

"I've got a white-noise app. That calms me," I said. "I hope you can help me with a case."

"My purpose in life is to help others," Grbth said. "That way we can all achieve enlightenment."

I tipped my fedora in thanks. "I'm interested in one particular enlightened individual. Maybe he was a student of yours? I need to find an evil wizard who's reformed. According to rumor, he's gone straight."

Grbth's furry eyebrows rose up. "Evil wizard?"

"He went by the name of Oorgak," I said. "Did some terrible things when he was an evil man, and then did even worse things to make up for them. I need to find him, so we can make the world right again."

"Oorgak?" Grbth grumbled. "Ah, you mean Walter!"

"I'm pretty sure I mean Oorgak, but I'm willing to start just about anywhere."

The ogre guru stomped off, gesturing for me to follow him out the back of the open ashram to the beautiful, secluded gardens in the rear of the property. "Walter is a special student, undergoing directed studies. He is my personal pupil."

"Maybe Walter knows where Oorgak went," I suggested.

Grbth gripped the spiked club and swiveled his enormous shoulders as he glared at me. "Oorgak is gone forever."

That bummed me out. RRita and Prince Dirk would not be happy to hear that at all.

Next to a whispering fountain and delicately carved stone obelisks, we stopped in a Zen garden with smooth stones perfectly arranged on a field of white sand. A dark-haired man in a white robe stood by himself with his back to us. He held a Zen rake, marking paths in the smooth sand. As we came closer, I saw that instead of drawing calming designs, he had been playing a game of tic-tac-toe with himself.

"Walter!" Grbth said, and the man turned. I saw his shaggy black beard, his black eyebrows, an angular face that might have been considered a caricature of evil under other circumstances, but right now his expression was as placid as a square of drying concrete.

"Guru Grbth." Walter gave a formal bow. "I have continued my exercises as I take even more baby steps on the road to enlightenment."

Proud of his student, the ogre clapped an enormous hand on Walter's shoulder. "The road to enlightenment is not an interstate highway, but a rugged jeep road through the mountains. With my teachings, I intend to give you the four-wheel drive you need."

Walter turned his potentially fiery eyes toward me, but they were just dampened coals now. "May you find your own journey to enlightenment."

"It's a journey, all right," I said.

I introduced myself and explained that I was searching for

the evil wizard Oorgak. Startled, Walter spun, looking desperately toward the ogre guru.

Grbth said, "Deep breath, Walter. Impose calm. You can do this."

The man closed his eyes and let out a sigh before he turned back to me. "I was once Oorgak," he said, "but the unicorn changed everything. Once I laid eyes upon him, I shed my evil ways. I knew I had to atone. I had to change. So now, I prefer the name Walter instead of Oorgak."

I agreed that it sounded less evil. This man was exactly who I was looking for. "In your evil days, Oorgak—I mean, Walter—you were very naughty."

He hung his head. "I'm aware of that. It was bad parenting. It was society's fault. I couldn't help myself."

"Do you remember changing Prince Dirk into a frog?"

Walter grimaced at the memory. "That was a terrible day. I was so full of myself, but the spell was at hand, and I really wanted to use it. Boy, did it work! Poof! He turned right into a frog, and he hopped away. I felt triumphant … but it wasn't a very nice thing to do."

He raised his bearded chin, drawing strength. "But once I saw the unicorn, I also saw the error in my ways, so I atoned. I undid the evil wrongs, and I cast a restorative spell to make him a handsome prince again. He's all better now."

I said, "Unfortunately, he had fallen in love with a frog princess, and you ruined their romance. They've hired me to restore him to his frog form. You're the one who can do it, Oorgak. You're the formerly evil wizard."

He recoiled in panic, then swung his gaze to the looming ogre. "But I can't! I'm a good wizard now. I cannot cast any evil spells. It would ruin my karma."

"But it's the right thing to do, Walter," I insisted. "You

would bring two lovers back together and make them very happy."

Walter shook his head vigorously and squinched his eyes shut. "I can't! I've been enlightened by Grbth, and I have to eschew revenge. I cannot cause harm, and I won't cast any more evil spells."

"Yes, you'd lose points for that," Grbth said.

"Not even if Prince Dirk wants you to do it?" I spread my hands, hoping Walter would see reason.

"No, I've gone straight!"

I turned to the ogre guru. "Can you please talk to him? This is a special circumstance. The best thing for all concerned would be for Walter to cast that evil spell and turn the prince back into a frog. Happily ever after on all accounts."

"That would be very unwise, Mr. Shamble. Walter is an addict of evil, and he is struggling. It would be like asking an alcoholic to take one last drink for the common good."

"It isn't just Guru Grbth's teachings!" Walter said. "I've had a genuine, soul-deep epiphany. When I saw that unicorn, I decided never to be mean again."

I could see this would be a very difficult argument to make. Exasperated, I said, "But nobody's ever seen a unicorn!"

Chapter 11

The next morning, a real, live unicorn walked into our offices and turned my whole world on its head.

It was a calm Saturday. Robin was proofreading her brief on the skeleton indecent-exposure defense, preparing for her court appearance on Monday. Sheyenne busied herself filing papers, closing out cases, and sending threatening bill reminders.

Alvina continued her conspiracy-theory research on the dark web. Her latest fascinating discovery was that a secret group of unicorns had faked the Moon landing, because it would have diminished the magical perception of silvery moonlight. I was skeptical about that. When the kid showed me proof posted right there on the internet, I told her not to believe everything she read online.

I was standing around in the front office, pondering cases, which is an important part of a zombie detective's work. I thought about volunteering to join a drainage-canal citizen watch to prevent any hooligans from dumping more rubbish into Bilge Bay.

Those considerations went out of my mind, though, when the door swung open, and rainbows roiled inside like smoke from a colorful Pride bomb. Holding my *World's Greatest Zombie Detective* coffee mug, I just stared.

At the file cabinet, Sheyenne dropped the folder she held

in her ghostly fingertips. Late-payment notices fluttered to the floor.

Alvina cried out, "Wow, cool!"

The pointed ivory horn came through the door first, swirled like a loop of soft serve. Attached to the horn came a stunningly majestic snow-white horselike form. The unicorn's white mane had hints of silver, and his hooves were like polished pewter. The beast shimmered with an imposing, breathtaking presence unlike anything I had ever experienced.

After stepping into our offices, the unicorn just stood there as the air crackled with magic and peace. Rainbow effects hovered around my eyes. When the unicorn snorted, it sounded like choir music.

Like a sleepwalker, Robin emerged from her office and stared, unable to find the presence of mind even to gasp. Sheyenne glowed with a sense of wonder, and Alvina jumped up and down with glee. "I knew it! I knew it!"

I recovered my composure first and stepped forward. I could feel my legs trembling, but it had nothing to do with my rigor mortis. "Uh, welcome to Chambeaux and Deyer Investigations. How can we help you today, Mr. uh …?"

The unicorn turned toward me. His long horn was deadly sharp, but I felt no threat. "I am Arthur."

"Of course you are."

"I require your services. I need to hire a detective."

I found the most inane comment possible. "Then you've come to the right place!" It didn't even occur to me to wonder how a unicorn would pay for our services. Maybe Arthur had a rainbow line of credit.

"I have lost something—something very important to me," the unicorn said. "I need you to find it."

"Then it'll be my top priority," I promised. I said that to every client, but I really meant it now.

Arthur lowered his voice. "I also need you to be very discreet."

I thought of the divorce cases I had worked, the secret photography that captured soon-to-be ex-spouses having illicit affairs. I had caught embezzlers. I had investigated corrupt politicians. "Discretion is my middle name," I said, then felt the need to add, "Not actually, like on my birth certificate, but I promise I'll be discreet." For some reason, the unicorn made me want to tell the absolute truth.

Exploding with joyful vindication, Alvina ran to the side table and snatched up her iPhone. "This is a perfect opportunity! I need to take a selfie with Arthur and prove to Miss Nifflesmoth that there are unicorns. Then I'll get an A!"

"Good idea, kid," I said.

Arthur shook his horn from side to side. "I'm afraid not."

I felt as deflated as a slug monster in salt water. "But it would help our vampire girl restore her honor from an evil spelling-demon teacher. Couldn't you do us that favor?"

"Not possible." Arthur snorted and tossed his head. "Unicorns must keep a low profile. We are rarely seen. Our existence must not be proven. It is the Horn Brother and Sister Code."

Alvina's shoulders slumped. "That code sucks."

Robin got down to business. "Exactly what services do you need from us, Arthur?"

"What did you lose?" I asked. "I have many connections, and I can help you find whatever it is."

Arthur lowered his head. "My beloved pet unidog Urmin has gone missing."

"Urmin!" Alvina squealed. "We saw the little horn dog. He's so cute!"

"He is magical and a great source of power, but now he has disappeared." Arthur snorted, and again it sounded like a church choir. "Other unicorn familiars have likewise gone missing. This is a terrible crime, and I have no choice but to seek outside help. Dan Chambeaux, I task you with locating Urmin."

I love it when the cases really do solve themselves. "You're in luck, sir. I know exactly where to find him."

"Good. Prompt attention to this matter would restore peace and unity among unicorns."

"Otherwise known as unicornity," I said, nodding.

The wondrous creature continued, "Unidogs are the true underlying source of unicorn magic."

"I thought the horn was the source of your magic?" Alvina asked. "That's what my research showed."

Arthur snorted again. "Horns are overrated."

Sheyenne began filling out a new client intake form. "We'll need your address and phone number, Arthur."

"Not possible," he said with another shake of his horn. "Unicorns are neither seen nor heard. It's part of our mystique. I am not allowed to leave a callback number."

"But when I find your unidog, how should I let you know?" It wouldn't take me long to go to the UQ Animal Shelter and retrieve poor little Urmin.

"I will be in touch," Arthur said. "I miss my puppy unidog. Please make sure he's safe and bring him back where he belongs."

"We're on it," I promised.

Sheyenne drifted up from her desk, shining brightly. "Are you sure you won't stay for a cup of coffee? We also have chilled water in the fridge."

"I must be back before others notice me. It's a terrible secret." Arthur turned with smooth grace, throwing off more subliminal rainbows and shedding pleasant spring-blossom scent into the air. We were all left breathless with a sense of wonder as the unicorn strolled out of the office.

In the hall, the shambling ghoul Renfeld was working his vacuum cleaner. His gray jaw fell open, and drool ran down onto his chest. Arthur pranced past him and went down the stairs that led out of the building.

My undead heart was beating rapidly. "Looks like we've got a new case."

Chapter 12

At times, I really *do* know what I'm doing—it's a good feeling. I knew exactly where to find our unicorn client's lost horn dog, thanks to McGoo, and I didn't want to waste any time.

When I set off for the Unnatural Quarter Animal Shelter, Alvina, not surprisingly, insisted on going along to see the cute kitties, puppies, and other cuddly larvae. Sheyenne accompanied us to take care of any necessary paperwork, but I think she just has a soft spot for lost causes, which is probably why she likes me so much.

"If we're going to get Urmin, can we adopt a pet for ourselves?" the kid asked, as she had done many times before.

"Not today, honey. This is part of a case," Sheyenne said as we headed down the boulevard. It was a beautiful day for a walk together.

"I think we should have a new case," Alvina said. "The case of the lovingly adopted pet for our offices!"

"I've got a full caseload right now, kid."

Alvina trotted ahead of us, as if she already knew the way. As soon as we turned the corner, we could hear the increased yipping and growling. "This isn't a shopping trip, just a quick in and out to get Urmin," I reminded them.

Sheyenne slipped her glowing, insubstantial arm through

mine as we moved toward the door. "We still have to figure out how to contact Arthur."

"If he's magic, he'll know when we have his unidog back," Alvina said.

"If his magic was strong enough, he wouldn't have lost the dog in the first place," I muttered, even though I knew puppies could be unruly creatures, and horn puppies might be even more rambunctious.

At the animal shelter door, a sign showed a fierce, spiky demon with smoke curling out of its scaled, pointed ears. In his scaly arms, he cuddled a purring kitten. "Everyone needs love," said the sign. "A lifetime of love is available here. Adopt a pet now."

Alvina pointed. "See, I told you!"

I nudged her to the door. "Don't believe every sign you read, kid."

"Is that why you never come to a complete stop at a stop sign?" she asked.

Sometimes my half-daughter pays too much attention to things.

From inside, the barking, yipping, growling, hissing, and hooting was a deafening cacophony, but the stony gargoyle at the front desk seemed deaf to it all. I'd had experience with deaf gargoyles before; maybe that was an advantage in the job here.

The shelter had several sections designated by species and temperament. Sheyenne was drawn immediately to the spectral pets section, which featured ghost cats and dogs. "Beaux, can we look in here? Just for a minute?"

"I thought we were only—" I cut myself off, knowing when to listen to my ghost girlfriend.

After opening the heavy door, we entered a lead-lined menagerie with cages full of glowing basset hounds and calico cats. Adorable puppies that had unwisely bounded into the street now ran around barking in their ghostly forms, filled forever with canine energy. Animal shelter attendants—also ghosts—frolicked with the animals, throwing intangible balls so the dogs could chase them. Bouncing around the lead-lined room, kittens batted a loose strand of thick spider web that dangled from the ceiling, while others were curled up in a mass of insubstantial fur.

Sheyenne drifted to a ghostly mutt and rubbed its spectral ears. It yipped as it circled her poltergeist form. I could see the thoughts turning in her head, so I cautioned her. "Renfeld doesn't allow pets in the building."

"I'd take care of it," Alvina pleaded. "I'd pick up all the ghost poop."

"Ghost dog turds are insubstantial, but still potent," I said. "They might be invisible, but you can still smell them."

"Like a fart," Alvina said.

"I had a puppy when I was a little girl. I loved that dog," Sheyenne said in a wistful voice, then heaved a sigh. "I just wanted to reminisce." She rubbed the ghost puppy's ears again, then it bounded off as the attendant tossed the invisible ball. "We could come here on a date sometime to pet the puppies and kitties, give them some love."

"Let's see the arachnids," Alvina said. "They have interesting species here, depending on whatever animal control catches out in the streets." Her brow furrowed as a thought occurred to her. "Or maybe I can just adopt those friendly leeches from Bilge Bay. I could put them in the same tank with my pet piranha."

In the next wing, the shelter's reptile section featured snapping turtles, Gila monsters, poisonous horned toads, venomous cobras, and fer-de-lances (marked with a two-for-one special). Larger tanks held estate-sale and owner-surrender pythons and boa constrictors. The snakes were kept alarmingly close to cages filled with adoptable lab rats.

Intent on wrapping up our case, I pulled us toward the dog section, where I expected to find the lost canicorn that McGoo had turned in. There, we found dozens of barking mutts, from hounds to German shepherds to tiny yap-yap dogs, and even a few fiery-eyed hellhounds.

But no unidogs.

"I don't see Urmin here," I said. "How are we going to solve our case?"

"We could ask at the front desk," Sheyenne suggested. I agreed since that would have been my idea in the first place.

In the main reception area, the hearing-impaired gargoyle was filling out an order for generic animal chow and a bulk purchase of spiked collars.

"We're looking for a lost dog," I said, hoping the gargoyle wasn't actually deaf, just disinterested. "With a horn?"

The attendant stretched her greenish-black wings, then tucked them back against her shoulders. Her lips didn't even crack a smile to show fangs. "You're here to report a lost dog?"

"Not a dog," Alvina said. "A unidog. We want to adopt one."

"Did you look in the canine section before bothering me?" she asked.

"We petted every puppy," Sheyenne said.

"The unidog we're looking for isn't there," I said. "The true owner hired us to retrieve it. We know it was brought here two days ago by Officer McGoohan of the UQPD."

"I can provide a copy of the police report if necessary," Sheyenne said.

"We have lists. We don't need police reports," said the

gargoyle. "Once they arrive here, our animals are on a quest to find their forever homes and their forever masters."

"This one already has a forever master," I said. "He had a tag around his neck with his name, Urmin."

"And a cute horn," Alvina added.

"We'd just like to retrieve him," Sheyenne said. "We'll fill out the paperwork and pay the adoption fee." She glanced at me. "We can charge it back to Arthur."

The gargoyle clacked on her computer keyboard, calling up records, scrolling through lists of exotic animals. "I'm reviewing past unidogs that have come through here. Not a very popular item." She clicked to a different screen, then nodded. "Ah, yes, one brought in just recently."

"We know," I said. "We'd like to get him back to his owner."

The gargoyle pressed her angular face closer to the screen, squinting her demonic eyes. "Oh, it seems that unidogs are more popular than I thought. This one was adopted right away."

"Adopted?" I straightened. "But he already has a legitimate owner."

"Sorry, our creatures are first come, first served. You'll have to move faster next time."

I pulled out my private investigator license, ready to use my heavy influence. "I was hoping we could resolve this amicably, but my lawyer partner is prepared to file paperwork. We need to know where that unidog has gone."

The gargoyle's bat-like wings twitched in annoyance. "It is not our policy to reveal the names of adoptive parents."

I thrust the P.I. license closer, and the gargoyle's wings sagged in defeat. "But we are a non-profit organization, and we don't have the funds or resources to combat a lawsuit. I'll let you work it out yourselves." She typed again and pulled up an address. "It says here that a dragon adopted the unidog as an emotional-support animal."

"A dragon?" I asked. "Why does a dragon need an emotional-support animal?"

"It's not our business to worry about someone else's emotional problems," Sheyenne said.

"The dragon has a gambling addiction," the gargoyle said, "and she thought the unidog would bring her good luck."

"Not sure that's the way to combat a gambling addiction," I mumbled.

The receptionist turned the screen to show us the address. Sheyenne was surprised. "That must mean the Renaissance Faire is back in town!"

"Can we go again?" Alvina asked.

"In fact, we'll go there right now, kid—even before they open." I remembered Alice the surly dragon, who was the main attraction at Dredd's Real Renaissance Faire. "We'll have to make our case that the horn dog belongs with a unicorn instead of a dragon."

CHAPTER 13

Once a year, the traveling spectacle of the Real Renaissance Faire arrived in the Quarter. After traveling around the country from city to city, they received their warmest welcome here, where the mythical creatures and other open-minded unnaturals felt right at home.

The traveling camp was in the process of setting up on the fringes of the Magic Kingdom district, which made good business sense, since that was where their largest customer base lay. According to the signs posted all around, the Faire itself would not open for another week, but the setup and rehearsals were already well under way.

Robin joined us as we headed to the Magic Kingdom, since we might need to do some legal arm-twisting to resolve this case. Robin is usually fiery, determined, and optimistic, but now she sounded surprisingly subdued about our prospects. "Getting Urmin back might be a challenge, Dan." She frowned. "Because Arthur and unicorns in general are so secretive, there's no paper trail. Arthur gave us no ownership certificate or unidog license when he engaged our services. We can't even demonstrate tangible proof that he hired us to retrieve his pet."

Alvina was disappointed. "That sucks. If Arthur had let me take a selfie with him, that would have been proof."

"We know we're in the right." I offered a different approach. "If the law isn't on our side, maybe BS will work."

"Once we explain the situation, I'm sure Alice will be reasonable and return the cute pet," Sheyenne said.

I thought back to my previous encounter with the dragon at the Renaissance Faire while solving a golem murder, and I couldn't forget her fiery temperament. "Reasonable wouldn't be the first word I'd use."

As we passed through the Magic Kingdom district, we were charmed by the elves and their cookie factory and the dwarves at their blacksmith shop. A pretty young woman sat on a bale of straw, working an old-fashioned spinning wheel in front of a boutique shop, Rumpelstiltskin's Fine Yarns and Macramé. We bought Alvina a cold treat at Geppetto's Gelato.

Soon, the commercial zone of the Magic Kingdom gave way to the dusty, bustling fairgrounds. The Ren Faire monsters had pitched large tents that could hold crowds for the show, while vendors set up carnival games for prizes, including Throw the Severed Head or Dunk the Desiccated Mummy. Trolls erected split-rail fences to enclose a jousting arena. Igors were setting up a Talbot & Knowles concession, but with medieval trappings and a sign that said "Ye Olde Blood Bar."

By now, the sun had set, and dusk was setting in, but the workers seemed prepared to continue well into the night, which wasn't surprising, because many of the species were nocturnal creatures. The traveling members of the Renaissance Faire were like vagabonds, moving from venue to venue in pickup trucks or Airstream trailers (which were especially favored by the vampires, because the gleaming aluminum coating reflected all sunlight).

Three burly ogres in ill-fitting iron-plate armor tossed long jousting lances at one another as if it were a game of lawn darts. A crew of furry werewolves sat in a circle around a campfire pounding on bongo drums, while a tentacled creature in black hose, a leather vest, and a jaunty Robin Hood cap played a lute.

A big golem security guard blocked our entry into the camp. "The Renaissance Faire opens in a week. Participants only."

"I'm a ghost," Sheyenne said. "How do you know I'm not from the real Renaissance period?"

That confounded the golem, who wasn't used to being asked challenging questions.

"I'm here on official zombie detective business," I said. "We're going to see a dragon about a unidog."

"I'll fill out an application for a special permit if necessary," Robin said.

"Pleeease?" Alvina said. "Can we go in?"

The latter argument convinced the golem, and he gestured us inside. "Just don't bother the rest of the crew. They've got work to do."

Inside the venue, painted wooden signs showed a fire-breathing dragon facing down not-so-brave knights above a list of showtimes. A cook tent advertised a nightly knight roast, but I figured it was probably just pork, or maybe even the artificial Mystery Meat that's become so popular.

On the fairgrounds, the dragon's tent was unmistakable—larger than a circus tent to accommodate the big reptile's wingspan. The marketers had decorated it with colorful pennants, windsocks, and pinwheels. In old English letters, a sign warned, "Beware ye of dragon."

I stood before the tent flap, not sure how to knock on a canvas door. Fearless, Alvina just ducked inside the flap. "I want to see the dragon."

With Sheyenne and Robin following me, I entered the dim

sulfur-smelling interior, raising my hand in a calming gesture. "Hello, Alice," I called out. "We're here on official business."

As my eyes adjusted to the gloom, I saw the huge curled-up dragon, with her long serpentine neck bent and her wedge-shaped head resting on an enormous, clawed forepaw. Smoke wafted from her nostrils.

Then, I heard the charming sounds of a yipping unidog. Alvina called out, "Here he is! I found Urmin!"

Alvina ignored the sleeping dragon. Instead, she chased the delighted horn dog. Urmin shed magical delight as he rolled on the ground and jumped into the vampire girl's arms. "Good puppy! Good puppy!"

With a loud snort, the dragon grumbled deep in her throat. Thick black smoke spurted from her nostrils, and her eyes opened, showing orange fires of inner magic. Awake now, Alice lifted her big head and opened her hinged jaw to show fangs nearly as long as the jousting lances we had seen out in the tournament field. "Trespassers! You've come to steal my treasure!"

Her barbed tail twitched and curled around a disappointingly small pile of treasure chests, piled gold chains, urns, and costume jewelry.

I pushed my way forward, hoping Alice wouldn't just torch us without a little ice-breaking conversation. "We're not here for your treasure, I promise."

Urmin yipped and yapped, and the noise calmed the big dragon, at least enough to talk.

"Good." The dragon used her tail to brush the mounds of valuables closer. "This is all I have left. Been on a losing streak." She shook her enormous head. "But it's bound to change. I can feel it! I have good luck now. I have a gambling-support animal."

Alas, the Renaissance Faire dragon still suffered from the

gambling addiction that had caused her so much trouble before. She snorted again. "Wait … I remember you. Back when I lost Excalibur in a poker game to that gremlin."

"And I remember you." I smiled.

"Dragons are quite memorable," Alice said, raising her head.

"And so, I hope, are zombie detectives," I said. At the end of that case, Alice had actually won the ownership of the Renaissance Faire, but she'd lost it again in the intervening time. "Pleased to come back and chat with you again."

Alvina kept playing with the unidog, and the dragon growled. "Leave my lucky dog alone."

The kid squared her shoulders and faced Alice. "He's not your unidog. He belongs to a real unicorn named Arthur."

Indignant, Alice shook her head. "What are you talking about? I adopted that unidog fair and square from the animal shelter! I filled out the paperwork … though I hate when they make you use digital pads, because my claws don't work."

I could only imagine this dragon trying to hold an iPad in hands the size of an Apple Store.

"Urmin already has an owner," Robin explained. "There's a collar around his neck, and we've been hired to bring him back to his true home."

The dragon squirmed, obviously agitated. "But I need that unidog! I've struggled with gambling addiction for years. I try to stop, but I … just can't. So, I may as well win. And a unidog is good luck."

Urmin let out another pleasant musical yip.

Robin gave me a troubled look. She lowered her voice. "We don't really have a legal leg to stand on, Dan, unless Arthur comes here himself and produces ownership papers."

I answered quietly. "Let me try something else." I stepped closer to Alice and tried to sound enticing. "If you've got a gambling addiction, then let's play to your strengths. I'll play you a round of whatever game you choose. And whoever wins gets to keep the dog."

"Horn dog," Alvina corrected.

Now the dragon was interested. "You'll play me a round? Winner take all?"

"Winner take all," I said.

"And my choice of game?"

"As long as I know the rules," I said. "I'm pretty good at Go Fish or 52-Card Pickup."

"Not checkers, though," Alvina said. "I always beat him."

The dragon stewed on that for a long moment. "Then my game of choice is … Farkel."

"A dice game?" I asked.

Then I noticed that the dragon's treasure mound contained several dice the size of shipping boxes. Alice reached over to scoop up all six in her reptilian hands. She pointed her snout down to the hoard. "There's a normal-sized set down there somewhere, Shamble."

I rummaged among the gold brooches, jeweled chains, dented royal crowns, and gilded letter openers until I found six glittery novelty dice. "You're on," I said.

Sheyenne drifted close. "Beaux, what are you doing? What if you lose?"

"Don't worry, Spooky. I've got a plan." I was taking a gamble of my own, but I knew the odds were in my favor.

Urmin sat down, wagged his tail, then bobbed his head from side to side so that the stubby horn moved like a metronome.

Robin sounded tense. "Good luck, Dan."

"You roll first," Alice growled, rattling the huge dice in her hands. I could see the eagerness in her huge eyes. Flickers of flame curled up from between her fangs.

I took the normal-sized set in my gray palm and tossed the dice on the ground. I'm not a professional gambler, and some games are highly nuanced, but I was familiar with the ways of Farkel. I plucked out the ones and a trio of sixes, which was sufficient to get me into the game.

Alice rattled the cubes in her palms and hurled the giant dice onto the ground. We had to dive out of the way as they bounced and rolled, giving the dragon only two fives and other garbage dice.

Frustrated at the lackluster roll, the dragon reserved a five, then rolled the rest of the dice, scoring only another five, and rolled again, but it wasn't sufficient to get her into the game.

I took my turn and got two pair. Urmin yipped, and I felt a rush of happy rainbows flow over me. The critter was rooting for me. Alvina cuddled the unidog, then let him go so he could trot over and lick the side of my gray hand.

Alice rolled once more and still failed to get into the game. Next, I achieved an astonishing six of a kind. Robin diligently kept score.

After several more rounds, Alice hurled the six dice in another roll, then groaned in dismay. "Farkel!" she cried, snorting fire from deep in her throat.

"Now then, rules are rules," Robin said. "Don't make trouble."

The game didn't get better for the dragon after that.

When it was all over, Alvina cuddled Urmin. "Now we'll make sure you get back to Arthur."

Even as the dragon roiled with her anger, Urmin continued to wag his tail and shed waves and waves of pastel rainbows, which made Alice dizzy. She sighed with a sound like a deflating zeppelin. "I've gambled enough to know when I lose. I'll have better luck next time."

I doubted that would be the case, because we were taking

away her good luck support unidog. We hurried out of the giant tent before her moods could shift.

As we left, Robin spoke to me in a scolding tone. "That was an extreme risk with so much at stake! What would make you gamble on something so incredibly uncertain?"

"I had no doubts," I said. "I was counting on the dragon's well-established bad luck."

CHAPTER 14

We could wrap up Arthur's case now that we had found the magical unidog, but Robin said she needed to take care of another urgent matter before we left the Renaissance Faire. When I saw the uncomfortable look on her face, I remembered our woefully malfunctioning restroom in the Chambeaux & Deyer offices.

Wearing a tight expression, Robin rushed to the line of plastic Tow-a-Toilets used by the Renaissance Faire crew. "Dan, please take Alvina and the unidog over to the drum circle and keep them occupied. I'll … be a few minutes."

She ducked into one of the blue plastic enclosures that reminded me of a TARDIS for human waste. I doubted, though, that they were bigger on the inside than on the outside.

Robin had tried Sewer Sweeties twice more for an emergency service call, to no avail. I had told her she could use the bathroom in my upstairs apartment, but it's cramped and filled with guy stuff and zombie stuff, and Robin didn't want to intrude on my privacy. Renfeld had offered to let us use the toilet in the basement abode recently vacated by an unruly tenant. Robin had tried it twice, but the previous occupant had placed the bathroom under a terrible curse, which was why Renfeld had retained the security deposit.

The situation must be truly dire if she was willing to use

these old Tow-a-Toilets. The plastic door squeaked shut, and she turned the latch to Occupied.

Alvina played with Urmin, giggling as she chased him around in circles. The horn dog sniffed a clump of thistles, as if making a very difficult decision, then he squatted and left a pile of rainbow-colored poop. I won't say that it smelled like roses, but it was definitely an improvement over most of the steaming piles of shit I had encountered in my life.

Alvina dropped to her knees in the dry grass, and the horn dog placed his little paws on her shoulders and licked her cheek, making her giggle all over again. Still, she seemed troubled. "Are you sure we have to give him back to Arthur?"

"That unicorn is our client, honey," Sheyenne said. "Urmin belongs in his loving home."

I said, "We have to wait for Arthur to get back in touch, though, since he didn't leave a contact number. Urmin stays with us in the meantime."

Finally, the plastic Tow-a-Toilet door creaked open, and Robin staggered out, letting it slam behind her. Her expression looked less distressed now, but more disgusted. Urmin bounded up to greet her, shedding shimmers of rainbows and barking like musical chimes, which brought relief to Robin's face. "Let's get back to the offices," she said. "I'm going to call Sewer Sweeties again—right away."

The horn dog needed no leash as he trotted along, accepting us as his new guardians. When we reached the office building and climbed the stairs to the second floor, Renfeld was pushing a hissing and burbling carpet machine that fumigated the stained rug. As soon as the carpet was fresh, though, mucus dribbled out of his nose and fell onto the damp fibers, then he trod across the ooze, grinding the stain in deeper. He probably considered it ghoul job security.

Urmin ran ahead, barking at the infernal machine. A

broad grin split the ghoul's face. "Cute puppy," he said, then hardened his expression. "No dogs allowed."

"It's not a dog. It's a canicorn," I pointed out.

Robin added, "I reviewed the building handbook, and there is no specific regulation against canicorns or unidogs."

"Or horn dogs," Alvina said.

"Okay," Renfeld drawled. "Have a nice day."

Urmin barked at the carpet-cleaning machine two more times for good measure, and then we retreated into our offices.

Sheyenne said, "I can call Sewer Sweeties if you like. I have their number."

"Oh, I have their number, too," Robin replied with an angry tone. "I may need to threaten legal action." She stalked off into her office.

In the kitchenette Alvina filled a bowl of water for Urmin, who lapped it up, wagging his tail the whole time. I brought out a few case folders and sat in the main reception area so I could watch the kid play with the unicorn dog.

"You're my special detective assistant," I told Alvina. "I'll need your help watching Urmin until Arthur comes to pick him up."

"Oh, I like to help," Alvina said. "And I'm also going to help you solve the frog prince case." Determined, she ran to our shelf that held legal volumes, phone directories, local takeout menus, and the stack of spiral notebooks and used spellbooks we had recently bought for her at the Unnatural Quarter flea market.

"I don't know how you're going to help me on that case, kid," I said. "The formerly evil wizard refuses to cast his evil spell again and make everything right."

I was flustered that the wizard Oorgak, or Walter, was being unhelpful. Robin already had an appointment with

RRita and Dirk the following day to discuss relevant legal issues, and I would have to give them the disappointing update.

Alvina plopped down at the little table and began paging through her used spellbook. Urmin sat next to her, wagging his tail, then he wandered around the office, sniffing at our plastic potted plant and the chairs in the conference room.

The vampire girl scrutinized a diagram on one of the pages, mumbling the words to herself. "Does it have to be Oorgak who works the enchantment? What if I can find a way to turn evil myself? I could cast a wicked spell and make Prince Dirk into a frog again." She turned the page and read a different section on dark magic. "Maybe I can practice the spell on my teacher, since she still won't change my grade on the unicorn report."

I wasn't sure I wanted my half-daughter to turn evil and cast a twisted spell, even if Miss Nifflesmoth deserved it. After Arthur had come to our offices, Robin called Nosferatu Academy and left a sternly worded message for the spelling demon, insisting that we had all seen an actual unicorn, who was now a client of Chambeaux & Deyer. But the teacher had dug in her horned heels and said, "Pictures, or it didn't happen." I was so upset I even considered joining the PTA.

Overhearing the conversation, Sheyenne drifted over and took the spellbook away from Alvina. "Now, honey, you don't need to turn evil just to do a good deed."

Robin emerged from her office in a huff. "They refuse to do anything! Sewer Sweeties never showed up for their earlier appointment, and now the next available one is in two weeks." She growled deep in her throat. "Satisfaction guaranteed or your sewage returned at no charge! Ha! I am going to file a sternly worded complaint with the UQ Chamber of Commerce."

Urmin trotted around the office and came up to sniff Robin's ankle. A wash of relief crossed her face from the horn dog's warm fuzzies. "I guess it's not so bad," she said. "I can start calling other plumbers."

Alvina followed the curious unidog down the narrow hallway. He poked his snout into the small restroom, where Sheyenne had taped a professional-looking "Out of Order" sign to the door.

"You don't want to go in there, puppy," I said.

But the critter paid no attention as he ducked inside. Faint rainbows wafted out of the room—and then I heard the startlingly unexpected sound of a toilet vigorously flushing.

Robin gasped as she hurried down the hall. "But the toilet's backed up. We can't—"

Urmin emerged from the restroom, wagging his tail, turning those big, brown eyes up at us. His little horn glowed with pearlescent light.

"The toilet is fixed!" Robin called.

Leaning over the commode, she watched sparkling clean water fill the bowl. When it was done, she pushed the flush lever again, and the water went down with a satisfying gurgle and roar. Her face filled with wonder. "It really is magic."

I patted Urmin on the back. "Good horn dog."

Urmin rolled over on the floor and bounced back up. Alvina swept him into her arms and cuddled him. Chambeaux & Deyer was back in business, and any of our clients could *do* their business without fear of bathroom retribution.

Chapter 15

y the following day, Arthur still had not gotten in touch to reclaim his horn dog, but Urmin caused us no troubles. Alvina loved having a temporary pet, and she was sad when she went off to school by herself.

Meanwhile, I turned my attention to our other most important case. Prince Dirk and RRita took their seats in the conference room, joined by me and Robin. This was a legal meeting rather than an investigative one.

Robin tapped her finger on the conference table while her magic pencil tapped its lead tip against the yellow legal pad. "Dan, can you fill us in on the status of this case?"

"I'm working very hard on it," I said, leaning back in the chair. "And I've made some progress."

"Progress?" Dirk grinned at his glistening frog lover. "Progress means moving forward, and forward is a very good direction."

"It is," RRita said. I was glad that she wasn't sobbing this time. "When can my Dirk be a handsome frog again?"

"Well, that's the disappointing part." I filled them in on my visit to the Wham-Bam Ashram and how Oorgak insisted on using only kinder, gentler magic now, refusing to cast another evil spell, no matter how beneficial it might be to others.

Now, RRita began to sob all over again, and her rounded throat belled in and out. Devastated, Prince Dirk wrapped a comforting arm around the frog demon's slimy, spotted shoulder. Using a corner of his purple cape, he dabbed away tears from her large, yellow eyes.

Beforehand, Robin had suggested more serious legal options, such as suing the evil wizard for the grievous bodily harm he had done, but Walter had seemed so centered and stable in the ashram's Zen garden that I feared we would inflict significant harm ourselves if we made him fall off the dark-magic wagon and down into the cycle of addiction again. There had to be a better solution.

I tried to reassure the clients. "Don't give up hope, you two. Zombie detectives are very persistent."

"You two obviously have a fairy-tale romance," Robin said, "but some domestic issues won't be solved by magic. No matter how much you're in love, you can't assume you'll live happily ever after." She pulled out a stack of documents. "While we're here, we have some important legal housekeeping to take care of, especially since Prince Dirk is the legitimate heir of the local royal kingdom. He is a wealthy man, and the previous king set up trust funds and money-market accounts." She withdrew a document—a credit report that Sheyenne had run.

Befuddled, Prince Dirk picked up the paper. "I knew there was a royal treasury, but I could never make heads or tails out of the checking statements."

"I'll do all the accounting in our relationship," RRita said. "I helped balance the books for my parents' pool equipment and chlorine-distribution business." She sniffled again, and more ooze trickled down her wide smooth face, but at least she was distracted by practical matters.

Robin warned, "Have you filed documentation on how Prince Dirk's fortune will be jointly accounted? Whether or not you're legally married?"

"But we're so in love!" RRita said. "Isn't that good enough?"

"Certain rights exist for a domestic partner," Robin said as her magic pencil scribbled notes on the yellow legal pad. "But everything could be challenged in court unless you have a prenup agreement or some other paperwork."

Alarmed, RRita burbled like a croaking frog. "Prenup? Prenup?"

Dirk looked like a deer in the headlights. "But, she's my frog princess."

"And he's my prince," RRita said.

"And the law is the law," Robin said. "That's why we're here. I can help you consider your options and file the proper paperwork. These matters must be resolved, regardless of how the evil wizard situation turns out, and there's no time like the present to create a domestic partnership agreement, open joint accounts that draw on the prince's royal treasury." She paused to look at Dirk. "If that's what you'd like?"

The prince looked baffled and helpless. "I'd like whatever RRita wants."

The frog demon's throat swelled and deflated in amphibious hyperventilation. "I want my frog prince back!"

"I'm working on that, I promise," I said, afraid that this would get out of hand. "There may be some dark-magic alternatives."

Robin continued to be pragmatic. "Have you considered making a will? Sometimes life is short in the Unnatural Quarter, and probate is long."

RRita sniffled. "I wanted to have Dirk help me run the family's pool-supply business. Bubo and Lubo and Son-in-Law's Aquatic Supplies. But since he's not a frog anymore, they won't accept him. They'd never let him be a part of the operation."

"In-laws take a while to come around," I said, remembering my own newlywed years. Her unpleasant parents had never liked me, and the feeling was very mutual. I had been too smitten at the time to see all the warning signs.

"Wills?" Dirk looked even more alarmed as he tried to catch up with the conversation. "Aren't those only for when we die? Like, who will wear the crown?"

"It's about the disposition of the entire royal kingdom," Robin said, glancing at both clients. "As well as the pool-supply business. Have you considered having children? Children change the entire dynamic of a relationship, and it's important to decide the inheritance and guardianship details. Your marital status will be relevant, along with your present inter-species status, though obviously we hope that will change soon."

Now RRita flashed her yellow eyes toward the prince's. "Children?"

They both looked away, embarrassed. It was quick, but I caught the unspoken exchange. This wasn't just a hypothetical question to them. Something was going on here.

Considering how sappy and romantic they acted toward each other, it didn't surprise me that they were having sex, though I didn't try to imagine the specifics. It must have been much more convenient and compatible when Dirk was in his frog form. Still, love always finds a way.

"We've talked about having children," RRita admitted. "It's very important to us."

"In fact, we've already—" Dirk began, but RRita raised a squishy-fingered hand. He clamped his mouth shut under the frog princess's spell.

"I'm not worried about that right now!" she said, flicking her tongue in and out. "We need to convince Oorgak to turn bad again, so I can have my handsome Dirk back."

"There may be an alternative solution." Robin raised her eyebrows. "Transformation can go both ways. Have you considered the opposite spell?"

I said, "Oorgak was being vindictive when he turned the prince into a frog. What if we find a way to turn RRita here into a beautiful human princess instead? That might save your relationship."

The frog demon opened her wide mouth. Her tongue flashed out and then snapped back inside in a horrified gasp.

Dirk said, "But she's already beautiful."

"And she could be human," Robin suggested.

I pressed, warming to the suggestion. "If Oorgak believed that would be a *good* deed, he might do it. In that case, you could be a beautiful couple, prince and princess, both human. And if Walter wouldn't do it, maybe I could convince the fairy godmother to work a spell or two."

Dirk draped his now slime-stained cape back over the arm of the chair. "As long as we're together, I'll be content."

RRita, though, seemed unsettled and alarmed. "That's a radical suggestion. And my parents …"

"Don't your parents want you both to be happy?" Robin asked.

I wondered if we should bring the horn dog into the meeting and let the rainbows settle everyone down.

"We'll think about it." RRita was clearly anxious to leave. "You've raised a lot of questions, Ms. Deyer, and we've got legal paperwork to consider. Do you have a brochure we could study?"

Grinning, Dirk nodded. "RRita likes to read brochures to me."

I was still trying to figure out the mood between these two. "Dirk, how would you feel about your frog demon girlfriend turning into a human princess? Would you like that?"

"I ..." the prince began, then ran out of vocabulary. He looked at RRita, then finally found his answer. "I want to do whatever makes RRita happy."

Sheyenne drifted into the room, glowing. "Then you've already found the key to a good relationship."

Chapter 16

Now that we knew unicorns were real, and we even had a horn dog in our offices, there was magic in the air. I wanted to use that rainbow connection to help our other fairy-tale client. I had high expectations for the fairy godmother.

On my previous visit to Betty Bibbity's event center and glass-slipper warehouse, I'd been trying to track down an evil wizard, but with all the chaos of setting up the bat mitzvah, the fairy godmother had been too frazzled for much conversation. I hoped the situation might be calmer now. Maybe I could convince her to work a spell of her own, wave her star-tipped magic wand and transform Prince Dirk back into a beloved frog. Failing that, perhaps she could zap RRita into a beautiful princess, although it was clear the couple preferred the former outcome.

I arrived at the front of the venue, which was quiet now that all the Jewish vampire decorations had been taken down and the banners removed. It was a blank slate for whatever shindig Betty Bibbity would run next. In the rear of the big building, delivery trucks had pulled up to the warehouse loading docks.

On the front courtyard, folding chairs were stacked in racks next to boxes of paper products—industrial napkins and nonabsorbent toilet tissue in rolls the size of barrels. A gremlin with a carpenter's toolbelt stood on a stepladder, using a wrench and screwdriver to tighten the fittings on the ornamental gazebo.

I caught his attention. "I'm looking for Betty Bibbity. Is she inside?"

The gremlin eyed me up and down. "Want to book a fresh funeral? Looks like you're a little late."

"I'm considering certain other services."

"Ah … *services,*" the gremlin said, with a knowing wink. He twisted the big wrench. "Fairy godmother isn't here right now, but go through the front office. Maybe Dava can help you out. I think she's in the warehouse."

I doubted the stylish Pegasus could cast any spells of her own, but she might have access to Betty Bibbity's appointment calendar. I opened the main entrance to the reception area, which had a desk, a conference table, and a consultation room. A bubbling fountain filled with suds popped small soap bubbles into the air, and a cloyingly sweet lilac scent wafted from an air freshener on top of the file cabinet. Against the wall, a low set of cubbyhole shelves held shiny, transparent footwear, along with a size chart and a price list.

I picked up a colorful folded brochure showing the fairy godmother and the preening flying horse. *With our help, yours will be the most talked-about event in your life or afterlife. From baptism to cremation to exorcism.*

But no one was around. I looked for a bell to ring for service. "Hello?" I called. "Zombie detective here on official business."

A half-open door led to the giant warehouse in back, from which wafted the thrum of forklift engines, the *beep-beep-beep* of backup warnings … then the crash of a heavy crate on the floor and the tinkle of broken glass, followed by angry shouts.

I pushed my way into the warehouse annex, which

reminded me of a big-box store. It was filled with endless shelves of inventory stacked with packages of crystalline footwear arranged by size, style, price, and design, each with a different SKU number. There were glass work boots, glass jogging slippers, extremely fragile pumps, and an entire children's line of glass sneakers. I was sure Alvina would love a pair for herself, but she was enough of a princess already.

The place was so huge, I couldn't even see the back of the warehouse, which extended like a maze all the way to the loading docks. A blue-collar Igor hunched over the controls of a forklift, revving the engine, as he rammed into a pallet full of sport-model glass slippers. Fairies buzzed around, identifying product numbers, pulling orders, and carrying boxes to shipping centers.

Not far from me, a plump, red-headed fairy hovered in the air on her break. She smoked a cigarette as she drifted there, bored. I tipped my fedora out of politeness. "I wonder if you could help me, ma'am?"

"Can't you see I'm on a break? Union rules."

"The fairies are in a union?" I asked.

She sucked in a long drag from her tiny cigarette and blew out impressive little rings. "They've got us on a multi-year contract, and we can't strike."

"Is there someone else who could help me?" I asked.

"I can't help you with that." The surly fairy fluttered her transparent wings and spun around, ignoring me.

I dodged another forklift driven by yet another nearsighted Igor, who didn't even notice me standing there. I walked down the lines of towering shelves until I came upon the glorious Pegasus scolding two trolls who had dropped a crate and shattered the glass footwear. "Those profits will be docked from your wages!"

"Yes, Dava," said one of the trolls.

"Thank you, Dava," said the other one.

A hardworking fairy janitorial crew swooped in with little push brooms and dustpans to clean up the shattered glass slippers from the broken crate. As the trolls looked solemn and guilty, Dava pawed the floor in frustration with her front hoof, showing off her stylish glass horseshoes.

When the flying horse noticed me, her eyes met mine beneath the gaudy, decorative crown that covered her forehead. "Are you looking for a job? Or looking for trouble?"

"I'm looking for Betty Bibbity, actually," I said, and introduced myself.

"She's not here today," said Dava. "She's filming a special segment for the HCN Charity Week. That fairy godmother's got a wickedly good heart." She huffed. "It's amazing we're still in business."

"Well, I'm looking for some magical advice, and I have a client who'll pay. I'd like to contract the fairy godmother to work a nice spell."

"Nice?" The Pegasus snorted like a cranky old mule. "That woman's got *nice* in spades!" She said it like an insult.

I nodded to her glass horseshoes. "I see you're a satisfied customer of your own line."

"Product placement," Dava said. "I have to be seen wearing these damn things, or no one will buy them." She tossed her mane. "But I am so beautiful, I draw attention wherever I go."

As I looked more closely at the Pegasus, I recognized a scar down her left flank and I remembered videos from the corrupt nightmare races I had investigated in a recent case. "Didn't you used to be a star—"

The Pegasus took offense. "I'm still a star!" She turned her gaudy crown bandanna toward me, as if to emphasize the fact.

"Of course you are," I said in a mollifying voice. "I mean a star from the nightmare races."

"There was a terrible accident caused by saboteur bats." Dava snorted again in annoyance. "I should have won that race. It ended my career at the Underground Downs." She lifted her feathered wing to look back at the scar on her flank. "And look what it's done to my perfect, luxurious hide!"

"I think it adds character," I said. "I'd call it a beauty mark."

Now Dava beamed. "I like you, Dan Shamble. I'll let Betty know you stopped by to see her."

A fairy whizzed up with a clipboard, pausing in front of the Pegasus. "We need your signature, Dava. A nose print will do."

Dava tapped her nose to the signature line of the clipboard form, and the fairy flew away.

"So much paperwork, so much nonsense, all these business routines," Dava muttered. "I remember simpler, magical times, when a fairy tale was a real fairy tale."

I commiserated. "Once upon a time."

The Pegasus looked at me. "I prefer original pretty fantasy instead of dingy, gritty urban fantasy."

"It's the Unnatural Quarter. That's my life every day," I said, even though the Magic Kingdom district had a different vibe altogether. "What do you think of genre crossovers?"

Dava snorted. "They hardly ever work."

Chapter 17

hadn't planned on spending the afternoon in the swamp, but Robin wanted me to join her at Bilge Bay, and I never let my lawyer partner down.

"Gil and Finn need us there for moral support," she said. "They've been open for early-bird customers for two days, and I think they're discouraged." Despite her tough exterior, she has a big heart and truly cares for our clients.

The unidog wagged rainbows behind us as we left the offices, making us feel content, although the warm fuzzy wore off by the time we reached the Pro Bono Mobile, our rusty Ford Maverick parked on a side street. Robin had papers to file with the court clerk immediately after our visit to Bilge Bay, so we didn't have time for a leisurely walk or shamble.

The car had once been lime green but was now leprous with rust patches. The engine still ran—or limped, depending on whether it was having a good day—but Robin had owned it for years, and we just didn't have the heart to upgrade to a flashy new company vehicle. Personally, I approved of keeping a decrepit old thing that was long past its prime and should have been put out to the junkyard or the graveyard.

Robin needed to proofread her lava monster brief on the way, so I drove. I started the engine, which seemed to be snarling at me, and shifted the Pro Bono Mobile into gear. The car was surprisingly powerful, especially with its recent tune-up and enhancements, although the muffler wasn't improved. As we drove past a small mom-and-pop convenience store, a dark-furred werewolf proprietor slapped his paws against his ears, cringing at the noise.

As she concentrated on her reading, Robin used a red pen to mark corrections. I saw that one entire paragraph was in bold letters, and that convinced me she would win her case in court.

When a trio of zombie teen slackers shuffled across the street in front of us, I blatted the horn, which didn't speed them up at all. The horn blast did, however, startle a banshee window washer, who yelped in surprise and shattered the store windowpane in front of her. One of the zombie teens flipped a finger at me, and the finger fell off. I drove on, letting him deal with his own digital experience.

Eventually, we reached Bilge Bay. The swamp resort's guest parking lot was disappointingly empty, so I pulled the car right up to the first spot next to the gate. Robin closed her folder and tucked the edited brief back into her case. "That was helpful, Dan. Now I'm ready for my court challenge after we check on Gil and Finn." We climbed out of the sagging Ford Maverick, and the engine sighed at us in dis–appointment.

Fresh signs at the gate announced "Grand Opening," "Early Bird Special," and "Slimy Fun for All Ages and Species." That was just hyperbole, though. All species? I couldn't imagine dry old mummies would enjoy the saunas or hot pools.

The ticket kiosk was empty. "Gil and Finn need to hire some other employees," I said as we walked right in.

"They're under tight budget constraints," Robin said,

shaking her head. "I've seen their financial sheets, and it's not good."

Bright Caribbean music emanated from speakers hidden inside the mangrove trunks and up in the tangles of Spanish moss. The duckweed-covered spawning pools were undisturbed, and the lazy river was quiet. "Not much of an early bird extravaganza," I observed.

"They sent out coupons, but the response is disappointing," Robin said. "They're still having trouble with trespassers and vandals, and I think rumors have spread."

At the one open massage cabana, a forlorn tentacled creature stood in a loose calypso shirt behind an empty table. He raised a hopeful tentacle. "Massage, ma'am? Massage, sir? I've got magic fingers." He twiddled his numerous tentacles.

"Tempting," I said. "But not today, thanks. We're here to see the managers."

There was activity in the picnic pavilion up ahead, and I smelled pungent smoke from charcoal briquettes at barbecue grills. A dozen tall, shaggy figures hung out together, chatting as they opened up packs of hot dog and burger buns and set out Jell-O salad, while two males monitored the meat on the grill. A poster announced it was the "Bigfoot Recognition Society Annual Mixer."

A Bayou Bigfoot ran and dove into one of the duckweed-covered pools with a loud bellow followed by a splash. Two other tall, hairy creatures swam along the lazy river, though I hadn't noticed them before.

Before I could pay much attention to the Bigfoot picnic, the two lagoon-creature proprietors walked up to us, clearly agitated. They frowned with their big fish lips, showing needle-sharp teeth.

"Ms. Deyer, Mr. Chambeaux," Gil said. "Thank you for checking on us."

"We were hoping for bigger crowds." Finn gestured toward a nearby shaved-ice stand with sample cones propped up on the counter, all of them melting in the humid heat. Mosquitoes buzzed around.

I tried to sound hopeful. "Maybe it's just a slow time of day."

"Every day's been a slow day, even with our coupons." Gil flexed his webbed hands. "Who doesn't want a free muck massage?"

"It's not my sort of thing," Robin said, "but I'm sure others would enjoy it. We'll try to spread the word."

"Who could resist a miasma like this?" I asked.

"You need to spread the word fast," Gil said in despair. "There's nobody here! We're losing our shirts."

In the picnic area, one of the Bigfeet called out from the charcoal grill, "Burgers are ready. Come and eat!" In the lazy river, two other Bigfeet splashed around as a third one fumbled blindly toward them with his eyes closed, waving about and yelling, "Marco!" The other Bigfeet responded, "Polo!"

I ignored them. "So you haven't had any customers all day?"

"Not enough to pay the bills," Finn said. "This is going to be a disaster. Our investors will be very upset."

"Maybe they need a muck massage to relax," I suggested.

"Who brought the potato salad?" called a shrill-voiced Sasquatch woman.

I glanced up again and realized I had forgotten that the hairy group was there. I pointed toward them. "Wait, isn't that a group of Bigfeet? They're customers, aren't they?"

The lagoon creatures blinked their fishy eyes at each other, then turned to the picnic pavilion, puzzled. "Oh, yeah. I forgot they were coming today. They're so quiet, nobody notices them."

"Did they at least pay a deposit?" Robin asked.

"I … think so."

"I hope they clean up after themselves," Finn said.

The Bigfoot Recognition Society had brought coolers filled with liter bottles of soda. They got rowdy as the picnic went on, but I lost focus and turned back to the real problem. "Have you considered advertising? Television commercials? Billboards? Newspaper flyers?"

"We took out radio ads," Gil said, "but no one listens to commercial radio anymore."

"And we do have a spot coming up on the Home Capitalism Network," Finn said. "But we've lost so much money already, we don't have an advertising budget left."

I drew upon my great commercial wisdom. "You've got to spend money to make money."

Gil countered, "But you need to have money to spend money to make money."

"That is a good first step," I admitted.

"Has the illegal dumping calmed down?" Robin asked. "There are stern prohibition signs on the drainage canal, and the neighborhood swamp watch has been alerted."

"We still get trespassers," Gil said with a burbly sigh. "But at least that means somebody's coming to Bilge Bay."

Robin and I did our best to cheer up the lagoon creatures, but Gil and Finn would have to sink or swim on their own. Having made our dutiful appearance, we said our goodbyes and headed back toward the exit. As we passed the picnic pavilion, one of the Bigfeet offered me a hot dog fresh off the grill, but I wasn't hungry. Their entire social mixer had slipped my mind somehow.

Distracted, Robin said to the hairy guy, "I'm glad your

group is here patronizing Bilge Bay. It's good to build up the customer base."

The Bigfoot lifted his grill tongs in a salute. "It's a nice place. We like it really quiet, where everyone leaves us alone."

Robin and I had already forgotten about them by the time we got back to the Pro Bono Mobile in the empty parking lot.

Chapter 18

When RRita and Prince Dirk barged into our offices, they were both so panicked that even Urmin's rainbow fuzzies could not calm them down. The frog demon wailed, moaned, and sobbed—but we were used to that by now. This time, though, even the handsome prince was crying his eyes out.

"Help us, please!" Dirk clutched his amphibious lover's hand.

"Please do something!" RRita wailed. "It's an emergency!"

Robin dashed out of her office. "What is it? What can we do?"

A glob of the frog demon's tears dropped on the carpet, and the horn dog came up to give it a sniff.

"Our babies!" RRita wailed. "They've been kidnapped!"

Dirk swallowed hard. "Our precious children have been stolen. All of them!"

"That's terrible!" Sheyenne gasped, grabbing the phone to call the UQPD.

"You have children?" I asked.

Being a lawyer, Robin asked a follow-up. "All of them? Children as in plural, meaning more than one?"

Also agitated, Urmin barked, and musical notes filled the air of the office.

In her abject misery, RRita flicked her tongue in and out. "Of course it's more than one! It's an entire clutch of eggs!"

I looked at Dirk for further explanation. "Eggs?"

The prince looked away, embarrassed as well as befuddled. "That was our dark secret."

"But we were in love!" RRita continued weeping.

Dirk squared his shoulders. "We are still in love, despite the tribulations, my dear, and don't you forget it!"

Robin got her legal pad. "We need more information before we can determine our next steps forward."

"I think we need *all* the information," I added. "I don't know what's going on."

Sheyenne returned from the kitchenette with a glass of water for each of them. RRita poured it over her head to remoisten her protective slime coating. To show his support, Prince Dirk dumped his glass of water on her head as well.

"You didn't say anything about children," I said, trying to sound stern. "If we're going to work on your case, we need to know important details like that."

"They hadn't hatched yet," RRita said. "We kept it a secret from my parents."

Dirk placed a hand on her spotted shoulder. "I am proud to have a family with you, my love. They would have been royal tadpoles."

I eyed the handsome human prince and questioned my understanding of biology.

"Now you know why Dirk *has* to turn back into a frog," RRita said. "What kind of father would he make looking like ... that?"

"We're supposed to live happily ever after," the prince said. "But RRita's parents were always skeptical of our relationship, so we tried to be careful. But, uh, we weren't careful enough, and I didn't really understand amphibious birth control."

Robin nodded, taking in all the information. "And RRita got pregnant."

Dirk's pale skin flushed a bright pink. "Well, I accidentally fertilized the clutch of eggs."

"And now they're about to become tadpoles," RRita said. "Our tadpoles. Our children!"

I suddenly understood why these two had looked so uneasy when we suggested transforming RRita into a human princess. If the two were going to be parents, a human prince and princess would have trouble managing a swarm of unruly tadpoles.

"My parents already didn't approve of us," RRita said. "And with this, they might even kick me entirely out of the pool-supply business."

Sheyenne glowed with empathy. "You might be surprised at how understanding parents can be when it comes to the welfare of their own precious daughter."

Remembering the big, colorful portraits of Bubo and Lubo from the pool-supply billboards, I realized I wouldn't want either of them angry at me.

Dirk hung his head and groaned. "Apparently even a royal prince isn't good enough for their daughter."

Urmin barked again, but the glimmer of rainbows faded without resolving the romantic distress.

I crossed my arms over my chest. "Okay, let's focus on the current crisis rather than the soap-opera aspects of the case. It doesn't matter whether they're tadpoles or human babies— the children are missing? What happened to them?"

"They've been kidnapped!" RRita said. "Our entire clutch of eggs. Stolen! Seized by truly evil people!"

"Anyone who would steal someone else's tadpoles is definitely evil," I agreed.

"Tell us what happened," Robin said. "We'll get to the bottom of this."

"They weren't at the bottom," Dirk said. "They were floating on top, the entire clutch of fertilized eggs. Sooner or later, they would have turned into cute little tadpoles as soon as they hatched."

"We were going to be proud parents, but now ..." RRita sniffled, then belled out her throat in an agonized sob.

Dirk said, "We searched all over the Quarter to find a perfect secret love nest, a place for our romantic trysts."

RRita interrupted him. "And also a place to raise a family, just the right environment. We wanted to make sure the babies were safe. And then, once Dirk was turned back into a ... a horrible prince, we were distracted."

The prince protectively draped the purple cape over her shoulders. "When we went to check on the eggs, they were gone!"

Though she already knew the outcome of the story, Sheyenne still gasped. For a cold ghost, she's very warm and sensitive.

"Are you sure you didn't just misplace them?" I asked. "Maybe you forgot exactly where you hid the clutch?"

"It was our nursery!" RRita said.

Dirk nodded. "We even decorated it in pink and blue, because statistically, our tadpoles are gender-neutral when they hatch, but they acquire sex as they mature." He nodded. "I read up on Wikipedia!"

I resolved to do the right thing. "I'm a detective, and I'm good at finding lost things. I'll track down where your children have gone. Where did you last see your eggs? Where should I start looking?"

"It was a perfect place," RRita insisted. "Moist, green, slimy, swampy."

"And a good school district, too," Dirk said. "Or so I hear."

I suddenly had an unsettled feeling. Robin shot me a glance even before RRita blurted out, "We hid all our eggs at the new Bilge Bay resort and spa! And somebody took them."

CHAPTER 19

What had been an enchanting case of a star-crossed romance was now an ugly custody battle.

The clutch of eggs remained at the troubled resort, "for safe keeping," and Gil and Finn insisted they would remain safe, as a bargaining chip, if nothing else. RRita and Dirk were also worried about moving their imminent children from the perfect incubator environment at such a delicate time, and they begged us not to call the police.

So, we had to work out a deal, somehow.

Since the Bilge Bay proprietors and presumed tadpole nappers were also clients of ours, Sheyenne simply assumed that everyone would do the right thing. My ghost girlfriend is adorable, but also naive. In custody battles, people often become irrational and rarely take the best interests of poor innocent tadpoles into account.

Such negotiations were Robin's bailiwick, though, and she assured the distraught prince and frog princess that the lagoon creatures would not harm their beloved tadpoles. I knew she would be able to work out a decent resolution.

In the meantime, I wanted to wrap up our other odd custody case—Urmin the horn dog—but I couldn't return him to his owner. Arthur had not contacted us again, and we had no idea how to find him (or any unicorn, for that matter). The majestic mythical creature had been so concerned about his missing pet that I figured he would call us daily. (I didn't worry about how a unicorn with hooves could use a cell phone.)

When Alvina came home from school, she threw herself upon Urmin, who barked and frolicked and wagged his entire body. The vampire girl rubbed the critter's belly and polished his horn, which sent sparkles into the air. I knew she was secretly hoping that Arthur took a long time to call back, so she could keep the horn dog.

In the near term, however, we had more practical unidog concerns since we didn't know what to feed the critter. I presumed the knowledgeable experts on mythical pets had taken care of Urmin at the animal shelter, and after Alice the dragon adopted him, surely she had fed her gambling-support animal. But now that we had the cute horn dog, none of us knew what he liked to eat. Sheyenne and Alvina had picked up a bag of monster chow at Barney and Clyde's unnatural grocers, but Urmin just turned up his nose at the disappointing brown kibble.

Alvina took him on regular walks, skipping down the sidewalk. Urmin left rainbow-scented little poops, which Alvina picked up in a plastic bag, so we knew his digestive system was still working. But he hadn't eaten in more than a day, and we were growing concerned. We didn't want Urmin to be starving when Arthur finally showed up to reclaim his magical pet.

Sheyenne had researched unidogs and canicorns, collecting cross-cultural references and folklore. In myth and legend, the horny little creatures were fantastical familiars, reservoirs of a special kind of magic. Some online encyclopedia entries even suggested that the horned pets were like batteries, serving as the true source of unicorn powers. Despite all of her research, as well as Alvina's wicked internet skills, we still had no idea what to feed the guy.

Then Alvina came to me, bouncing with excitement. "It's so obvious! What else would you feed horn dogs? *Corn dogs,* of course!"

"Corn dogs?" I already felt queasy. That was definitely an unnatural food group.

Urmin yipped and barked in agreement.

I looked at Sheyenne, and we both shrugged.

Since we don't normally keep corn dogs in the office freezerette, Sheyenne whisked off to the grocery store to pick up a trial pack while I stayed behind with Alvina and the unidog.

In order to keep both kid and puppy occupied, I decided to earn some brownie points with our building superintendent. We trotted down the hall, where Renfeld's apartment door stood half open. The fetid odors of the ghoul's cooking, or his decomposition, wafted out into the office building.

"Hey, Renfeld," I asked, "could we take our magical unidog down to the basement abode? The one where the previous tenant left a curse?"

The ghoul looked at me with his slack face, trying to understand. "Do you still need to use the bathroom, Shamble? I thought you got yours fixed."

"I'm doing a public service," I said. "This cute little unidog might be able to get rid of that bathroom curse with a wag of his tail and a rainbow or two."

Renfeld handed me the key. "Be my guest." Urmin barked at him, which brought a foolish grin to the ghoul's gray face.

Down in the dank vacant unit, I smelled cobwebs and disappointment wrapped up into a snarky vendetta. This office had been a temporary IRS auditing office, and it still held an unpleasant stink of tax accountants. When Renfeld had kicked them out for nonpayment of rent—which seemed odd for stickler auditors—they had left behind a threatening notice, as well as a curse on the bathroom facilities. Now, spectral gloom roiled around the atmosphere, strongest near the unit's restroom.

Urmin sensed the curse, too, but felt no threat. Instead, he trotted ahead into the bathroom, with Alvina trotting after him. The cheerful unidog wagged his tail, and like an excessive burst of spring-rain air freshener, the IRS curse dissolved into nothing. The air lightened, and the sink and toilet were restored to the same clean purity I would expect from any public restroom.

"Mission accomplished," Alvina said.

When I returned the key to Renfeld and reported our success, he offered to scoop up an extra bowl of his simmering stewed flesh so I could join him for dinner. "It's been seasoning in the composter for four days."

I declined, though, with the bright reassurance that I would soon have corn dogs waiting for me up in the office. Renfeld's eyes lit up at the suggestion, but we departed before he could invite himself to join us.

Sheyenne was already in the kitchenette, opening packages and placing corn dogs in the toaster oven. "These were on special—a new brand of Mystery Meat corn dogs."

"Mystery Meat keeps expanding their product lines," I said, though I had no interest in eating them. From a previous case, I knew what Mystery Meat was made of.… Then again, I had a general idea of what real hot dogs were made of, too, and it wasn't any more appetizing.

Sheyenne heated up two corn dogs apiece for Alvina and for Urmin. The vampire girl sat cross-legged on the floor under the small table. When she offered a corn dog to the horn dog, he gobbled the entire thing right off the stick. Alvina savored her own unhealthy treat, twirling the stick until she finished every bite. Then each of them ate seconds.

"That's one problem solved," I said, relieved. "Now if only we can find Arthur ..."

Because it was getting late and Alvina had school the next morning, we sent her upstairs to bed, where Urmin would curl up with her in the air-conditioner box she used as a cardboard coffin. After Sheyenne and I read her a quiet and comforting tale of cosmic horror from *Lovecraft's Big Book of Bedtime Stories*, we tucked her in.

I decided to rest for a while, which meant that I stood quietly in a dark corner and loomed relaxingly. Even as I dozed like a character from Poe's "Premature Burial," I had warm dreams of sweetness and light, giggles and rainbows. I saw unicorns and fairy dust in my imagination. I felt the warmth of magic spells, blooming flowers, pixies, and starshine. I awoke grinning, but still feeling oddly unsettled.

Alvina also had a wonderful night's sleep, and she was in a great mood as we gathered the next morning. I served her a bowl of her favorite Unlucky Charms cereal, where the artificial dye turned the milk in the bowl a bright arterial red. She was sad to leave Urmin behind for the day, but we reassured her and sent her off to Nosferatu Academy with her unicorn backpack.

Before I could start work on my cases, though, I received a phone call from McGoo. A very grim phone call. "Shamble, I need you here right away! It's a crime scene."

I was instantly alert. "I'll be there, McGoo. What is it?"

He gave me the address of a vacant lot. "We found your unicorn early this morning. He's been murdered."

Chapter 20

fficer Toby McGoohan has been with the Unnatural Quarter Police Department for as long as I've been a P.I., but he'd never before had a dead unicorn on his hands. The procedures manual did not give him any specific guidance. He looked more befuddled than usual when I arrived.

The vacant lot had once been a drive-up VHS rental store, which folded when videotapes went out of fashion and when schlock horror films seemed too similar to daily life. The original building had been torn down, but incomprehensible city ordinances had prevented any new business from opening up there. Dry thistles poked up through the cracked asphalt, and tumbleweeds bounced against a sagging chain-link fence.

The site was surrounded by squad cars with flashing red and blue lights. Gremlin evidence techs unrolled yellow crime-scene tape, decoratively festooning the fence poles and a dead tree in the corner.

I flashed my private investigator's badge as I pushed my way forward. If I hadn't already been undead, my heart would have stopped at the sight.

A majestic white unicorn was sprawled on the cracked asphalt in a pool of blood. His silvery mane was matted. His head was cocked up, and his tongue lolled out of a partly open mouth. The knurled horn pointed impotently toward one of the nearby tumbleweeds. One foreleg was raised, as if the unicorn had reared up trying to defend himself. A deep red wound in his pristine white side showed where the mythical creature had been stabbed through the heart.

Squatting beside the body, McGoo looked up at me. "He never had a chance, Shamble. One strike, deep—clearly a mortal wound."

I bent down next to my best human friend. "His name is Arthur. He's a client of mine."

"*Was* a client," McGoo said. "Looks like he should have worn a tactical-armor saddle."

The gremlin evidence techs had used playground chalk to mark a bold outline around the dead unicorn.

I removed my fedora out of respect and sadly shook my head. "Alvina is going to be devastated. He was magical." My eyes were stinging. I couldn't believe such a thing could have happened. Not too long ago, I didn't believe that unicorns even existed. "Who found him?" My voice was rough and hoarse.

"I got a call late at night about barking dogs near the edge of the Magic Kingdom district," McGoo said.

"A noise complaint?"

"Not a complaint. In fact, the caller said the barking was soothing—but it was unusual. I came out here to investigate, and something caught my eye over at the old VHS store. That's where I found the victim."

The evidence techs scurried about, pulling out big cameras to take crime scene photographs, as well as selfies with the murdered unicorn. I felt a pang, remembering that Arthur hadn't allowed Alvina to take a picture.

I pulled out my phone and snapped a quick shot for our own records. If nothing else, we could show it to Alvina's obnoxious teacher as proof of unicorns, although Miss

Nifflesmoth would probably double down because the photo showed only a *dead* unicorn. I decided that gruesome crime scene photographs were not appropriate for a class report anyway.

"You better tell me all you have, Shamble," McGoo said. "This is no longer just a cute little fable. It's a murder investigation."

"Well, Arthur is the owner of the horn dog you brought in. He hired us to find the critter—which we did. But once we reclaimed Urmin, we had no way to contact Arthur, because he wouldn't leave his phone number. We've been waiting to hear from him." I shook my head. "I can give you a copy of our client intake form, but most of the lines are blank. Arthur was a very private unicorn."

"That's peculiar. Do you think he was in the unicorn protection program?"

"Is there such a thing?" That would explain many of the missing details.

"Such things are above my pay grade, Shamble."

I bent down to trace my fingers on the white hide, but I felt no lingering magic there, no answers popping up. "Arthur didn't want anyone to know where he was or who he was."

"Unicorn killers feel the same way, apparently," McGoo said. "There's no evidence at the scene."

A crowd had begun to gather outside the chain-link fence. An elderly vampire held up his frequent-customer punch card from the old VHS rental shop, as if that would give him crime-scene access. Police officers shooed the spectators away, but the unnaturals were very persistent and curious. I even spotted a tall Bigfoot using his camera to take pictures as proof of the strange dead cryptid.

As McGoo stood, he let out a groan from his stiff joints.

"We'll have to do an autopsy on the unicorn. I've already let the coroner know."

A UQPD motorcycle cop rolled up, escorting the ramshackle coroner's wagon, which doubled as a glue-factory truck. The evidence techs hurried over to join their morgue counterparts, and the furry creatures scurried into the vacant lot, circling the dead unicorn, taking notes, pulling out tape measures, and jotting down numbers. They swung open the back of the dead-meat wagon, removing a stretcher that was obviously too small, then a black body bag that wouldn't fit, and finally a tarpaulin with ropes. Two of them hooked chains through grommets in the corners of the tarp, then operated a power winch.

I'd seen enough. The stakes had just gotten higher, and I was more determined than ever to solve this crime.

Chapter 21

Sensing the terrible fate that had befallen his master, Urmin was more clouds than rainbows, and he sulked under Sheyenne's desk.

Still shaken by the murdered unicorn, I had to concentrate on another crisis in the office. Tension in the conference room was as thick as a swamp and smelled just as rank, the fishy tang of a clash between opposing aquatic parties. The lagoon creatures had come to face off against Prince Dirk and RRita. If anybody could find an amicable resolution, Robin Deyer could. I felt nothing amicable in the air, but I was there for moral support.

The lagoon creatures were in high dudgeon over the continued illegal dumping and vandalism that plagued Bilge Bay, but they were taking out their anger on RRita and Dirk, who were understandably upset themselves.

"We won't do it!" Gil flapped his gill slits in frustration.

"We've been through enough!" In frustration, Finn scratched the armored laminate of the conference room table with his hooked claws.

"You stole our babies!" the frog demon wailed.

"You're kidnappers!" Prince Dirk pounded his fist on the table. "And that's against the law in my royal kingdom."

"Bilge Bay is outside of your royal kingdom," Gil said. "Your princely decrees have no jurisdiction over us."

"I can call in the UQPD any time," I said. "I know people over there."

Dirk flushed. "I'd rather do it by royal decree. Wouldn't that work better?"

RRita belled her throat out as if pumping up a balloon, then she blurted out, "You're tadpole molesters!"

The lagoon creatures took great offense, rising up from their moist chairs.

Robin interrupted in a calm but firm voice. "Let's just take this down a notch."

Sheyenne entered the room, wearing a forced smile and a bright poltergeist glow. In her ectoplasmic hand, she carried a tray with a pitcher of ice water and glasses. "Here are some refreshments, so everyone can cool off."

I said, "I know you're all good creatures of various sorts, and I know you want to do the right thing."

The lagoon creatures looked at each other and blinked their fish eyes. "The right thing is for them to pay a massive fine to compensate for their crimes," Finn said.

"Dirk and I are just trying to have a family," RRita sobbed, "and the whole world is trying to stop us."

The prince put his arm around her slimy shoulders, rocking her back and forth. "Love will conquer all, my dear. My minstrels sing that all the time."

"This isn't a minstrel song." RRita flicked her long tongue while glaring at the scaled lagoon creatures. "This is reality."

As they argued, my mind churned. I couldn't stop thinking about the dead unicorn. Who would want to murder Arthur? I had given McGoo all available information for his police investigation, but I would continue my detective work as well. I feared that we had a unicorn serial killer on our hands, although that would require the existence of more than one unicorn.

I steeled myself and turned my attention back to the bickering at hand. The tragic case of the seized frog demon eggs took priority now.

Robin spread paperwork on the table and scanned the notes written on the yellow legal pad. "You have all expressed valid concerns, and I'm sure each party believes they have a legal leg to stand on."

"My leg is stronger," Gil said.

"And I can jump higher," RRita countered.

"It's not a competition," I said.

All four clients glared at one another across the table.

Robin said, "RRita and Dirk, you clearly violated the private property of Bilge Bay, and you left your eggs where they didn't belong."

"We have 'No Trespassing' signs everywhere!" Finn said. "Can't you read with those big eyes?"

"*You've* got big eyes!" Prince Dirk snapped, demonstrating his royal powers of diplomacy.

"We needed a place for our babies," RRita said. "The environment is perfect, and it's not right that you keep it all for … hedonistic customers."

"What customers?" Gil asked with a sad undertone.

"It goes against the laws of nature," said the human prince, who had fertilized the eggs of an amphibious female.

"Other laws take precedence," Robin said, then turned to the lagoon creatures. "Gil and Finn, you snatched this couple's children. They don't belong to you."

"Not cool," I added.

"Our resort keeps being vandalized by hooligans just like these two. Having sex, spawning outside of the designated spawning pools!" Gil's gills were upright with indignation.

Finn said, "And you didn't even pay for admission! You snuck in through the back fence."

RRita rested her round, smooth head on Dirk's purple-caped shoulder. "We didn't want anyone to know …"

"There's nothing to be ashamed of, my love," Dirk said.

Gil continued, "We're going to be ruined by all the trash and magical debris just being dumped." He shook his hideous head. "Fortunately, someone bought that contaminated spellbook and a few magical artifacts at our rummage sale, but who knows what kind of stain they left in our beautiful resort? What if someone gets a rash?"

Robin cut him off. "We aren't here to discuss the discarded magical garbage. These two are not responsible for that. Let's focus in on the clutch of eggs. I'm sure RRita and Dirk would issue a sincere apology."

"Not good enough," Gil said.

"They have to pay damages! Restitution!" Finn cried. "And a lot of money. He is a prince, after all. Have him open the royal treasury." Both lagoon creatures crossed their scaly arms over their scaly chests. "That'll keep Bilge Bay afloat a little bit longer."

I glanced at the handsome prince, then at Robin. "He does have a royal treasury …"

Dirk lifted his chin, highlighting the strong royal jawline. "I will spare no expense to keep my beloved RRita happy."

"We have a slight problem." Robin shuffled through the papers in front of her. "Because of Prince Dirk's transformation into a frog, and now his transformation back, the bank placed a hold on his basic checking account. They've frozen his money markets because his ID on file no longer matches his frog facial features."

"RRita had me take a new photo when I was a frog. I changed all the change-of-appearance papers," Dirk said. "But I'm human again."

"We'll refile for your change of physical appearance."

Robin slid copies over to Dirk, who gave them a bewildered look. "But it could take weeks to get everything resolved. It has to go through the DMV."

That made RRita even more upset. "But we're trying to get him turned back into a frog so we can have our family together! I don't want to change his ID."

"Then I'll file an amendment," Robin said. "But that will take even more time."

"All our eggs will hatch before then! We'll miss the most important years with our baby tadpoles. They could metamorphose into frog nymphs by the time we get them back."

"You shouldn't have put the eggs on our property in the first place," Gil hissed. He turned defiantly toward Robin. "You told us explicitly that anything trespassers left on Bilge Bay property was ours to keep, the right of salvage."

"I did say that," Robin admitted. "But my opinion applied to inanimate objects."

"They were just eggs," Gil said. "And they seemed pretty inanimate to me."

"We should fry 'em up," Finn suggested.

RRita shrieked.

I said, "They're not that kind of eggs."

"Then we'll serve them as caviar," Gil said. "Hold a swanky fundraiser to raise money for Bilge Bay." The lagoon creatures looked at each other and nodded at the brilliant idea.

"No one will eat them, or fry them, or harm them in any way," Robin scolded, then turned to the frog and her prince. "Thanks to several lawsuits filed by mad scientists, ownership of unnatural embryos is in a contested state. Experimental laboratories can be designated as nurseries under certain conditions. Abandonment of your eggs on private property, especially with the clear and threatening 'No Trespassing' signs, will not look good for you." She pursed her lips. "I can take your case to the courts, and I will win, but it will take months."

"They're going to hatch any day now!" RRita wailed.

Gil and Finn lurched up out of their seats. "We're not giving them back. Those tadpoles are ours now—unless you figure out a way to pay restitution."

The prince blinked in astonishment. "But what are you going to do with our cute little babies in the meantime?"

"Put them to work at the Bilge Bay concession stands!" Finn and Gil stomped off, flopping their flippered feet on the floor.

CHAPTER 22

After such a long and terrible day, I needed to blow off steam and down a pint or two at the Goblin Tavern. I always feel better sitting on the bar stool next to my best human friend and watching other monsters drink themselves into oblivion.

When I came in that evening, McGoo was already halfway finished with his first beer. I set my fedora on the bar as I lifted my stiff leg and climbed onto my usual seat.

McGoo was clearly having a bad day, too. A murdered unicorn would take the rainbows out of anyone's sunny disposition. "Hey, Shamble."

"Hey, McGoo." I raised two fingers to Francine, the hard-bitten human bartender. A lifetime of cigarette smoking made her face look like old leather, but there was nothing vintage about it.

Francine had already started filling my beer. The Goblin Tavern was familiar territory, and I felt like an appreciated patron rather than a hardened alcoholic. Since I had embalming fluid in my veins and a nonfunctional liver, I could drink as many beers as I liked, strictly as a social endeavor, without getting buzzed. As a zombie, I didn't need alcohol to make myself lurch and stagger about.

"You know how vampire investors get rich, Shamble?" McGoo asked, barely pausing for a reply. "From crypt-o-currency!"

"You're not making my day any better, McGoo," I replied, but it was nice to have some normalcy. "Any luck finding the unicorn murderer?"

"I'm surprised we found a unicorn at all," he said. "We combed the scene carefully, but there were no clues. The evidence techs secured some gravel and tumbleweeds, looking for fibers or fingerprints, but so far nothing."

"Did you check for hoofprints?" I asked. "The killer could have been another unicorn."

"What other unicorn? If we ever *find* another unicorn, he'll be the prime suspect," McGoo said. "But Arthur is the only one ever documented."

I took a long drink of my beer and glanced to my left, startled to find a big hairy figure already sitting on the stool next to me—a tall, shaggy Sasquatch with his elbows resting on the bar surface. He waved for Francine, but she continued washing glasses, then wiping down an empty section opposite us. She didn't notice him.

Deciding to help the Bigfoot, I called out, "Francine, you've got a customer here."

She came over to me, questioning. After a moment, she spotted the Sasquatch. "Sorry, didn't see you there. What can I get you?"

"A rum and Coke," he said. "No, make that a Diet Coke."

"Coming right up." Francine turned back to the bar, filled a highball glass, and poured two shots of well rum. She paused, as if trying to remember what she'd been doing, glanced up at me. I pointed to the Bigfoot next to me, and she blinked. "Right." She finished filling the glass with Diet Coke and handed it to him.

"Who's your new friend, Shamble?" McGoo asked. "When did he come in?"

"I don't think we've met." I turned to the creature and hesitated. "Or have we?"

The Bigfoot extended a huge, hairy hand. "Philip. I come in here often."

I had an idea. "Hey, you might be able to offer some insight into a conversation we're having."

"I certainly have my opinions," said Philip.

"They're like assholes," McGoo said.

The Sasquatch's brown fur ruffled. "Are you calling me an asshole?"

McGoo sipped his beer and didn't respond. He probably hadn't heard Philip.

I tried to remember what I'd been thinking of, then snapped my stiff fingers. "So, Philip, what are your thoughts on mythical creatures and cryptids? Until a few days ago, we weren't sure unicorns existed, and now we have a dead one on our hands."

"Ah, cryptids!" The Bigfoot had a rich, resonant voice. "Strange, mysterious creatures lurking about—but many people don't notice what's right in front of their eyes."

"It's rather hard to miss a unicorn," I said. "Prancing about and sticking its horn up in the air, shedding rainbows all over the place."

"People really aren't very observant," Philip said. "They often don't see things that are plain as day."

McGoo watched Francine stir up a mojito for a chupacabra who took a seat at the far end of the bar. "The Big Uneasy made everything possible," he observed. "The human imagination can come up with anything." He drank from his beer again, then belched. "I've seen some batshit crazy stuff that goes beyond imagining."

"Me, too." Our Bigfoot friend raised his rum and Diet Coke, sipping from the little red drink straw. "Cryptids are underappreciated, even in the Unnatural Quarter. Take Bigfeet, for instance. You might think you know everything about us—tall, hairy forest creatures skulking about, rarely seen. But we're pervasive in human culture. Think of the Yeti or the Abominable Snowman up in the Himalayas, or the Bayou Apes down in Louisiana. We're called Sasquatches or Bigfoots, though we prefer Bigfeet as the plural. Our species just hasn't warranted much study, though we leave footprints and droppings all over the place."

Philip slurped more of his drink, then rattled the ice cubes at the bottom of the highball glass. "My people have been using public restroom facilities more often now, though."

"Interesting," I said, but I wasn't really paying attention. I turned to McGoo. "You're due to watch Alvina for the next couple of nights. She usually looks forward to staying with you, but her heart's been broken because of Arthur."

"I like having Al stay with me," McGoo said. "I even wash the sheets in her cardboard box. But if you think she'd rather stay with you and take care of the horn dog ...? She might feel better."

"We can ask her," I said. "Sheyenne is doing deep searches to find if Arthur had an established will. We don't know who Urmin legally belongs to. Robin thinks Arthur's entire estate might have been left to his pet."

"What kind of an estate can a unicorn have?" McGoo asked.

I just shrugged and sipped my beer, staring ahead in deep thought.

The Bigfoot finished his rum and Diet Coke and stood up from the barstool. He waved to get Francine's attention. "Thanks! Let me get the beers for my two friends here." He pulled out a couple of twenties and laid them on the bar.

Francine took his empty glass and snatched up the bills, putting them into the cash register.

The Bigfoot left, but no one turned their heads as he passed.

McGoo and I sat in comfortable silence for a few moments, then I looked at him. I glanced at the empty barstool to my left, trying to remember who had been there. "What were we talking about again?"

"We never talk about much of anything, Shamble," he said.

I finished my beer and turned to go. In the back of my mind, I thought I remembered that someone had paid our tab, but McGoo just laughed when I asked. "You're trying to pull a fast one!"

Francine came over, her brow furrowed in concentration. "I would remember if somebody paid for you, Shamble!"

I picked up my fedora and tapped the middle of my forehead. "My memory hasn't been the same since I got this big hole in my skull."

Francine took my pint glass and wiped down the bar, as well as the empty spot next to me.

McGoo stayed. "I'm having another one, so I can continue my detective work."

Chapter 23

This was not my first autopsy, but it was my first one with a unicorn. These things never get easier.

McGoo had invited me to join him at the coroner's lab, and I felt an obligation because Arthur had been my client. I couldn't forget the white unicorn's glorious presence in our offices, and I wish we had seen more of him. But now, as I saw the mythical beast spread out on the slab, I hoped he had gone to someplace better, somewhere over the rainbow. McGoo and I shared a grim glance as we stood together, paying our respects and doing our duty.

The coroner's operating theater was kept extremely cold, which was the preference of the UQ's new coroner, a looming necromancer named Durgolon. My skin was always gray and numb, so the cold didn't bother me. McGoo hunched his shoulders in his blue patrolman's uniform and exhaled a curl of white steam as he sipped from a Styrofoam cup of bad coffee.

Durgolon wore a surgeon's gown over his embroidered black velvet robe. He sported an unstylish black hat contraption that looked like it had been rejected from a Catholic Church fashion show. The necromancer's large hands and long arms gave him a scarecrowish appearance, as if someone had stretched his arms, legs, and chin during his formative years.

He paced slowly around the autopsy table, circling the

dead unicorn like a vulture considering his next meal. "A very interesting specimen." His long face held a studious expression. Next to his dissection implements was a thick coroner's tome with stained and yellowed pages. With a vigorous snap, Durgolon pulled on a pair of latex rubber gloves, then used the extra traction on his fingertips to page through the tome. "Scanty information on unicorn baseline data in my coroner's handbook." He flipped to the index in back, scanned down the listing of topics, then turned to another page. "Unicorns … Ah—see Alicorns for a more comprehensive study." He paged to the front section of the book.

"What are alicorns?" I asked.

McGoo looked at me, relieved that I had asked the question, so he didn't have to appear ignorant.

"Unicorns are pretty basic mythical creatures," the coroner said. "Alicorns are far more advanced fairy tales. Winged unicorns. Frequently evil, though."

He set the book aside and mounted a transparent splatter shield in front of his piercing golden eyes. He ran his palms over the white unicorn's hide, studying the spine and shoulder blades. "I see no evidence of wings, however, so I conclude that this specimen is not an alicorn."

"I could have told you that," I muttered. "Arthur was just your basic unicorn."

"Yes," Durgolon said. "Otherwise known as the common unicorn."

McGoo snorted, making more white steam curl out of his nose. "If unicorns were common, our little girl wouldn't have failed her school report."

"We shall take measurements and do what we can for science and for the art of necromancy," said the coroner.

He took out a tape measure and asked me to hold one end

at Arthur's tail as he unrolled the tape and measured to the point of the horn. Then he measured the horn itself and wrote the numbers down in a ledger book. "The specimen is definitely not a pony."

I had hoped the autopsy would yield more meaningful results.

Durgolon measured the forelegs and the rear legs, took samples of hair from the tail and mane. I noticed that he tucked a few strands into the pocket of his surgeon's gown.

McGoo turned his head away, and even I felt queasy as Durgolon withdrew blood samples, took hide scrapings, poked around in the unicorn's mouth. He marked all of the samples and arranged them in a holding tray.

The coroner used a magnifying glass, tweezers, and the zoom function on his phone camera to inspect the gaping wound in Arthur's side. He poked and probed, then thrust his index finger deep into the hole, wiggling it around. "I suspect this was the mortal wound." Staring at us through the plexiglass splatter shield, Durgolon said in an ominous voice, "I conclude that he was … stabbed."

He waited for our surprised reaction. McGoo nodded to me. "See? I told you, Shamble."

"The weapon appears to have been a spear of some kind," he continued. "A long but circular stabby thing that was pointed at one end, but I can't speculate on what it might be."

McGoo straightened. "Wait, I have an idea! A sharpened pool cue, just like at the Goblin Tavern!"

The coroner blinked in surprise. "I had not considered that." He jotted down a note.

"A pool cue? That would have been my … second choice," I said.

"I'll run further analysis." Durgolon took out his bone saw, circular saw, scalpels, forceps, and even a few rusty medieval torture devices. He clicked the power button on the spinning circular saw. "This is the fun part," he said.

He used a felt-tip marker on Arthur's white hide, then made a careful Y-incision for the main autopsy. He used spreaders to crack open the unicorn's ribcage, so he had elbow room to rummage inside and inspect the internal organs.

Durgolon removed and weighed the unicorn's lungs, kidneys, and liver, and kept a careful record. "Lots of good stuff in here." He was very enthusiastic about his work. The Unnatural Quarter had bad experiences with previous coroners, but Durgolon seemed to be well-liked by the UQPD, as well as all of his prior customers. He claimed that this was a dream job for a necromancer.

With bloody latex gloves, he held up Arthur's heart as if it were a trophy. "See this right here? That big hole in his heart? That looks like a stab wound to me."

"Put it in your final report," McGoo said.

Durgolon set the organs in separate stainless-steel trays, humming to himself as he went about his work. He paused, then turned to me and McGoo. "Do we have any word on the disposition of the remains?"

"We're still looking for next of kin," I said, "although we do have his unidog."

"If nothing turns up, there's a big aftermarket on these organs, especially that unicorn horn. Lots of collectors out there."

I stiffened. "We don't want Arthur or any of his parts to be sold on eBay."

The coroner sighed. "I can keep the cold cuts in the morgue refrigerator for the time being, but after a while there'll be space considerations." He finished his official work. "I have a lot to clean up here. Would you gentlemen care to help?"

"Other priorities," McGoo said uneasily. "Important police work."

"The cases don't solve themselves," I said. "I better get back to wandering around the Quarter."

We hurried out of the city morgue and into the warm gloom of the hazy afternoon. McGoo removed his cap and wiped his forehead. "I'm glad to be out of there."

"Me, too." I remained deeply troubled. "I need to find more clues. It's not as if the solution is going to walk right in front of us."

Just then, two fairies buzzed past my face, like aggressive hummingbirds. I heard a tinkle of crystalline horseshoes and saw Dava strutting along the boulevard with an entourage of fairy workers from the glass-slipper distribution warehouse. They flitted around the preening Pegasus, and she fluffed her lavender-feathered wings, showing off for us.

McGoo's eyes opened wide. "Now that's something you don't see every day."

I said, "I haven't seen her since two days ago."

Dava cantered up and huffed at me. "You're that zombie detective."

"And you're that Pegasus," I countered.

"But not a unicorn," McGoo said observantly.

Dava turned toward him, showing the gaudy gold crown that covered her forehead. "Pegasi are much more noble creatures than unicorns. I am not afraid to be seen. In fact, I love the attention." She spread her wings, and her fairy entourage swirled about, devoted and adoring.

"You are the most impressive Pegasus I've ever seen," I said.

"And I will always be," Dava said. "That's why I'm such a star on television."

McGoo leaned close to me and asked, "Is she in that college-dorm reality show?"

I shook my head. "No, the Home Capitalism Network."

Dava sniffed. "Unicorn culture is insular and secretive. They refuse to join the normal world, even after the Big Uneasy, when unnaturals can come out of the closet and express themselves."

"Sounds like unicorns are similar to Amish," I said.

Dava snorted again at the comparison. "Yes, but without the quilts and the cabinetry. Pegasi are much more outgoing."

McGoo raised a hand to stop her. "You should come down to the station so we can ask you more questions about unicorns."

But she strutted away with her crystalline shoes clinking on the sidewalk. The fairies swarmed ahead to clear gawking pedestrians out of the way. Dava looked back over her shoulder and folded her wings. "As soon as I can fit it into my schedule, of course. Kisses!"

Chapter 24

hen I finally got back to Chambeaux & Deyer, the offices were on fire.

I pushed open the door and got a face full of smoke and brimstone. I waved my fedora in front of my face, trying to see.

Sheyenne sat at her desk, typing on her keyboard, seemingly unperturbed. As the smoke cleared, I could make out a glowing orange-and-red figure filling the main room. The burly thing had broad shoulders and cracked magma skin, a head like a half-melted boulder, a gaping mouth that flickered with flames, and deep eye sockets full of bright coals.

Dressed in a charcoal-gray blazer, Robin pulled out our office fire extinguisher, which we had installed according to code, and blasted the carpeting that had begun to smolder at the lava creature's feet. "Excuse me, Erwin."

"Sorry," rumbled the fiery beast. "My temperature rises when I get upset."

Robin blasted with the extinguisher again. The lava creature moved its feet, and I saw blackened marks in our already much-stained carpet.

"We'd better upgrade to higher asbestos content in the rug, considering our clientele," I said.

"Dan, this is Erwin Bush. He's hired me to challenge several overly restrictive fire codes."

"I'm usually called Burning Bush," he said. "It's my nickname."

The lava monster extended his hand in greeting, but I was wise enough not to take it. "I've heard about your case, sir. You can count on Robin to do her absolute best."

"I can't do my business with all these absurd regulations!" the creature growled. Flames flickered from his gravelly skin.

Just then, the smoke alarm sounded with a shrill, pulsating beep, and the ceiling sprinklers deployed, spraying jets of water across the paperwork on Sheyenne's desk, as well as dousing Robin and the lava creature. Erwin groaned and cringed as steam erupted from his molten skin, turning the offices into an unpleasant sauna.

"Damned nuisance!" the creature said. "That stings!"

Aiming to protect her client, Robin snatched an umbrella from the stand and opened it to shield Burning Bush from the downpour. I put my fedora back on my head for protection, since I hate it when water dribbles into the bullet hole in my forehead.

Sheyenne flitted up to the ceiling and used her poltergeist powers to fan away the smoke. Eventually, she cleared the sensors enough to shut off the shrill alarm and the sprinklers. As the last dribbles of water trickled down from the ceiling nozzles, Robin continued to hold the umbrella so the lava monster could fume and dry off.

The sodden office smelled like wet ashes. While Erwin seemed embarrassed, Robin blasted the smoldering rug one last time with the fire extinguisher. "We may need to reconsider the parameters of our case. I doubt you'll get a sympathetic jury in such an inflammatory case. Even if the harsh restrictions cause you personal inconvenience, there are reasons for the fire code."

The lava monster balled his magma fists in frustration, but

hung his molten head dejectedly. "This business has always been my dream! Where do I even start? I can't get the basic permits."

"What business are you in?" I asked.

"He wants to open a bookstore," Robin said.

"It's called Burning Books," Erwin said. "We want to cater to right-wing extremist clientele."

I frowned. "I don't generally approve of burning books."

Robin offered a possible solution. "You could focus on ebook delivery and also stone-tablet novels."

"That would be old school," he said.

"And you could build the entire shop out of nonflammable materials," she continued. "I might be able to get exemptions for that in the building code."

The lava monster seemed slightly mollified. "Thanks for considering alternatives and helping me out."

The door opened, and Alvina trotted in, leading Urmin on a leash. The horn dog yipped and yapped as he smelled the smoke in the air. When the lava monster turned toward the cute critter, Urmin strained against the leash as he pulled forward to greet him, shedding rainbows.

"Be good now," Alvina said. "Don't jump up on strangers."

The lava monster crouched and extended a molten hand to pet the unidog, but Urmin squirmed back. "Cute puppy." Finished with his business, the smoldering creature lumbered out of the office.

Sheyenne fetched paper towels from the kitchenette to mop up the sprinkler water on her desk. Alvina unclipped Urmin's leash, and he trotted around the office, spreading a little magic everywhere. Soon enough, the wet ashes and smoke smelled like honeysuckle, and the heady steam filling the air was reminiscent of a fresh spring shower. Even the damaged carpeting sparkled as if it had just been steam cleaned. The lava monster's burned footprints had become part of the muddled, indecipherable pattern.

"You're handy to have around, Urmin," I said.

The horn dog let out an exceedingly pleasant bark.

"Does that mean we can keep him?" Alvina asked, then sniffled. "Now that Arthur is … gone."

"He has a home here until we know where he really belongs," Sheyenne said. "But Arthur must have had family."

"Can I take him to school and show my teacher?" Alvina asked.

"If anything could sour this cute little critter, it would be Miss Nifflesmoth," I said.

Robin, Sheyenne, and I were all concerned. We truly didn't know how to care for a unidog, though Urmin was good at caring for himself.

"I'll make us some corn dogs," Alvina said. "I'll bet Urmin's hungry."

She ran into the kitchenette and preheated the toaster oven. The Mystery Meat was precooked and heavily processed, so it was perfectly healthy for the kid to eat the corn dogs cold. Urmin yapped and trotted after her.

"Be careful not to poke someone in the eye with the corn dog stick, honey," Sheyenne said.

"I'll be careful," Alvina said. "Urmin and I have eaten enough corn dogs to be professionals by now." She grinned at me, showing her baby fangs. "Should I make you one, Half-daddy? You can eat corn dogs with us."

I was about to brush the offer aside, but I had eaten nasty things before. "Why not, kid? It'll be a treat."

"We could have used that lava monster for a real weenie roast," Alvina said.

"Maybe next time," Robin said. "I'm sure Erwin wouldn't mind."

Later, we sat around the little table, holding our sticks and enjoying our corn dogs. The Mystery Meat was rather good, so long as I didn't think about it too much. Our makeshift dinner felt like a family picnic.

CHAPTER 25

still needed to see the fairy godmother, but maybe that was wishful thinking. I had encountered the dazzling Pegasus twice now, but Betty Bibbity was the one who could work the magic. I went straight to the studio of the Home Capitalism Network, because Betty and Dava were due to film their weekly fragile-footwear segment.

Cases had taken me to TV studios before, and I knew that despite the glamour shown on a television screen, the places were usually cluttered and dingy. And they were not open to the curious public, not even to zombie detectives on the job.

Fortunately, one of the front-office workers recognized me from my P.I. credentials. She was a short-statured troll with fanlike ears, and she wore far too many garish necklaces, dangly earrings, and gaudy rings—all of which I presumed she'd bought from HCN.

She gasped when she saw my name, starstruck. "You're the real Dan Shamble!" Trolls usually have rough gravelly voices, but hers was high-pitched. "I've read all your books. They're compelling and hilarious adventures." She lowered her voice in commiseration. "Don't pay any attention to the Amazon reviews."

I always felt awkward when someone brought up that subject. "Those books are only loosely based on my real cases, written by a ghostwriter, Linda Bullwer—you can find her name in the fine print on the copyright page."

Howard Phillips Publishing had been successful with the book series, and in exchange for letting them use my name, I received a monthly maintenance spell from the Wannovich sisters, skilled witches who were also lead editors for the publishing house. Being a well-preserved zombie doesn't happen all by itself.

"But it's you! It's really you!" the fangirl troll blurted out. "I just can't believe it! Is there going to be a new novel soon? I finished *Bats in the Belfry* as soon as it came out!"

"That was a ridiculous one," I admitted.

"I'm so pleased you're here!" said the troll. "Are you going to be one of the new presenters on HCN? Selling all those books—ooh, and autographed, too!—would be a big hit on the network."

"Sorry, that's not why I'm here," I said. "I understand that the fairy godmother and Dava are here filming a segment? I need to talk with them." I lowered my voice conspiratorially. "It's for a case."

The troll's ears fanned out, which made the gaudy earrings jingle. "Ooh, am I going to be in it? Will this scene be in the new book?"

"That depends on how the chapter pacing turns out," I said. "And whether they need to pad the word count."

Bouncing along, she hurried me to the studio in back. "You should join Betty Bibbity on her show. It would be a nice matched set—wear your new glass slippers while you enjoy the new Dan Shamble novel!" She cackled. "Read a good mystery and feel like a princess."

I wasn't sure about the crossover marketing, but I told her I'd consider it. Regardless, the licensing aspects for the book series were controlled by the publisher.

The cluttered studio was chaotic in preparation for the filming. The stage had been dressed up to look like a homey living room with a coffee table for product display and a comfortable seat from which the fairy godmother would give her maternal sales pitch. On the opposite side of the coffee table, where a co-host would normally sit, the area had been cleared so that Dava could strut about in her glass horse slippers.

Goblin camera techs hunched on tall seats behind their large video cameras, swiveling them around, pulling in to test the focus. A set director, a human woman with long dark hair and an angry expression, stared at her clipboard, working out the shot list.

Betty Bibbity and Dava stood off to the side of the stage going over the script. The unionized service fairies flitted about, delivering boxes of glass slippers for display on the coffee table. They removed the lids and lifted out the transparent footwear, arranging them for the best sales effect. Preoccupied, the fairy godmother waved her star-tipped wand to create soap bubbles in the air.

One of the fairies flitted closer, bearing a white paper cup twice her size, but the dragonfly wings were strong enough to carry even a grande coffee. "Here's your pumpkin spice latte, Betty."

The fairy godmother accepted the drink with a nod of thanks. "I appreciate it very much, dearie."

Surprised that pumpkin spice was already in season, I let her take a sip before I interrupted her. "Excuse me, Miss Bibbity, I need to ask you a few more questions."

Her brow furrowed as she tried to remember me. "Oh … you're the zombie rabbi from the bat mitzvah."

"I'm the zombie detective," I corrected her. "Thanks to you, I was able to find the evil wizard Oorgak, and he's definitely given up evil for the foreseeable future."

"Oh, that's nice to hear," she said.

Dava tossed her mane, annoyed that I had interrupted their rehearsal. Her crown was slightly askew, and I reached forward to adjust it across her forehead. "There, now you look even more beautiful," I said, and the compliment mollified her.

"We have to start filming soon, Betty," she snorted. "No time for helping people."

"There's always time to help people, dearie," the fairy godmother said, adding a tsk-tsk before she turned back to me. "Oh, that's right! You're working with dear Prince Dirk. It's so nice that he's cured from being a frog."

"It's not nice, actually," I said. "While under the spell, he fell in love with a frog demon, and now they're no longer physically compatible. I was hoping you might have a spell that would rectify the situation."

She became formal and businesslike. "I charge for my spells, dearie—as well as for my glass slippers."

"He does have a royal treasury," I pointed out, though I didn't mention that he might not have immediate access to the funds.

Betty twitched her wand to release a burst of silvery soap bubbles that drifted around the studio area. "Bring Prince Dirk back to my event center along with his frog girlfriend. We'll have a consultation. The prince was already a client, so I have a file on him."

I took heart from that. "You think it's at least possible?"

"Anything's possible, dearie," the fairy godmother said. "If you feel the magic. But I should warn you, amphibious transformations aren't really in a fairy godmother's repertoire."

Dava strutted around the stage, then paused as a gremlin makeup technician whipped out a large bucket of powder and began dusting blemishes and spots on her hide. The makeup tech spent a lot of time covering the scar on her lavender flank from the tragic injury at the nightmare races.

"Not too much, you idiot!" Dava snapped. "Or I'll figure out a way to turn *you* into a frog! There must be some evil wizards still out there."

The gremlin shrank back, terrified by the insult, but Betty stepped in, chiding, "Now, Dava, get yourself in the right mood. You need to have a sparkling personality for the taping."

"I always have a sparkling personality, damn it!" said Dava. "I just wish we were living in a real magic kingdom, like in the fairy tales. Then I wouldn't have to deal with all this bullshit." She twitched her wings, then went to the craft-services table to nibble on a white powdered-sugar donut.

Betty Bibbity clucked her tongue. "That Dava … always wishing for something she can't have. You can't teach an old Pegasus new tricks."

Dava glared at her with powdered sugar all over her nose. "I'm not old!"

The fairy godmother's attention remained on me, though. She strolled over to the display table, where the worker fairies had built up a pyramid of different sizes and shapes of perfect transparent footwear. "Hmm, I wonder if a glass slipper would fit this frog princess. I don't know that we have any amphibious designs, although with enough slime, she could slip into one of our larger models."

"Would that work the magic spell?" I asked, imagining RRita going through the motions of trying on one glass slipper after another.

"No, but it would be fashionable," Betty said.

"I'll see that those two book a consultation appointment with you, ma'am. Rather than changing RRita into a human princess, they really want Dirk turned back into a frog. And now there's an added complication with an entire clutch of fertilized eggs."

"Children always complicate a relationship," said the fairy godmother. "But they're also quite adorable."

I couldn't envision a human prince and princess raising a swarm of tadpoles, but that certainly wouldn't be the weirdest thing I had seen in the Unnatural Quarter. RRita seemed more worried about how her parents would react to seeing their daughter in a human body.

A loud bell rang, and the set techs scuttled about. The fairies placed a final glass slipper on the display, then buzzed away from the cameras.

Dava pawed the rug with her glass-covered hoof, and Betty Bibbity gave a vigorous flourish with her magic wand, spewing fresh soap bubbles into the air.

"Quiet on the set!" the dark-haired set director shouted, then stepped back as the goblin camera operators rolled in. The fairy godmother took her seat, focused on the filming process.

I ducked out of the studio, vowing to follow up with her, but I wasn't interested in watching the entire filming. I had other cases on my mind, including a murdered unicorn.

Before I left the station, my troll fangirl intercepted me with a battered trade paperback copy of one of the Dan Shamble mysteries, *Tastes Like Chicken*, and asked me to sign it. It was just another one of my duties as a zombie P.I.

CHAPTER 26

'm not the sort of guy who's good in a social situation, but I agreed to have dinner with RRita's parents, Bubo and Lubo. I thought it might help our distraught clients. Sheyenne joined me as my date, since she's a lot better at these things than I am.

She chose a bottle of wine to bring along, saying that white zinfandel was the safest alternative, although we didn't know what dish would be served. I suggested picking up a pack of chocolate chip cookies, since cookies are always a safe alternative.

We arrived at the home of the wealthy frog demon pool-supply specialists, a nice sunken rancher in a boggy area. The yard featured ornamental ponds dotted with lily pads. A decorative lawn gnome stood cute and cheery among the greenery, but when he moved, I realized he wasn't there as eye candy. Two other lawn gnomes moved along the side of the house with rakes and hedge trimmers, clearly a gardening service.

Standing on the front porch with Sheyenne, I rang the doorbell, which let out a loud *ribbit* like a croaking frog.

A squat frog demon opened the door. She wore a pink blouse, a bracelet on her slimy wrist, and a large amount of peppermint-pink lipstick spread across her extensive lips. "You must be Mr. Shamble! I'm Lubo."

When I introduced Sheyenne as my associate, she

promptly corrected, "I'm his girlfriend." She slipped her ectoplasmic arm in mine.

Lubo led us inside. "Pleased to meet you. Come, we're sitting out in the back. I've got an hors d'oeuvre tray ready." She waddled as she walked, as if anxious to be back out into the sun.

The back patio featured a shallow pool and a Jacuzzi under an awning, where sprinklers sprayed cooling mist to keep their bodily slime fresh and perky. Lounge chairs had been set up in a semicircle around a glass table.

Prince Dirk and RRita were already there, sitting close and holding hands. Across from them, lurking like a king on his lawn-chair throne, Bubo was a squat, warty male frog demon, with black speckles and brown age spots, as well as lumpy encrustations around his eyes. His huge, dry lips were stretched downward in a frown.

Lubo sounded saccharine sweet. "Bubo, these are our guests, Dan Shamble and his girlfriend associate, Sheyenne."

I reached out to shake the bull frog's squishy hand. He didn't seem impressed by me.

Too late, Prince Dirk mumbled, "Careful you don't get warts."

"I thought frogs and warts were just a myth," Sheyenne said.

"It's toads," Bubo corrected. He gripped me tighter to emphasize his handshake.

"I thought that was a myth, too," I said, finally reclaiming my hand from the frog demon.

"After the Big Uneasy, lots of myths came true," Lubo said.

"Unicorns did," I admitted.

Changing the subject, Sheyenne offered the bottle of wine. "We brought white zinfandel."

"And cookies," I added. We placed them on the patio table next to a big bowl of still-twitching flies and fresh guacamole dip.

"We're so glad you came," RRita blurted out. She sounded desperate.

Bubo's voice was like a deep burp. "We were just having a conversation."

"Oh, won't it be good to hear some fresh opinions, dear?" Lubo said.

Her husband just let out a "Hrrummph."

My stiff lips aren't good at smiling, but I made them work. "It's nice to see the family all together."

Prince Dirk looked shell-shocked in his chair. The tension in the air was palpable.

Lubo took a seat in the lawn chair next to her husband, and she struggled to find fresh pleasantries to add. "Nice weather we're having …"

"Too hot," Bubo said.

"My Magic Kingdom always has nice weather," Dirk observed.

RRita clutched his hand. "It's a sunny day whenever I'm with my prince."

"Human prince," Bubo grumbled.

"That's not his fault, dear," Lubo said.

"We're trying to fix it, Daddy!" RRita said. "You liked him when he was a frog."

Bubo let out another all-purpose "Hrrummph."

"I can't wait to meet our sweet grandtadpoles," Lubo said. "They'll be little slimy bundles of joy." She elbowed her husband, and he let out a belch-like grunt.

"That boy misled my daughter," Bubo said. "And now there are illegitimate babies involved. A lot of them!"

"Daddy, I love him!" RRita insisted. "You said you accepted him."

"That was when he was still a frog." The bullfrog yanked a can of beer from the holder in the arm of his lawn chair and drained it in one long pulsating gulp. He crushed the empty and reached down to a cooler beside his chair to snag a second beer.

"It's not my fault the spell wore off," Dirk said. "It was a malicious good deed perpetrated by a formerly evil wizard." I could tell he had rehearsed the big words. "I love your daughter for who she is, and she loves me for who I am *inside*."

"It's the *outside* that causes problems," Bubo said. "I've got an image and a reputation—and a pool-supply service to run. When potential customers see you two as a couple, think of the scandal!"

Lubo scuttled away from the patio. "I'll go check on the casserole."

"We're attempting to rectify the situation, sir," I interrupted. "We have located the evil wizard to see if he'll redo the spell and turn Dirk back into a frog. As an alternative, we've contacted a fairy godmother specialist to see if she can turn RRita into a human princess."

"My daughter—a human?" Bubo said with a loud gasp. "Never!"

RRita crossed her arms over her chest. "I'll do anything to be with my prince."

"Then who'll raise the children? Tadpoles don't belong with humans."

"What do you care, Daddy?" RRita said with a daintier *hrrummph* of her own. "You told us you wanted nothing to do with the children."

"Illegitimate children! What will the church congregation

think?" His throat belled out again, and he glared at Prince Dirk. "I hope you got genital warts."

"That's just a myth," Dirk said.

Lubo came back out from the kitchen. "Still another fifteen minutes. I just crumbled potato chips on the top, to make it nice and crispy." She nudged the bowl of flies and the guacamole closer to me. "Have some hors d'oeuvres, Mr. Shamble."

I didn't know what to say, but Sheyenne tried to break the ice. "It looks delicious, but I'm not much for solid food."

"Oh, are you on a diet, dear?" Lubo asked. "You look beautiful."

"Yes, she does," I agreed.

"Did I hear you mention church, dear?" Lubo turned to her husband, then back to us. "We sing in the choir."

"We may have to find a different church now," Bubo said. "How can we bear the shame of this doomed romance? Our daughter is ruined by this … cad."

"I'm not a cad, I'm a royal prince," Dirk said. "And I'll take my beloved RRita back to my Magic Kingdom. I'll install a fresh moat in front of my castle so that our baby tadpoles will have a nice place to play."

"If we ever get them back …" RRita sobbed. "Daddy, you could be helping."

"Why should I have anything to do with this mess?" Bubo's tongue flicked in and out of his mouth as he snatched squirming flies from the appetizer bowl.

"Because they're still our grandchildren, dear," Lubo scolded him. "We can use the influence of our pool-supply service, encourage our fellow frog demons to boycott Bilge Bay until we get the babies back. That might make those nasty lagoon creatures relent. Think of the children."

He responded with another "Hrrummph."

"Why don't I open the white zinfandel?" I suggested. I was ready to drink it right out of the bottle. Fortunately, we had chosen a brand with a twist-top instead of a cork.

"After dinner, we could play card games," Lubo suggested. "Wouldn't that be nice?"

I glanced at my watch. We had only been there ten minutes. It was going to be a long night, and I braced myself to endure a zombie social apocalypse.

Chapter 27

After seeing RRita's unsupportive amphibious parents, I felt more determined than ever to return Prince Dirk to his frog state. It was the only way I could restore harmony to the lily pad and the Magic Kingdom district.

It was clear now that transforming RRita into a human princess was not going to fly (not that I had ever imagined frogs flying). This would take more than a nice fairy godmother spell. I had to get Walter to become evil again, at least briefly, so that as Oorgak, he could work his dark magic and save the lovestruck couple.

In order to do that, I had to appeal to his true personality, his "inner self" as the Wham-Bam Ashram would call it. I needed to understand the psyche of an evil wizard.

I went to the headquarters of Howard Phillips Publishing, where I could discuss the matter with the two most knowledgeable witches in the Unnatural Quarter.

I've had dealings with the Wannovich sisters for as long as I'd been a zombie detective, as was dramatized in my first fictionalized adventure, *Death Warmed Over*. The names had been changed to protect the innocent, as well as those who were guilty as sin. Notwithstanding what was written in the novel version, I knew that Mavis and Alma would be willing to help. If nothing else, it would guarantee them an appearance in the next ghost-written Dan Shamble, Zombie P.I. book.

After entering my name on the clipboard for a guest badge at the publisher's front desk, I worked my way past cubicles of designers, marketing experts, social media influencers, and nearsighted proofreaders until I finally reached the corner office.

Mavis and Alma Wannovich were now senior editors of many successful titles—not just my own silly zombie detective books, but the classic reissue of the original *Necronomicon*, as well as the new authorized sequel. Howard Phillips was also known for their culinary guides to the Unnatural Quarter, with special editions for different species, as well as a human survival guide in times of monsters.

When I knocked on their office door, Alma Wannovich let out a squeal of delight—a literal squeal. It's her natural mode of communication ever since she'd been transformed into a large sow as the result of a love spell gone horribly wrong. The subsequent lawsuit against the publisher had been one of Robin Deyer's most prominent cases. In recompense, Robin had made Howard Phillips Publishing hire the two witches as editors, and it was a dream job for both of them.

Now, in their shared corner office, Alma wallowed in the slush pile, which she had brought with her into a shallow kids' wading pool filled with a muddy slurry. That was how she liked to read manuscripts.

Mavis looked up from her desk and smiled, showing her snaggly teeth. "Why, Mr. Shamble! So good of you to visit." Unlike her porcine sister, Mavis was a more traditional witch with a long, hooked nose, including a decorative wart, and a lumpy chin, from which sprouted a few wiry hairs. Her tangled mop of black hair stuck out from beneath her pointed black hat. She swiveled toward me in her expensive, ergonomic, Herman Miller office chair.

"Right now we're gathering your royalty numbers for *Bats in the Belfry*," she said. "It did rather well. I think it was the excellent cover painting."

"That was a good one," I admitted. The likeness of me seemed even more handsome than reality, and I was fine with that.

From her slush pile pool, Alma used her snout to shove an unsuitable manuscript out of the mud and onto the floor.

Mavis's eyes were shining. "When should we get Linda Bullwer started on the next book? Are you embroiled in any sexy and action-packed cases right now?"

"How does a unicorn murder sound?"

"Oh, dear! That sounds delightful."

I frowned. "It wasn't delightful for Arthur, but I'm determined to find the culprit."

"Do you have any idea who the killer is?" she asked. "Or is it a plot twist?"

"I'm still working on it. No suspects yet. I may not even have met the killer, but I'll track him down." I removed my fedora. "Or her. Or it."

Mavis finished what she'd been typing on her keyboard, then hit enter. "I'm just posting anonymous five-star Amazon reviews," she said. "It helps the algorithm."

"I don't understand the publishing business." I shook my head. "But that's not my field. I'm a zombie private investigator, and I need your expertise."

I had both witches' full attention now. "I'm afraid we don't know much about unicorns," Mavis said.

"This is about a different case," I said. "A prince who was turned into a frog and found true love."

"Oh, my!" Mavis said. "Your novels could definitely use more romance."

Alma snuffled, then adjusted herself to a more comfortable position in her muddy pool.

"I need to get into the mind of an evil wizard," I said. "Originally, he cast a dark spell on the prince, and then he cast an even worse do-gooder spell. I need to convince him to make amends for making amends, to undo the damage he tried to undo."

"But we're witches, not wizards, Mr. Shamble. Our local coven is very tight-knit and helpful—a support group. But we only know about witches. Wizards and warlocks are entirely different things, even if they do begin with the same letter."

"I've been to a meeting of your Pointy Hat Society," I reminded them, "but I'm hoping you can still shed some insight on what makes an evil wizard tick. His name was Oorgak, and he lived in the Magic Kingdom district."

I told them all the details I knew, embellishing a little so I could entice the Wannoviches. Mavis gave a solemn nod. "Medieval evil wizards are the worst."

Alma snorted in agreement.

"I was afraid of that, but this one has gone straight. He's now enlightened, and I need to convince him to work just one more evil spell."

Mavis waved a long-nailed finger at me. "*Just* one more, Mr. Shamble? Evil spells are like potato chips. No one can work just one."

I remained determined. "But if we don't, then the prince and his frog will not have a happy ending."

Now the witches understood the gravity of the situation. "And that will affect the plot structure of our next book!" She set to work on her desktop computer, calling up the catalog of Howard Phillips publications, including guidebooks and user's manuals for all the witches, warlocks, and other magic users who were registered in the Quarter. "Evil wizards seem to be quite scarce these days.… Ah, here's our old listing for Oorgak!"

I leaned close to her screen to follow along. "Wizard for hire. Dirty deeds done dirt cheap. That sounds heavy."

"Oorgak has a dark heart, specializes in astrological disasters, unscheduled eclipses, and general mayhem. But he only has a three-star rating," Mavis said, "so he couldn't have been entirely evil."

"Or successful," I said. "But this listing isn't accurate. Once Oorgak was enlightened, he closed down his business, shuttered up his evil lair, and changed his name to Walter."

"We've been meaning to issue a new guide." Mavis sounded apologetic.

Alma leaned out of the mud pool to a stack of manuscripts on her left. She nuzzled the pile of papers and pushed out a manila folder that contained a printout. Mavis snagged it before it could fall into the mud and opened it up. "Yes, here's the draft manuscript, only partially complete. There's a lot of fact-checking involved."

Knowing that I liked hard copies, she printed the online listing from their database. "These are some of Oorgak's past clients and cases, his successes." She lifted her warty nose. "Maybe you could remind him of his glory days, and he'll want to be evil again, out of nostalgia."

I took the papers from the printer tray. "Thanks. I'll go talk with him in his Zen garden."

"Make the encounter exciting," Mavis suggested as I turned to leave. "The book will be more commercial that way."

Chapter 28

Back in the offices, I was about to settle in for an afternoon of hard pondering over the printouts Mavis had given me, but a panicked phone call always messes with the day's plans.

Robin's office door was open, and I could hear her intense discussion with her skeleton client, who was due to have his indecent exposure hearing in court that afternoon. Sheyenne was away from her desk heating another Mystery Meat corn dog in the kitchenette so Urmin could have a puppy snack.

When the main phone rang, I answered it from Sheyenne's desk. "Chambeaux and Deyer—Dan Chambeaux speaking."

"Help, Mr. Shamble! It's a disaster!"

I recognized the raspy, burbly tone. "Gil? Or is it Finn?"

The voices overlapped as the lagoon creatures shouted in panic. "It's both of us. Come to Bilge Bay quick. It's a disaster!"

"More vandals? Should we call the police?"

"It's a domestic issue," Gil said. "But they're ruining the place. Come right now."

Finn shouted, "The tadpoles have hatched."

I couldn't see how that was such a dire emergency. "Congratulations on the blessed event."

"It's not blessed," Finn replied. "It's a nightmare! They're monsters."

RRita and Dirk would have found the comment insulting. I said in a firm voice, "Then maybe you should just give the tadpoles back to their real parents."

"We need you here right away, Mr. Shamble!" Gil wailed. "We're in fear for our lives!"

I heard a splash and a sound like a growling burp. Then the line went dead.

Hearing the commotion, Robin had emerged from her office. "I heard you say Bilge Bay. Is it another crisis?"

"Yeah, another crisis," I said in a deadpan voice.

She looked concerned. "I should go with you because Gil and Finn are important clients. But right now, my priority is with Archie here."

The anxious skeleton defendant had followed her out of her office. He wore a long trench coat and a knitted beanie cap pulled down over his bare skull. Rubber galoshes covered his bony feet. Archie was clearly doing his best to cover most of his body parts, which was probably a good idea for a skeleton accused of indecent exposure.

"I really need you, Miss Deyer," he said in a rattling voice. "If you aren't with me, who will argue my case?"

Stoic and determined, Robin said, "I won't leave you behind, Archie. We've gone over your testimony, and you know which trigger words to avoid. This is going to be a close one, and it'll be hard to get sympathy from the jury."

"But I'm all covered up with my trench coat. There's nothing showing!" He turned his skull eye sockets toward me. "I keep getting a boner."

"That's more information than I need," I said.

Making up her mind, Robin turned to me. "You'll need to resolve the issue, Dan. I can't go with you."

"It seems to be a security concern," I said. "I'll handle it, don't worry. Go knock 'em dead in court."

"I'm already dead," Archie said.

"And you're also accused of a serious crime," Robin scolded him. "Now come back into my office, and we'll go over this one more time. I'm basing my entire case on a loophole, but we'll only have one shot. We have Judge Angela Stone, and she's a real hard case." She narrowed her dark eyes. "And even though my strategy is on solid legal grounds, I have a moral responsibility, and I need to know that this will never happen again. You understand that what you did is wrong?"

"I've been through therapy," Archie said. "My counselor is convinced that I know the difference between a scapula and a hip bone and a coccyx, and what's appropriate and what isn't."

"Good," Robin said. "Now let's go prepare for court, Archie."

"I'll bring McGoo for moral support. The two of us can handle any swamp emergency." When I called and asked him to meet me at Bilge Bay for a domestic disturbance with one of my clients, he perked up at the idea of going to a water park, though I doubted this would be what he expected.

When I arrived at the resort gate, McGoo was already pacing back and forth, frowning at the "All Welcome" and "No Trespassing" signs. He waved his hand in a vain attempt to scare away the bloodthirsty mosquitoes. "Hey, Shamble. I could sure use a dip in the lazy river right now. I brought my official police department swim trunks."

I thought of the scum-covered pools and the spawning ponds, and McGoo swatted bugs away again. Before I could answer him, we heard a scream, a growl, and a splash from inside the park. We ran inside.

One of the shaved-ice carts had been overturned, and towels lay strewn about. The tentacled masseuse stood under the thatched palm-frond roof of his cabana and used multiple wormlike appendages to play a game on his smartphone. He still had no clients.

I heard a raspy outcry from deeper inside the recreational swamp. "Watch out, Gil!"

I gestured for McGoo to follow me. "Sounds like they're at the lazy river."

"Sounds like it's not very lazy," McGoo said.

We ran down the crushed-gravel path to reach the shore of the lazy river, where I saw Finn splashing about with his webbed feet and clawed hands. He scrambled onto the bank, panting hard through his gill slits. Gil grabbed him by the scaly arm and dragged him away from the current. "You're safe now, Finn."

Something dark, like a rubbery, slime-covered torpedo, ducked under the murky water and swam away.

"Safe?" Finn gasped, flapping his gill slits again. "Nothing is safe! They're monsters. They're evil."

McGoo drew his police special revolver, and I pulled my .38, looking around for attackers. "A public facility like this should at least have rent-a-cops on duty," McGoo said.

"We called the Temporary Security Agency," Finn wailed. "But there's a waitlist!"

Gil blinked his fish eyes. "They said too many members of their staff were eaten in recent weeks."

"Hazards of the job," I said.

In the lazy river, a rounded, black, eyeless head poked up, wobbled around in the current, then ducked down again.

"Whoa, was that a tadpole?" I asked.

"It's a monster!" Finn cried. "That entire clutch of illegal eggs hatched!"

In the adjacent spawning pool where Alvina had played with the cute pet leeches, duckweed and pond scum stirred to indicate numerous creatures swimming around under the water.

The scum parted, and more tadpole heads popped up, like round-nosed blind sharks. The resident leeches, as large as snakes, scurried away in panic, but the tadpoles darted after them and chomped down on the squirming bloodsuckers.

"Those kids don't look anything like either RRita or Prince Dirk," I said.

McGoo was amazed by the size. "You said they just hatched! How did they get so big?"

Gil slapped his hands on the side of his head. "The water must be contaminated with all the magical junk that was dumped here."

I thought of the sodden spellbook with the strange symbol on the cover, which they had sold at their rummage sale. "That's really toxic magic." The mutant tadpoles splashed and frolicked among the duckweed, then dove under the water in pursuit of more hapless leeches.

"Have any other customers turned into monsters?" I asked. "I mean, the ones who weren't monsters in the first place?"

"We haven't had enough customers to know for sure," Finn groaned.

"They might have been more susceptible to dark magic contaminants in their embryonic state," I said.

I slid the .38 back into my pocket, sure that the baby tadpoles were not going to lunge out and attack us. After all, they were just kids.

McGoo kept his revolver drawn, though he looked ready to start firing at the ubiquitous mosquitoes in the air instead.

Though I could see the damage the rowdy tadpoles were causing, I felt little sympathy for the lagoon creatures. "This is your own fault, you know. If you hadn't kidnapped the eggs and held them here for ransom, then RRita and Prince Dirk would have taken their children safely away, and they wouldn't be your problem."

Finn flared his fins and Gil gaped his gill slits, both of them incensed. "And now those two are going to have to pay even more substantial damages if they ever want those delinquents back!"

A monster tadpole sprang out of the spawning pool and arced over the dry walkway to plunge into the lazy river with an enormous splash.

"So you won't surrender the tadpoles?" I asked, not hiding my impatience. "We could resolve this situation here and now."

"Not until those two trespassers pay!" Gil insisted.

"Then it's your problem." I pointed a stern finger at both lagoon creatures. "And don't you dare let any harm come to those little ones, or Robin and I will make sure you sit in a very dry prison cell for a very long time." I sighed and turned to go. "We're done here, McGoo." I had wasted the best part of the afternoon here and it was already sunset.

We left Bilge Bay behind, though the mosquitoes followed us out the front gate.

Chapter 29

cGoo suggested that we stop for a cup of coffee at the Ghoul's Diner, but then the police radio sent out an urgent call about a drunk centaur making a horse's ass out of himself. "Sorry, I'm on duty, Shamble. You'll have to endure the coffee all by yourself."

We parted ways, and I headed into the miasmic streets of the Quarter. As the gloom of dusk set in, the light had that peculiar tinge that makes you wonder if you need glasses. The old brick buildings and shops created a tangle of dark, narrow alleys, adding a sinister tinge to the local neighborhoods, but that was part of their charm.

I know all these dark streets like the back of my hand. Unfortunately, I don't know the back of my hand very well. Who looks at the back of their hand? Knowing the general direction back to our offices, I chose a likely alley, hoping it would be a shortcut. I forgot the well-known Boy Scout adage that shortcuts rarely are.

Preoccupied with the lagoon creatures and their doomed aquatic park, I didn't pay a lot of attention to my surroundings. What was I going to tell RRita and Dirk? A shadow passed in front of the alley opening ahead of me, a dark equine form that I could barely see in the gloom. Maybe I did need glasses.

The air suddenly had a weighty crackle, like a looming thunderstorm. I heard a noise ahead of me, and my cold, insensitive skin crawled. It was the sound of clomping hooves, followed by a whinnying snort. Ahead, I could see the distinctive silhouette of a horse—but with the added attraction of a long, pointed horn on its forehead. Another unicorn blocking my way!

I spun in the opposite direction to see the shadow of a second unicorn cutting off my exit.

I faced the first unicorn as it stepped closer, where I could see it better. This was not a majestic, white steed like Arthur. Rather, the creature was coal black with a dangerous-looking bronze horn. He clearly wouldn't let me past him.

Additional hoofbeats came from the alley entrance behind me, and now four unicorns crowded my exit—an ash-gray, a dappled brown, and a dingy white one that could have used a bath. The unicorns pushed forward into the alley, coming up from behind. The black unicorn stood his ground in front of me.

Uneasy, I slipped my hand into my pocket, felt the comforting grip of my .38. I couldn't stop thinking about how Arthur had been senselessly murdered in the vacant lot … but Alvina would never forgive me if I shot a unicorn. I released the gun.

A small black form scuttled through the shadowy garbage on the alley floor, bounding toward me in a racket of growls and barks. It was another unidog, like Urmin, but this one was black with a stubby, dark horn in the middle of its forehead. The critter's snarls didn't sound particularly musical.

"Good doggie," I said. "Good little horn dog."

The black unicorn strode toward me, his head lowered and sharp horn extended. A second gray unicorn followed him. They were closing in, and I had no escape.

I raised my hands. "No need to get ugly."

The gray unicorn closest to me said, "We're not ugly. We're unicorns."

The black unicorn stopped and stood his ground. He was apparently the leader. "You stumbled upon things you shouldn't know, Dan Shamble."

"It's Chambeaux," I said, out of habit, though it was a losing battle. "I'm a private investigator. My job is to solve mysteries."

The black unidog growled again, very intimidating and obnoxious, though he seemed too frightened to come within reach.

"Don't we want him to solve Arthur's murder?" said the brown dappled unicorn behind me. It was a female voice.

"It's none of his business," said the black unicorn. He lowered his head until his long horn touched the back of the growling unidog. "That's enough, Gurmin. We've got him right where we want him."

One of the two gray unicorns said, "I thought we wanted to take him to our secret clubhouse."

"The HornPub," said the other gray.

"Don't tell him the name!" the black unicorn snapped. "It's not a secret if you tell him the name."

"I didn't give the address," said the abashed unicorn. I think the two grays might have been twins.

When I faced the black unicorn again, he held a dark fabric sack in between his teeth, and I had no idea where it had come from. He spoke around the fabric. "Put this over your head, Shamble, so you don't see where we're taking you."

Cautiously, I took the black bag. "You mean like a hostage situation? I'm supposed to put this over my head and trust you?"

"You're supposed to put it over your head, *or else,*" said the black unicorn.

I held open the sack, uneasy. "It's not big enough to fit over my fedora."

"One size fits all." The gray unicorn behind me pushed close. "You can take it off when we get to the clubhouse."

"Squash the hat," said the black unicorn.

The horn dog, Gurmin, snarled with a sound more like thunder than rainbows. Dutifully, I pulled the black bag over my head, and I couldn't see anything.

The unicorns led me along. I fumbled and held onto the tail of one of the mythical creatures. They led me on at a deliberate, confusing pace, turning into other alleys, passing down ramps or creaking staircases into echoing tunnels and cavernous chambers. My sense of direction isn't great, even when I have my eyes open and I'm holding a map; I was completely disoriented by the time the unicorns brought me to the destination. I'd never be able to find their HornPub again—which was the point.

One of the unicorns used its teeth to yank the black sack off my head and knocked my fedora loose. I straightened the hat to recover my dignity, brushed down my stitched-up sport jacket, and looked around.

The unicorns had taken me to a gloomy, windowless pub decked out in dark wood with a bar with several tap pulls featuring British beer. There were tables for patrons to have conversations as they drank their beer, but no chairs because a secret clubhouse for unicorns did not need seats. An unused dartboard hung on the wall.

The dirty white unicorn clomped around to the back of

the bar and used his horn to knock one of the tap pulls forward, then leaned down and slurped the warm, flat brew that came out. After drinking his fill, the beast nudged the tap closed again without offering to pour for his buddies.

"I could pour you all a pint," I said, raising my hands. "After all, I do have fingers and opposable thumbs." I wanted some answers, and these unicorns could explain a lot.

"It's not a social event," the black unicorn said.

"But it *is* a pub," the dappled brown unicorn pointed out.

"I wouldn't mind a beer myself," I said. "Then we can talk about your concerns, and I've got some questions to ask, too."

"That would be nice," the two gray unicorns said in unison.

None of them stopped me as I went behind the bar, pulled a pint glass for myself, and then found tin pails that were suited for unicorn guzzling. I filled a pail for each of the five unicorns, randomly pulling different beers. I chose the bitterest one to give to the black unicorn.

As I slipped into my role as tavern wench, delivering the sudsy pails, I couldn't block out my questions any longer. "Okay, you all know who I am—now tell me who you are." I looked from the gray unicorns to the dirty white one, the dappled brown, then the black.

"Why should we trust you?" asked the black unicorn.

"You brought me here," I said, "and I am a certified zombie private investigator. We value client privacy and confidentiality." I raised my pint glass and took a slurp of the foam. "In fact, for the price of a pint of beer, you can hire me on retainer." I had learned legal tricks like that from Robin.

"Arthur did hire him," the dappled brown unicorn pointed out. "I'm Melissa."

The two gray unicorns glanced at each other. "I'm Clyde," said one.

"And I'm Dale."

The dirty white unicorn said, "And I'm Pirouette." Her voice had a flirtatious lilt.

The black unicorn huffed, looking indignant. He thrust his nose into the pail and slurped his bucket of bitter without introducing himself.

Clyde said, "He's Midnight Pete."

Melissa added with a whicker and a snicker, "He was called Stinky Pete because his manure is so foul."

The black unicorn blew beer foam from his nose. "I stamped that out."

Dale added, "Then he wanted to be called Black Pete, but the other unicorns thought that sounded racist."

"I'm *Midnight* Pete," the black unicorn said, "and I run security for the Secret Society of unicorns."

"The Horn Brothers," Clyde said.

"And Sisters," Pirouette amended.

"Arthur was in charge of us," said Dale, "our brave leader, but … he's been murdered."

"His own damn fault," Midnight Pete said. "He exposed himself, and all of us, to danger."

Gurmin, the horn dog, growled at the very idea.

"So, are you all the unicorns that remain? Five of you?" I asked. A few days ago, I wasn't sure I believed in one unicorn.

"We're just this branch of the Horn Brothers and Sisters," said Melissa. "There are clubhouses everywhere, but you have to be a member to know about them."

"Unless our security lapses," Midnight Pete snapped. "Arthur let himself be seen, and now people are asking too many questions. We're not ready to come out into the world yet."

I wet my mouth with another gulp of beer. "But why not?

The Big Uneasy was thirteen years ago. All the monsters came back, and everyone already believes in unnaturals and mythical creatures."

"Unicorns aren't like other mythical creatures," Pete said. "We're majestic and glorious, and we deserve the full awe and adoration of the public, like in magical medieval times."

I admitted that we all had nostalgia for the good old days, whenever that was. I had liked my normal suburban life at times.

Midnight Pete pawed the scuffed floor of the HornPub with his front hoof. He was growing agitated. "Arthur should not have engaged your services. He revealed our existence and left a paper trail."

I felt defensive. "He hired us to find his pet horn dog, Urmin. He was a good pet owner."

Pirouette looked away from her pail of beer. "My unidog is gone, too. It's like a part of me is missing."

Clyde and Dale snorted. "All our pets ran off."

"There's been a string of unidog-nappings?" I asked.

"None of your business," Midnight Pete said. Gurmin squirmed and barked as if pleased he was the only unidog in the secret club.

I did not like this black unicorn. "Well, we take pride in our work and our reputation at Chambeaux and Deyer. We did find Urmin, although it was too late for Arthur. Maybe I could find your other horn dogs, too."

The unicorns suddenly looked very interested in my services.

"Never!" Midnight Pete glared at the other unicorns. "Do you all want to be murdered like Arthur?"

They were aghast.

I couldn't understand why Pete was so surly and

intractable. "Are you still angry because unicorns were left behind on Noah's Ark?"

"That's just a ridiculous story," said the talking black unicorn.

"It's my job to dig into unanswered questions," I said. "I found Urmin, and I'm going to find Arthur's murderer."

Midnight Pete stomped on the floor again as if he had lost his temper. "The only way unicorns can be safe is if we stay hidden until the world is a fairy tale again and ready for us. We need to let this blow over." He was so loud and dominant that he cowed the other unicorns into submission. "Now get that sack back on your head, Shamble, and we'll take you out into the streets. We're finished with you."

I convinced them to let me finish my beer, and then I complied.

Chapter 30

Knowing about the Secret Society of Horn Brothers and Sisters changed my entire worldview. After I told my harrowing tale, Sheyenne and Robin were amazed.

Alvina was even more enthusiastic. "Can I bring you to school for show-and-tell? You can explain to all my classmates and to Miss Nifflesmoth that you saw a whole bunch of unicorns."

"I don't have any proof, kid. Your teacher is a spelling demon, and she's a real stickler."

Still, I vowed to dig even deeper into Arthur's death, which had been deemed a unicide in the official police report. After seeing all of those sinister pointy horns in the HornPub, I was sure I knew the murder weapon, but since the mythical creatures were so secretive, I wasn't close to naming a suspect.

Alvina seized on a different aspect of the case, however. Even though the Secret Society of Horn Brothers and Sisters had not officially engaged our services—which meant that Sheyenne couldn't send them a bill when it was over—the kid insisted that we find the missing horn dogs.

Alvina took photos of Urmin in cute poses, then used an easy graphics app to design *Lost Horn Dog* posters. Since Urmin was light brown and Gurmin was black, we assumed the other unidogs were a variety of colors. Alvina used image-processing tools to produce different colored critters for the posters.

"The important part is that the little dogs have horns in the middle of their heads," Alvina said. "We can sort out the colors when we find them."

Sheyenne printed a stack of the flyers so we could put them on lampposts and street corners in the old-school way; Alvina posted on the UQ social media pages for lost pets. She was determined to add "reward if found" on each listing, but Sheyenne cautioned, "Honey, we don't have the funds to pay any large rewards."

Alvina shook her head. "If they find a lost horn dog, they will feel a natural reward. Look at how good we feel just from petting Urmin."

I would have asked Robin for her legal opinion, but she'd been holed up in her office writing an appeal. Her skeleton indecent exposure case had resulted in a hung jury with half of the jurors wanting to hang Archie. Robin argued that even if they hung the skeleton, it would only result in separated vertebrae, and she was asking for community service instead.

So, Alvina and I decided to hit the streets. Once the flyers rolled out of the color inkjet printer, I took a stack while the kid grabbed a fresh roll of tape.

While Urmin let out his musical yips, Alvina clipped the leash onto his little collar. "Let's go for a walk and find your friends."

Even if we did locate the missing pet horn dogs, I had no way of contacting the Horn Brothers and Sisters, nor could I locate their HornPub. It was the same predicament we'd had with Arthur, but we could worry about that once we solved the first part of the case.

We left the offices with Urmin trotting in front of us. "Let's go wander aimlessly around the Quarter, kid," I said. "You'll see what it feels like to be a real detective."

It warmed my cold heart to walk along with my vampire half-daughter and the cute little pet. The horn dog sniffed at the ankle of a mummy pedestrian, but we nudged Urmin away before he could yank on one of the loose linens. We bumped into a werewolf walking her large pet Komodo dragon, and Urmin and the dragon sniffed snouts, then butts.

At each lamppost, we taped a *Lost Horn Dog* flyer, which had the phone number for our offices. I hoped someone would call.

Because we were looking specifically for unicorn dogs, and because Alvina had a hankering for another tasty Geppetto's Gelato, we headed in the direction of the Magic Kingdom district.

The Renaissance Faire was almost ready to open, with tents and bleachers set up and concession stands loading. Orc parking attendants laid down white chalk lines a car width apart on the empty field, though from prior experience I knew that no one would park within the lines. The Faire would open this weekend.

A shadow drifted overhead, and I glanced up to see the winged form of Alice the dragon, practicing test flights. I quickly moved us along, not wanting Alice to spot the cute unidog. "Let's head into the town square, where there's some shade."

Walking through the quaint medieval streets, we stepped aside to let a determined group of dwarves march past, singing "Hi-ho, Hi-ho!" as they headed to work in the sewer tunnels.

A withered, evil-looking crone stood behind a stand trying to sell Red Delicious apples. A puppeteer did a tiny performance, twitching the strings of her little marionettes so that they bashed and bonked one another. Alvina found it hilarious.

One of the town attractions was a large boulder with a sword thrust into it. For twenty-five cents, you could try your luck at pulling it free. Alvina was intrigued, and I indulged her, as always. I plunked the quarter into the box, and the vampire girl sweated and strained, but could not budge the sword. I wondered if Prince Dirk would do better.

After the dragon had finished her practice maneuvers and returned to her tent in the Renaissance fairgrounds, I took Alvina to the wishing well in the center of the town square, where we put up more *Lost Horn Dog* posters.

I glanced over to Oorgak's evil abode, surprised to see the shutters open and fresh sheets hanging on a clothesline. The evil wizard was back home, perhaps open for business; at the very least, he was airing out his lair.

I studied the dark sorcerer's personal logo, an oval with the dot in the middle, and remembered where I had seen that symbol before: The stylized *O* for Oorgak had been embossed on the cover of the leather-bound magic tome among the garbage washed up in Bilge Bay. Was that what had contaminated the waters and mutated the poor, innocent tadpoles? And who owned it now, after the lagoon creatures' rummage sale?

I wondered if Oorgak had dumped out his contaminated evil items when he became enlightened.

I took Alvina's hand and led her toward the imposing sinister lair. "Come on, kid. We're off to see the wizard."

Oorgak's front door was indeed wide open, though the air smelled musty and moldy. The "Closed for Business" and "Got Enlightened" signs had been torn down, though the neon "Open" sign was still switched off.

Urmin trotted forward, leading the way. I heard voices from inside, rising louder, as if in an argument. "Just one more time! Come on, you know it'll feel good!"

"No, I can't!"

The first voice was female, and I thought it sounded familiar. "You know you want to, Oorgak."

"I'm Walter!"

"Well, we can fix that. I really need you to do this for me. You can't let me down."

The evil wizard's voice was quavering. "No, I can't! I've finished my twelve steps. I'm completely straight and good now."

Now I recognized the other voice. It belonged to Dava, the beautiful Pegasus. "I can't believe you'd let me down like this, Oorgak."

"It's Walter!" he cried, his voice growing shrill.

"Think of how you could change the world. Just do this one little thing, and I'll leave you alone." I heard a soft, crystal chime; Dava must have struck her glass horseshoe on the wizard's flagstone floor.

"No! Leave me alone!"

It was time to interrupt. Accompanied by Urmin and Alvina, I strode through the front door into the torchlit dimness of the evil wizard's lair. "Hello! Excuse me!"

In the middle of the room the sparkling Pegasus flared her lavender-feathered wings. She stomped on the floor in a huff. The golden crown across her forehead reflected the torchlight as she turned toward me. "What are you doing here?"

The distraught wizard looked as if he were about to burst into tears. "Who are you? But I'm glad to see you."

Urmin let out a musical bark.

The diva Pegasus tossed her head. "This is a private matter."

"Private matters are better when they're shared with the public," I said.

In a huff, Dava stomped past us out the front door. "Think about what I said, Oorgak." We watched as she began to gallop, then leaped into the air, flapping her magnificent wings to fly off.

"Was she bothering you?" I gambled on his kinder, gentler name. "Walter?"

"It's so hard to be magically sober," he moaned. "Temptations everywhere. I got rid of all of my magical artifacts, my spellbooks, anything loaded with dark magic. I discarded them where no one would ever find them! But I can't get away from the addiction."

I narrowed my eyes. "Did you happen to dump your evil spellbooks in the drainage canal so that it washed up into Bilge Bay?"

"I don't know where the junk went, and I don't care," Walter said. "I cleared out my entire lair, every reminder, every remnant, no matter how rotten and evil. I threw them away."

I understood. It was like an alcoholic clearing his house of all the empty bottles, all of the trappings that reminded him and tempted him.

"After seeing that unicorn, I'm enlightened, and I have to hold on to that," Walter said.

"By purging all your magical artifacts into the water supply, you may have caused even more problems, sir," I said. "Now an entire generation of frog-demon tadpoles is mutated."

Walter wailed. "It's a curse. Everywhere I turn, there's more and more damage."

I thought of how desperately RRita and Dirk wanted to be

together again. "You could fix a lot of it if you'd just cast one more spell from your dark tome."

Walter's eyes went wide, and he became frantic. "Not you, too. Out! Out!"

He picked up a broom and swatted at us, chasing us back out the door. We fled, but Alvina managed to drop one of the *Lost Horn Dog* flyers, in case Walter had time to look at it.

CHAPTER 31

ime for another deep counseling session—not to find my inner zombie, but to consult with the enlightened ogre guru about Walter's karma. The pursuit of happiness and well-being is the right of any unnatural, and I didn't want to screw up any evil wizard's inner nirvana. But I also had a case to solve, a client to satisfy, and a fairy tale to end. If I could get Guru Grbth on my side, maybe he could convince Walter to do one last evil hurrah.

At the Wham-Bam Ashram, a pool-service van from Bubo and Lubo's company was parked in front, and a young frog-demon employee was conducting tests and maintenance on the ashram's koi ponds. Meditation sessions were on their midday break, so I wandered into the empty main building in search of the ogre guru.

Grbth received me with a smile as large as a Florida sinkhole. "Would you like to chant with me, Mr. Shamble? I have a catchy meditative tune." He raised his caterpillar eyebrows. "Or we could study some Zen readings."

"I'd rather just shoot the breeze." It would be like sitting down at the Goblin Tavern, only with more monastic undertones.

"Conversations lead to questions, and questions lead to understanding, and understanding leads to enlightenment," the ogre guru said.

That sounded pretty deep. He led me to the community

kitchenette in the back, where he put a kettle on to boil. As he waited, he set out an enameled teapot and unrolled a bamboo mat on the tile floor. "Have some tea with me, Mr. Shamble."

While Robin enjoyed a good cup of green tea, I explained that I was more of a coffee drinker myself. The ogre's heavy eyebrows drew together. "It is part of the process, Mr. Shamble."

"All right, then," I surrendered. "I would be honored."

After the water boiled, Grbth filled the teapot so the dried leaves could steep. Then he placed the pot on the bamboo mat between us and set out two delicate cups barely the size of shot glasses. Somehow, with his enormous sausage fingers, he was nimble enough to pour the tea into the tiny cup in front of me, then filled his own cup without spilling a drop.

I had enough trouble simply bending my legs to get into a lotus position across from him. Grbth motioned to me, and I picked up the cup. We both took a gentle, delicate sip. The tea was scalding hot and bitter.

"It's good," I said.

"What did you need to talk about?" the ogre asked. "The weather? Politics?"

"I avoid talking about politics," I said.

Grbth guffawed with such strength, he knocked my fedora askew. "Then you have already achieved the first stage of enlightenment. Oh, and avoid social media."

"Thank you for your wisdom, Guru Grbth, but I really need to talk about your acolyte, Walter, formerly known as Oorgak."

"I thought that might be the case." With a delicate little slurp, the ogre took another sip of tea. "That man had a transformative epiphany that made him eschew his former evil ways. Seeing a unicorn made him realize his many bad choices in life."

I got right to the point of the horn. "And that unicorn is now dead—murdered."

The news startled the ogre so much he rattled his tiny cup and spilled a thimbleful of tea. "Bad karma." He refilled his cup and offered me more, but I had only managed to swallow the first sip.

"Arthur's murder is one of my most important cases," I said. "That unicorn's path crossed Oorgak's, so there may be a connection. He's appearing in a lot of my cases lately. One of his evil spells messed up the lives of two other clients, and he has to do a good deed by being evil one more time. I talked to him twice, even went to his lair yesterday, but he won't budge."

Grbth nodded his shaggy head. "I am proud of my padawan. The twelve-step program really stuck. He is truly enlightened."

"But my handsome prince desperately needs to be turned back into an ugly frog. I've checked the Chamber of Commerce directory, I've searched the web, and there aren't any other evil wizards available. Oorgak is our only hope." I felt exasperated. "If Walter worked the reversal spell, it wouldn't be evil, because it would make a loving couple very happy. Now a whole clutch of tadpoles doesn't have the right role model for a father. Think of the children."

I didn't mention that Walter's contaminated magical trash had caused even more harm by turning those same tadpoles into unruly monsters.

"The web of existence is all connected," Grbth said, "and Walter has triumphed after a great struggle. You cannot ask him to forget all of his hard-fought sobriety for someone else's convenience."

"I wouldn't call it merely convenience...."

The ogre grew somber. "The addiction runs deep in his

marrow, Mr. Shamble. The dark side is strong in this one. His heart remains black, and the pull is constant. He fights the temptation all day, every day. Walter doesn't dare let go, even once, or he may be lost forever."

I had seen the wild desperation in the recovering evil wizard, and I hated even to ask it. Bracing myself, I drank the rest of the bitter tea in one gulp. "Are you saying the world is a better place if Oorgak doesn't fall off the wagon?"

Grbth reached behind him to grab his twisted club and pounded it on the floor for emphasis. "Exactly!" The ceramic teapot and the little cups jiggled with the vibration. "Walter must stay clean and in full possession of his fresh goody-two-shoes persona."

That was very unfortunate for RRita and Prince Dirk. But I realized that if Walter did go on a raging evil-magic bender, the white unicorn couldn't give him another epiphany. Arthur had been murdered.

"Maybe he needs a pet unidog for emotional support," I said.

"I have suggested it." Grbth levered himself to his feet, using the club as a crutch. "But he is allergic to pet dander."

The ogre dumped the rest of the teapot into the sink, then reached into a cabinet underneath to pull out a bottle of bourbon. "Now that we've finished the tea ceremony, how about a snort of the good stuff?"

Chapter 32

left the Wham-Bam Ashram feeling distinctly unenlightened. The meditation disciples were just arriving for early-bird services, and they gave me a happy "Om" as they climbed past me on the zigzag path to nirvana.

I still had no solution for the non-frog prince. I knew Robin was trying to set up another mediation session between the lagoon creatures and RRita and Dirk. Gil and Finn refused to budge, even though the mutant tadpoles were causing great mischief. I hoped that Tadpole Protective Services didn't have to get involved, because then all of the slimy black children would end up in foster swamp care.

As I wandered the streets of the Quarter again, I turned my thoughts to the Secret Society of Horn Brothers and Sisters. Were they paranoid enough to murder one of their own? Could it have been a vicious horn dog attack? I imagined snarling black Gurmin leaping into the air and plunging his stubby little horn into Arthur's side. No, that pointy tip would never penetrate deep enough to pierce the white unicorn's noble heart.

Of course, there was McGoo's theory of a sharpened pool cue as the murder weapon. Next time I went to the Goblin Tavern for a beer, I decided to see if a potential murder weapon was missing.

The full moon shone down from the open sky above. I cut

through another dark alley where some rats were having a picnic inside a rusty old coffee can. Two gremlins raided a dumpster, sorting out the good garbage, which they took home in eco-friendly fabric shopping bags. Seeing me, they grabbed their fresh haul and darted out of the alley. The rats packed up their picnic and ducked back into a dark hole in the brick wall.

Wandering the empty streets didn't prove fruitful, and I was fresh out of ideas. But at least I was getting my steps in.

Then one of the cases found me. A unicorn appeared at the end of the alley, blocking the exit. "Not again," I said. Then a second unicorn came in behind me. Both were ash-gray—Clyde and Dale. "We've got to stop meeting like this," I said.

The one in front of me, Dale, said, "Shhh, keep your voice down!"

The gray unicorns boxed me in, without any consideration for personal space. The pair seemed furtive, but not threatening. When I inhaled, I smelled something stronger than horse manure in the air—it was the stink of fear. Equine fear. I saw that their horns were trembling.

"We needed to speak with you, Shamble," said Clyde. "You're the only one we can trust."

"Sounds like you need to know more people," I suggested.

"We had to meet you here, out of sight from anyone else in the Horn Brotherhood."

"And Sisterhood," said Dale. "Melissa and Pirouette would completely agree."

"Unity among unicorns," I said.

"Except for Pete," Clyde snorted.

"Stinky Pete doesn't agree with anything," Dale said with a sad whinny.

Both unicorns hung their heads. Under the full moonlight, they looked pale and silvery, but they seemed diminished, nothing like the impression Arthur had given.

"I don't have the strength to deal with this much longer," Clyde said.

"We're both weakened," Dale added. "All unicorns are weakened without our horn dogs."

I thought of how Urmin was like an energy drink for all of us. "How could you all lose your horn dogs at the same time? Did somebody leave a backyard gate open and they ran loose?"

"They just disappeared," Clyde said with an annoyed whicker.

Dale added, "We think they were dognapped."

"Is there a black market for horn dogs?" I asked. "And how would someone even find you to steal your pets? My little vampire girl wrote an excellent school report on the subject. Nobody believes unicorns exist."

"Somebody does," Dale said. "And somebody has our unidogs and all the magic they contain. Please find them, Mr. Shamble!"

"Already doing my best," I said. "Alvina and I put up flyers all over the Quarter."

"We saw the flyers," Dale said. "Very impressive."

Clyde leaned close and spoke in a whickering whisper. "We've got to warn you about Midnight Pete. He'll do anything to maintain the mystique of unicorns. He's got his head stuck in the Middle Ages."

Dale added, "Pete thinks that unicorns belong only in a perfect fairy-tale world, and it would be beneath us to come out of the closet right now."

"The other monsters are out of the closet," I said. "It's not a perfect fairy-tale world, but we do our best. Though we could use more rainbows and glitter."

The two dejected gray unicorns hung their horned heads. "Oooh, rainbows and glitter."

Then a harsh yapping interrupted our illicit back-alley conversation. Startled, nervous Dale leaped half a foot off the ground.

The black unidog scuttled down the alley, defiantly challenging us with atonal, unmusical barks. "It's Gurmin!" cried Clyde. "We're caught!"

"We aren't doing anything," I said.

Spooked, Clyde and Dale turned to face the alley opening where the black unicorn had arrived. Midnight Pete strode toward us like a schoolyard bully, his hooves clomping on the debris-strewn ground. "What's going on here?"

"Oh … nothing," said Dale.

"Just out for an evening constitutional," Clyde said. "And we bumped into Mr. Shamble."

Midnight Pete made a grunting, chuffing sound. "And Shamble just happened to be here in a dark, shadowy alley under a full moon?"

"I was out looking for the horn dogs," I said, since honesty is always the best policy. "What better place to look?" Pretending to be brave, I stepped closer to the black unicorn. "But why do you still have your pet when all the other unidogs have vanished? Is it because nobody wants your mutt?"

He swung his horn toward me in a clearly threatening gesture. "Because I'm a good pet owner. My familiar doesn't go wandering off."

Gurmin snarled in agreement.

"We were good pet owners, too!" Clyde and Dale both said at the same time—unicorns in unison.

Midnight Pete huffed, as if he knew he couldn't win the argument. "You two, leave Shamble alone. He's got detecting to do. Can't have mangy, unruly unidogs running loose in the streets." He harassed the two gray unicorns to precede him out the alley.

"I promise I'll track down the missing critters," I called after them. "And I'll find Arthur's murderer, too! Rainbows or no rainbows."

I meant it.

CHAPTER 33

Every Friday, the Ghoul's Diner had a fish-fry special, so naturally, Gil and Finn wanted to meet there for a lunchtime conversation. The food at the diner was always fishy, slimy, or rancid, but on fish-fry day Albert Gould advertised that his meat came directly from the sewers, rather than being scraped off the street as roadkill. I hoped the lagoon creatures might have had a unicorn-level epiphany about their hostage tadpoles.

Robin was in court filing her appeal for Archie's indecent exposure case, so I agreed to meet Gil and Finn myself. And by myself, I meant that Sheyenne accompanied me. She even considered it a date, although if I had been serious about a romantic meal, we would have gone literally anywhere other than the Ghoul's Diner.

I drove us in the Pro Bono Mobile, and we arrived just before the big lunch rush. I pulled open the door in a gentlemanly gesture, motioning Sheyenne to drift inside. The smells hit me like a supernatural force, and Sheyenne's ectoplasmic form rippled.

Back in the kitchen, Albert slaved over his hot grill, sweating mucus down onto the food as he moved with slow, jerky gestures. Drool dribbled out the side of his mouth, and he wiped it off with the top of a bun, which he placed on a cheeseburger he was preparing. His discolored face was sagging, trapped in the middle of swift decomposition; his eyes were dull, and his words slurred. Like always, he raised a greasy spatula in greeting as he saw me.

"Smells good, Albert," I said.

"Special," the ghoul drawled. "Fish-fry special."

"That's what we're here for."

Sheyenne scanned the crowd, looking for Gil and Finn among the werewolves, vampires, Igors, necromancers, and other unnaturals. "I don't see them."

A mummy was straining a bowl of chicken soup through the gauze bandages across his mouth. A werewolf frowned at a strand of fur he had found in his chef salad. A pair of skinny human college students with backpacks sat at a narrow booth and studied the menu; beside them on the table was a guidebook of available hostels in the Unnatural Quarter.

"We're early." I motioned to an empty booth where we could use the time to plan strategy. Sheyenne picked up a menu with her ghostly hands, although both of us knew all of the selections by heart.

Esther, the annoying harpy waitress, swooped in like a bird of prey dive-bombing a helpless bunny. "Now what?" she demanded. "You can't take a whole booth for yourselves."

I looked up calmly. "We're expecting two more, Esther. I'll just have coffee for now."

"Coffee's not enough!" the harpy screeched.

I had long ago learned not to get riled up by Esther's foul mood. "I'm sure we'll be having the special."

"You better! And you better tip, too."

"How can I not reward such sparkling service?" I asked.

The waitress sneered at me with her sharp, angular face, clacked her beak, then swirled in a huff and a flurry of oily, iridescent feathers.

"I wish Mary Celeste was waitressing again," Sheyenne said with a sigh.

We had worked with the pleasant four-armed waitress during a previous case—a quiet, small-town girl with too many limbs who had come to the Unnatural Quarter seeking fame and fortune as a hand model. She had gotten a job at the Ghoul's Diner as a dishwasher, then worked her way up to waitress, which was an aggressive stance as far as Esther was concerned. I said, "She has her hands in many pies."

Esther slammed down my steaming, murky cup of coffee as if it were an insult, but I was looking at Sheyenne's glowing blue eyes.

After the waitress left, she said, "Alvina was asking about Arthur again this morning. Are you any closer to finding the murderer?"

"Only questions and suspicions." I had told her about my encounter in the alley the previous evening. "And I know McGoo would like to interrogate a few unicorns of interest, but I have no idea where to find the HornPub so he could serve a search warrant." I shook my head, but refused to give up. I placed my elbows on the table. "Today let's focus on our other case." I slurped the coffee, and it tasted awful. I nodded in appreciation. "Maybe we can convince Gil and Finn that their best course of action is to give RRita and Dirk their sweet baby tadpoles back."

Sheyenne sighed. "But we're still no closer to turning Dirk back into a frog."

"We're at a dead end, as far as Oorgak is concerned. He's just too mellow to do the dirty deed we need."

The door jangled, and the scaly lagoon creatures strode in on their wide flipper feet. Seeing us, they made their way past a towering troll who had been waiting at the cash register to pay his bill. Esther often ignored paying customers, hoping they would just drop extra dollars on the counter, which she could sweep into her apron and count as an extra tip.

Reaching our booth, Gil and Finn quibbled over which one would get in first, because neither of them liked to slide across the red Naugahyde. Their greenish bodies glistened with perspiration, or swamp water. I could see they were both short-tempered and frustrated.

Finn finally slid in. "I sure could use a fish fry."

"Best in the Quarter," Gil added, looking at me. "We come here every week."

"Glad you have low expectations," I said. "It's how Albert has so many satisfied customers."

In addition to the fish fry chalked on the board, the Ghoul's Diner also featured Mystery Meat fried steak and Mystery Meat corndogs (flagged with "Our most popular item!"—likely because they were preprocessed and prepackaged, and the ghoul cook could do little damage). The one I'd eaten with Alvina and Urmin hadn't been too bad, but I'd been with good company.

"Has business picked up at all at Bilge Bay?" Sheyenne asked.

"What business?" Finn grumbled.

"Those demon tadpoles scare away all the customers," Gil said in frustration. He left claw marks on the speckled Formica tabletop. "Or they would, but there aren't any customers in the first place. They've eaten all the leeches in the spawning ponds!"

"Those were special imports from Louisiana," Finn added.

Strutting over, Esther was about to accost the two lagoon creatures when they both glared at her. "Yes, we're ready to order. Two fish-fry specials."

Startled, she wrote the order on her pad.

"And a glass of milk," Finn added.

"Just water for me," Gil said.

The harpy waitress swiveled her searchlight glare to me. "Make up your mind, Shamble."

"I'll have a … corn dog. Those are tasty."

"Our most popular item," Esther said.

When she was gone like a passing thunderstorm, I turned to the lagoon creatures and used my most reasonable zombie tone. "Look, you two, cooler heads have to prevail. Many of your problems would be solved if you returned those tadpoles to their proper parents. I've been learning a lot about the benefits of good karma these days."

"If they want those tadpoles back, they need to do something for us." Gil pounded his webbed hand on the tabletop.

"Why would they even want those nasty vermin?" Finn added. "They're monsters!"

"Kids can be rambunctious," Sheyenne said. "But they're worth it in the long run."

"RRita and Prince Dirk don't want to be absentee parents," I said.

"They should have thought of that before they got those eggs fertilized out of wedlock," Gil said.

"That's a very medieval attitude," Sheyenne retorted.

"Bilge Bay isn't far from the Magic Kingdom district," Finn said. "It's a very conservative part of the Quarter."

Esther dropped baskets filled with battered, deep-fried fish heads, tails, and entrails mixed with golden crinkle-cut fries in front of each of the lagoon creatures. She handed me a corn dog on a stick, but I had to ask her for ketchup and mustard. When she came back with the condiments, I had finished my coffee and raised it, requesting a refill. The harpy acted as if I had declared war, but she came back and poured the volcanic hot black liquid into my mug, spilling half as much across the tabletop.

"And bring us some more napkins, please," Sheyenne asked.

Gil crunched on the deep-fried fish heads while Finn ate his fries first, dipping them into the tartar sauce. We ate in silence for a few minutes. I twirled the corn dog in a pool of ketchup and mustard, which I mixed together to form my own special sauce. The corn dog wasn't half bad, considering it was made from processed mutant worm meat. At least it wasn't vegan.

After Gil finished his second fish head, his posture changed. His scaly shoulders slumped, and he hung his head. "Our problem goes deeper than monster tadpoles, Mr. Shamble. I never thought it would be so difficult to get people to try a brand-new resort."

"All our coupons and marketing and specials haven't worked." Finn sounded offended. "Once they see what we have to offer, they're sure to come back. We just need to get over these opening jitters."

I had an idea. "Frog demons would be the perfect clientele. They love swamps, and they like to pamper themselves."

"How do we get them to come at all?" Gil wailed.

Finn ate another french fry.

"For one thing," I said in a stern voice, "maybe you should make friends with RRita. She's the daughter of the most powerful pool-maintenance frog demons in the Quarter."

"She is?" Gil asked.

"And you've made enemies out of her influential family by stealing her tadpoles. Not a smart move."

"Bubo and Lubo would do anything to defend their daughter and her handsome prince fiancé," Sheyenne added.

I doubted the parents would be inclined to do any favors, one way or another. But Gil and Finn didn't need to know that.

I set my half-eaten corn dog aside and leaned closer to the two lagoon creatures. "Would it hurt to be nice? If you make RRita happy, she can encourage her parents to spread the word among all the frog demons. Then Bilge Bay will be crowded."

Gil and Finn finished their fish-fry specials in silence. "We'll consider it, Mr. Shamble," Gil finally said. "Please tell Miss Deyer."

They got up to leave. Since they were in such hard financial circumstances, I offered to pick up the tab. Sheyenne and I looked at each other, feeling somewhat hopeful for a change.

I capped off the meal by eating the last few french fries from Finn's basket.

Chapter 34

After my diner corn dog meal, I felt more lethargic than ever, as if a fresh round of rigor mortis had set in. Sheyenne was as light and bright as ever, since she'd had only an insubstantial lunch. We left the Ghoul's Diner, happy to tell Robin about the minor progress we had made with the lagoon creatures.

Before walking back to where I had parked the Pro Bono Mobile, we watched a delivery truck pull up behind the diner. Mystery Meat from Gold Boris. The truck showed a large, tasty-looking corn dog. *Corn Dog Express!*

"I guess it really is the most popular item on the menu if they need a whole truck to deliver the week's supply," I said. If we were going to feed Urmin for quite a while, maybe we should start buying corn dogs in bulk.

A zombie in a grease-stained khaki jumpsuit and a green trucker's cap swung out from behind the wheel. I thought I recognized him. "Sheyenne, is that …?"

"Steve Halsted!" she said.

Steve was a zombie trucker based in the Unnatural Quarter. He had died, leaving behind a charming young boy and a shrewish, bitter wife. After the Big Uneasy, when Steve came back from the dead, his wife denied him visitation rights for his son, because he was dead. Robin took on the case, which turned out to be a very hairy legal battle, but in the end, Steve was reunited with his son so they could spend quality time together.

Sheyenne and I strolled over to say hi. Steve removed his trucker's cap and looked at me with a puzzled expression as the wheels turned slowly in his mind. "Oh, Dan Shamble! My dirt brother!"

We had both crawled up from the grave on the same night, so we had a certain bond. I shook his hand. "You're running Mystery Meat now?"

He screwed the cap back on his head and grinned with pride. "Not just any Mystery Meat—I'm the driver of the Corn Dog Express." He lowered his voice. "Beats long-haul trucking, and I get to spend weekends with Jordan."

Given our past acquaintance, being dirt brothers and all, I wondered if Steve might let a few corn dogs fall off the back of the truck for Urmin. As if she could sense what I was thinking, Sheyenne gave me a warning glance.

"I just had a corn dog for lunch," I said. "Albert advertises them as his most popular item."

"Yup, Ghoul's Diner is a regular stop on my route." Steve opened the back of the Corn Dog Express, which was piled high with cardboard boxes showing the cute corn dog logo. Steve picked up two boxes and staggered toward the rear door of the diner. The rest of the truck remained full.

I offered to help. "Need me to follow you with a few more loads?"

Steve paused at the door. "No, this is Albert's order. The rest of the cargo is for a specialty client."

I looked at the many remaining boxes. Just one client? "He must have a big appetite." I couldn't imagine who in their right mind, or with a functional digestive system, would eat that many corn dogs.

"Special delivery," Steve said with a shrug around his armload of boxes. "One client, one address, one truckload of corn dogs."

He nudged the door open with his steel-toed work boot and carried the box into the kitchen, where I heard Esther shrieking orders.

Something about this seemed odd. Sheyenne drifted beside me. "What are you thinking, Beaux?"

"I'm thinking that horn dogs eat corn dogs," I said. "And I'd like to find out where this big delivery is going."

Steve stood just inside the door with his clipboard, waiting for Albert's interminable signature. He tore off the top copy, left it on the counter, then headed back out to the truck. He closed the back of the Corn Dog Express and climbed into the driver's seat, giving us a parting wave. "Nice to see you again, Mr. Shamble. And you, too, Miss Sheyenne."

"Hey Steve, can you tell us where you're delivering all those corn dogs?" I asked. "Who's the big customer?"

He shook his grayish head. "Sorry, that's against company policy, and I don't want Gold Boris getting mad at me." He lowered his voice. "I've heard rumors that more than one misbehaving delivery driver has become worm food."

"No worries, Steve. I wouldn't want you to get in trouble." I made up my mind to surreptitiously follow him instead.

With the roaring engine of the Pro Bono Mobile, there was no surreptitious way to tail the Corn Dog Express, but Steve had cranked up the radio, blasting out Rush's greatest hits loud enough to cook the corn dogs in the back, so he didn't notice us. We could hang back a good distance, because it wasn't hard to keep an eye on the brightly painted delivery van. Of course, our lime-green, rusty Ford Maverick stood out like a rotting sore thumb, too.

The delivery truck meandered through the streets of the Quarter, which are never straight. (The unnatural highway department doesn't believe in expressways.) The traffic slowed down at the edge of the Magic Kingdom district, and I realized it was opening day for the Renaissance Faire, but we got rolling again as Steve turned a corner—and headed straight for Betty Bibbity's event-planning venue.

"A fairy godmother eats corn dogs?" I asked.

"Maybe she has a big event, like a wedding reception, with corn dogs for all the guests," Sheyenne said.

I felt the real answer was far more suspicious.

The delivery truck drove around to the back of the big warehouse, where the fairy godmother and her Pegasus partner distributed glass footwear sold on the Home Capitalism Network.

Cautious, I parked half a block away, where we watched the Corn Dog Express back up to the large delivery-bay doors. He honked his horn and waited. The big warehouse door rolled up as Steve climbed out of the truck and opened the cargo compartment.

A swarm of unionized worker fairies flitted out from the cavernous warehouse. Steve stacked the corn dog boxes on the asphalt, and the fairies worked together to pick them up and fly them inside. Sheyenne and I watched until the entire van was empty and all the corn dogs were safely delivered. One fairy pushed a red control button, and the segmented delivery-bay door rolled down and crashed against the concrete pad.

Content to be done with the day's deliveries, Steve started up the truck and rolled away from the warehouse. Betty Bibbity's glass-slipper warehouse was locked up tight.

"We need to have a look at what's going on in there, Spooky." I was always suspicious of corn dogs, but now the mystery was even thicker.

Chapter 35

eaving the Pro Bono Mobile parked out of sight, Sheyenne and I crept across the cracked asphalt delivery zone. The large building was imposing, but there had to be a way inside.

As a zombie detective, I'm willing to bend the rules, and that includes breaking and entering under extreme circumstances. But there are advantages to having a ghost girlfriend: Sheyenne could simply slip her spectral form through the walls and enter without breaking anything at all.

"I'm on it," she said.

"Go have a full reconnoiter," I told her, using the proper detective terminology.

Sheyenne blew me an air kiss, then her glowing ectoplasmic form passed directly through the brick wall. I waited outside, leaning against the wall next to the big delivery doors. I adjusted my fedora and tried to look like a common bum, so no one would ask questions.

Sure, maybe Sheyenne would find a completely normal and innocent explanation inside the warehouse. It was possible the loyal unionized fairies were just having a company barbecue with all those corn dogs. But I suspected something fishier than the fish fry at the Ghoul's Diner.

I just couldn't imagine that the sweet fairy godmother event planner was actually a twisted villain with a nefarious horn-dog-napping scheme. Then again, if Betty Bibbity really was evil, perhaps we could hire her instead of Oorgak to turn Prince Dirk into a frog again.

I always like to look on the bright side of things.

Sheyenne was gone longer than I expected, which gave me time to become paranoid. Considering all my prior experience, I'm good at coming up with worst-case scenarios.

Her spectral form slipped through the brick wall again, appearing in front of me with an urgent expression. "I found them, Beaux! They're all in there."

"It is a big warehouse. Glass slippers of every size and style."

"Not slippers," Sheyenne said. "Puppies! Cute little unidogs."

"Well, that explains the big corn dog delivery. How many did you see?"

"About a dozen unidogs—confined in little cages. It's like a puppy mill!" Her ghostly face was distraught. "Poor little horny things. We've got to free them."

I nodded. Clyde and Dale, Melissa and Pirouette would all be happy to have their magical familiars back, although Gurmin would no longer be top dog. But a dozen? That was a lot more than I expected, because I had seen only five members of the secret unicorn society in the HornPub. Then I remembered they had mentioned other branches of Horn Brothers and Sisters. Unicorns were a lot more common than I had thought.

I decided to call for backup. I pulled out my phone, and McGoo answered right away. "Hey, Shamble. I picked up Alvina from school, and we're going to make dinner. Macaroni and cheese with ketchup on the side."

"Sounds delicious, but we have an emergency here." I explained about the illegally caged horn dogs inside Betty Bibbity's warehouse.

"Okay, I'm up for some overtime," McGoo said. "You want this to be official, or you want it to be quick?"

Sheyenne glowed in front of me, pleading. "They look so miserable. We've got to free those horn dogs!"

"I'd rather have quick," I said.

"Good. I'll be right there, and I'll bring backup."

I knew exactly what he was suggesting. "Alvina?"

"Al's got a way with those little critters."

After I hung up, I pondered the fortresslike warehouse, but I didn't see a way to break in. Long past business hours, the warehouse looked sleepy and quiet on the outside. The delivery doors were secure, and the controls were on the inside. "Now we wait, I guess."

Sheyenne tossed her insubstantial blond hair. "We're not going to wait." She floated directly through the wall again, and seconds later I heard the hum and whirr of controls. She had used her poltergeist powers to push the big red button.

The slatted delivery door rolled up into the warehouse ceiling, and I stood in front of the yawning opening. "That's another way to enter without breaking."

Sheyenne drifted ahead of me. "Come on, follow me!"

Previously, I had seen only the front section of the hangar-sized warehouse as fairies and troll workers distributed units of breakable footwear. Now Sheyenne led me to the back section, which was a labyrinth of stacked wooden crates, tables, and decorations for different kinds of celebratory events, from weddings to graduation parties, Walpurgis Night social mixers, solstice dating hours, birthdays, and spawning showers.

Walled off and out of casual view, we found the puppy cages: wire structures that held pathetic but still adorable unidogs. They were dark brown, blond, smoky gray, or spotted like a Dalmatian. Sulking, the critters hunched beside water bowls and gnawed sticks from the corn dogs they had been fed. They looked gaunt and malnourished (and I knew that Mystery Meat is chock-full of vitamins and minerals, according to the advertisements).

Someone had snatched all of these unidogs, but for what purpose? The horn dogs yapped and barked and wiggled their entire bodies with excitement as they saw Sheyenne and me. A few of them cringed, which implied they might have been abused.

As they continued to bark, the sound was like soothing, easy-listening music, and rainbows sparkled in the air. I recalled McGoo mentioning a neighbor calling about mysterious and unexpected barking on the night of Arthur's murder. Maybe that had been the sound of these captive unidogs.

Crouching in front of the first wire kennels, Sheyenne used her poltergeist powers to work the stubborn latch. "Let's get them out of these cages!"

I used my stiff fingers to open another cage, and the first two unidogs bounded out, frisky and delighted. We each turned to another cage, frustrated by the stubborn latches. After two more puppies were loose, though, I heard an ominous buzzing in the air, like a squadron of toy bombers.

It was worse than bombers, though. A swarm of angry, unionized fairies hurtled toward us on the attack. Tiny, high-pitched voices shouted, "Intruder alert! Intruder alert!"

A fairy crashed into my fedora and knocked it off my head. Sheyenne swatted at four fairies swarming around her, but they couldn't harm her insubstantial form. The horn dogs barked even louder.

"Fairies united!" one of them called. The obnoxious creatures weren't just fanatical; they seemed to be bonded by some kind of spell, ridiculously loyal to their employer.

I flailed my hands, but the flying pixies were fiendishly fast and determined. "This is an illegal activity," I shouted, "and you'll all be under arrest. The police are on the way!" I'm sure Robin could have provided more appropriate threatening verbiage.

The fairies were not easily cowed, though, and they buzzed around, dive-bombing. The black-and-white spotted horn dog, freed from its cage, jumped into the air and tried to chomp down on a fairy, clearly having no love for these pesky Tinkerbell nightmares.

I smacked a fairy out of the air, and she went reeling and buzzing into the white latticework of a dismantled wedding arch. I used the brief respite to duck down and fumble with another cage latch.

Pissed off, Sheyenne drew herself up and gathered her poltergeist powers. With a whoosh of air, she unleashed ghostly ripples that knocked the fairies away from the cages. "I've got more hot air where that came from!" she said in a dark, threatening tone.

I managed to open another cage, and Sheyenne freed one more unidog. Half of them were loose now.

Suddenly, all the buzzing fairies drew back and hung in the air, as if waiting for something.

I huffed. "Maybe they learned their lesson, Spooky."

But all the horn dogs whimpered and cowered, and I had a very bad feeling. I turned slowly around to face the big open delivery doors and the expansive parking lot outside.

The black unicorn stood there with his snarling black unidog. Midnight Pete lowered his threatening horn, pointing it directly at me.

CHAPTER 36

The intimidated fairy workers ceased their attack and buzzed away from the black beast. The horn dogs shivered and trembled in terror. Two of the ones we had freed ducked back into the safety of their cages.

"I am Midnight Pete!" he said with great pride. "Fear my horn!"

I took charge of the situation, forcing a victorious smile. "Good news, Stinky Pete. We found the missing horn dogs. Another successful case."

"Stop using that name!" the black unicorn snorted.

Gurmin let out an ominous growl, making me fear that my ankles were about to be nibbled.

Pete slashed from side to side with his bronze horn. The rainbow shimmer from his dark coat was slanted toward the indigo and violet end of the spectrum. "I told you not to poke around in unicorn secrets, Shamble, and now you'll face the consequences."

"Chambeaux and Deyer is still sending you a bill," Sheyenne said. "Case closed."

"I solved another case, too," I said. I'm good at bluffing, especially when facing a dark nemesis, and this one was black as night. "You murdered Arthur, didn't you? I bet that horn of yours is a perfect match for the weapon that caused his fatal wound."

Pete let out another sarcastic snort. "Arthur was such a

cliché! Such a do-gooder, pure and white in this drab and dingy world. He thought he could prance around like a fabled unicorn. He had to be stopped before he ruined everything."

I was surprised the confession was so easy. I lowered my voice and said to Sheyenne, "I knew it wasn't a sharpened pool cue from the Goblin Tavern."

Sheyenne also faced the black unicorn. "Did Arthur try to stop you because he discovered you were kidnapping these precious unidogs? Is that how Urmin got away?"

Gurmin growled, as if the cute little horn dog was his mortal nemesis.

"There were so many reasons to kill Arthur. Why pick just one?" Pete said, thrashing his tail. He clomped forward into the glass slipper warehouse. "After we obtained that powerful spellbook from the lagoon creatures' rummage sale, I had everything I needed for my grand plan—except for the unidogs to power it all. I was going to unleash waves of fairy-tale magic, but Arthur wanted to throw the spellbook back into the drainage canal where he said it belonged."

"None of that magical garbage actually belongs in the drainage canal," I said. "The evil wizard dumped them, because he didn't want the temptation around."

"But now I possess them! And now I have the unidogs and all their magic. Unicorn magic!" He let out a sinister whinny. *"Fairy-tale magic."*

"The horn dogs really are cute," I agreed.

"What are you going to do with all that magic?" Sheyenne shimmered defiantly beside me. "These familiars belong with their own unicorns."

Midnight Pete raised his front hoof as if it were a clenched fist. "I will transform the world, using the evil wizard and his dark spellbook. With enough unidog magic,

I can make the Unnatural Quarter into a storybook fantasy world! Like Medieval Times, or a theme park. A place fit for majestic unicorns to live. When the world is a fairy tale again, we won't have to keep our existence secret anymore."

I tried to poke holes in his megalomaniacal twisted plan. "You don't have to hide right now. I'm sure I mentioned that before. Everyone will accept you for who you are."

"The world isn't ready for us!" Pete stomped his forehoof on the warehouse floor, striking sparks. Fortunately, he wasn't wearing a glass horseshoe slipper, or it would have broken. "Unicorns should be revered and worshipped as fabled creatures. Instead, we're used as logos and cartoon mascots."

"Otherwise known as cultural icons," I said. Alvina would never go to school without her cute unicorn backpack.

"Are you living in a fantasy land?" Sheyenne asked with scorn.

"Not yet," Pete gloated, "but soon."

I still didn't know how he was going to work that powerful spell, even if he had purchased the spellbook at the rummage sale. In my research for the case, and on all the unicorn conspiracy websites Alvina had studied, I'd never heard that unicorns were also sorcerers.

Behind the black unicorn, a gruff voice shouted, "Freeze! Hold it right there!"

With his police special revolver drawn, McGoo stepped through the open receiving bay door. He looked around, assessing the situation. "Who let the dogs out?"

Behind him, Alvina led Urmin on a leash, and the brown horn dog was so excited he yapped and bounced up and down. She unclipped the leash so he could run free.

"Good timing, McGoo," I said.

"Thought you could use some help, Shamble. I'm ready to make arrests," McGoo said. "Is the fairy godmother here?"

"Fairy godmother?" Pete's voice was filled with scorn.

"Isn't she part of this?" I asked.

"She is a fool!" the black unicorn snarled.

"Doesn't answer my question. One would have to be a fool to take part in such a crazy scheme," I said. "The jig is up, your goose is cooked, and all the other clichés have been retired."

"Oh, look at all the horn dogs!" Alvina and Urmin ran to the cages, where the other canicorns began barking. Entirely ignoring the threat of the evil unicorn, the kid petted the loose critters and then set to work on the rest of the cages. Sheyenne swooped in and began helping.

"Stop that!" Pete said, frustrated. "We are right in the middle of my grand finale! I am in command here."

McGoo waved his revolver. "My badge and my gun say otherwise."

Pete whickered with harsh equine laughter. "Ah, but my evil wizard says otherwise!"

He let out a shrill, commanding whistle. I didn't know that unicorns could whistle, but up until recently I didn't know unicorns even existed. I was learning more and more every day.

Alvina kept opening the puppy cages. When that vampire girl sets her mind to something, it's hard to distract her.

I heard a rumble of thunder outside and saw dark clouds gathering in the sky. With a loud boom for fanfare, a dark-robed figure stepped forward.

Right now, Walter did not look as mellow or karmically centered as he had been at the Wham-Bam Ashram. Despite the ripples of power that rose around him like body odor, his bearded face looked haggard. His eyes were bloodshot, his black hair was wild, and his hands trembled, like an alcoholic suffering from DTs.

"Oh good, there he is," Pete said. "Even after we bought his spellbook and paraphernalia from the lagoon creatures, we still needed him to work his dark magic again."

Black and obnoxious, Gurmin darted into the labyrinth of crates and event-planning items, barking and growling. Finding what he was looking for, the sinister unidog dragged a waterlogged, leather-bound spellbook onto the floor of the warehouse. I recognized Oorgak's signature logo on the stained cover.

"This is all an evil wizard needs," Midnight Pete said.

Walter stared at the book as if afraid to come closer. He took tentative steps, struggling with himself like a person on a strict diet walking past a candy store that gave out free samples.

"Do it, Oorgak!" Pete pressed. "You know you want to."

This was worse than I had thought. "Walter, you can't! Remember your Zen enlightenment. This is going to mess with your inner harmony."

Walter covered his mouth with his hands, terrified, and began biting his fingernails, but he couldn't tear his eyes from the evil spellbook. The temptation and the need were too much for him.

I saw the moment his resolve broke. Walter flung his arms apart and raised them toward the warehouse ceiling as if calling down the heavens. His dark robes rippled about, and more thunder boomed outside.

McGoo looked unsettled and confused. Sheyenne and I stared up at the roiling black magic. All the unidogs howled together.

The ominous wizard crackled with twice the self-confidence he had exhibited before. "I am not Walter," he said in a booming voice. *"I am Oorgak!"*

Chapter 37

or more than a week I had been trying every possible trick to make Oorgak return to his evil ways, so I should have been happy. But as he simmered and roiled before us, a mass of dark sorcery complete with a loud maniacal laugh, I didn't feel like taking a victory lap.

Midnight Pete cheered him on. "You tell him, Oorgak."

"Silence, horned minion!" the wizard snarled. "Behold, as I revel in my newfound evilness!"

The black unicorn looked annoyed. "That wasn't the deal."

Gurmin yipped at the raging sorcerer, and Oorgak made an offhand gesture. Static electricity and ozone rippled through the air, and with a sudden *poof!* the unidog's fur turned embarrassingly fluffy and frizzy, like an unruly afro on four legs.

Next to Alvina, Urmin let out a succession of barks that sounded like snickers.

"Let's take a breath and talk about this," I suggested. "Go over a list of unrealistic expectations."

McGoo clearly wished he had stayed home with Alvina to make mac and cheese with ketchup.

Oorgak seemed to gorge himself on his newfound black magic. Now that he had fallen off the wagon, he wanted to make up for lost time. "Disharmony feels so *good!*"

Pete stalked over to Oorgak. "Keep your eyes on the ball

and remember our objective! A fairy-tale existence awaits for all of us, but only if you use the unidog magic and unleash the terrible spell."

The wizard picked up the waterlogged spellbook that Gurmin had dragged out of storage. He cuddled it against his chest like a love letter. "Yes, I will create a fantasy land with wizards and unicorns and dragons, haunted castles and magic spells. It will be just like Medieval Times."

"Sounds like what happened after the Big Uneasy," I said. "But backdated."

McGoo's freckled face wore a perplexed frown. "Why in the world would anybody want to go back to life in the dreary Middle Ages?"

"Because it was magical!" Oorgak snapped.

"And mythical creatures had the respect we deserve," the black unicorn added.

"But stinky, drafty outhouses were the height of personal sanitation." McGoo is good at assessing criminal mastermind plots from a pragmatic perspective.

"Unicorns don't need to use outhouses," said Midnight Pete.

I spoke up. "And there was no indoor plumbing or electricity, no heat during the winter and no air conditioning on those sweltering summer days."

Oorgak/Walter began to falter. "Air conditioning is certainly nice...."

"And the class inequality back then was terrible," Sheyenne said. "Sure, everything was nice if you happened to be a noble lord with a vast estate, but if you were a squalid peasant, then life sucked. Serfs lived in ramshackle hovels and used manure for fires."

Oorgak opened the spellbook's stained leather cover and

began flipping through pages. "That is not the scenario I intend to create."

"Ooh, and there were lots of diseases," Alvina said. "I read about them for a school homework assignment. The bubonic plague and the Black Death, cholera and lice. Ick!" She shuddered so hard her blond pigtails quivered.

"But there were also brave knights," the evil wizard insisted, "and magic swords and dragon's treasure."

"We can find all that at the Renaissance Faire every year," I said. "You've been duped into thinking this is a good thing, Walter."

"I am Oorgak!" he roared.

Midnight Pete tried to regain control of the situation. "Do not get distracted—this is our chance! We have all the unidogs together, and their magic is concentrated in one place. We must use it now!"

"That's magic you stole," I said. "You had no right to those pet horn dogs. They belong to your Horn Brothers and Sisters. You're betraying the legendary nobility of your own species. Who is going to respect unicorns at all after this?"

"Good one, Shamble," McGoo muttered.

The frizzy black unidog whimpered plaintively up at Pete, hearing his master's threat to drain all the horned familiars. The black unicorn did not reassure him.

The recidivist evil wizard was clearly conflicted, though. He flipped through the pages of his spellbook, studying footnotes and commentary in an attempt to find insight.

"Don't do it, Walter," I repeated. "Don't make this a fractured fairy tale."

Clutching the spellbook, he squeezed his eyes shut, groaning—and then he snapped. "No! Leave me alone! I like being evil!"

A booming thunder crack of unleashed dark magic rattled the warehouse. Oorgak clearly intended to demonstrate his power and dominance, to keep us all cowering and in control, but the loud thunder had the opposite effect—the noise spooked the terrified unidogs and they bolted in all directions.

Out of control, Oorgak blasted a lightning bolt into the event planner's storage shelves, obliterating rolls of crepe paper and cardboard bells from a vampire's silver anniversary. Sparks, ashes, and debris flew everywhere.

Barking, Urmin ran after his fellow horn dogs, and Alvina squealed as she chased after him.

Midnight Pete pawed his front hooves on the floor. "Stop them!"

Some of the horn dogs scattered into the warehouse, knocking boxes of glass slippers from the shelves, but most of the horny familiars ran through the open bay doors and the empty parking lot outside.

McGoo swung his revolver around, looking for a target. The spellbound fairies buzzed around us, but I put them far down on the list of nuisances.

But Oorgak was not just evil—he was also flustered. When Pete kept demanding that he do something, the wizard retorted, "You can stick that horn up your ass!" He raised his arms to call the knotted thunderclouds in the sky.

Sheyenne and I ducked past Midnight Pete and escaped out into the open. Outside, the horn dogs ran loose, burning off energy from being kept in small cages.

"How are we going to stop them, Beaux?" Sheyenne asked.

"This is a little out of my wheelhouse," I said. "Someone must be better equipped."

Then a true worthy opponent arrived, a person who could confront the no-longer-formerly-evil Oorgak. The beautiful (sic) frog demon princess looked proud as she strode forward, arm in arm with her brave Prince Dirk, who wore his purple cape, his tight hose, his jerkin, and his crown. He carried a sword that I was sure he had pulled from the boulder in the town square.

Dirk lifted his square jaw defiantly and faced down Oorgak. "There you are! I've been looking for an evil wizard."

CHAPTER 38

We were facing a destructive, dark sorcerer who wanted to get all medieval on the Quarter, so I was more than happy to let some other hero take the hit. Prince Dirk was made for this sort of challenge, right out of a storybook. He had a crown, while I only wore a fedora. I had my .38 pistol, but Dirk held a royal sword.

"Foul Oorgak!" the prince roared. "You shall atone for the harm you have done—and the worse harm you have *undone*."

RRita blinked her lamp-like eyes at her beloved Dirk, adoring him even without his amphibious physique. "Antagonize him, my prince. Piss him off!"

"I am already pissed off," Oorgak said.

"Then I challenge you." Dirk held up his sword. "By the power of my princely blade Pointy Thing, I shall combat your dark sorcery."

This had all the hallmarks of a staged confrontation at the Renaissance Faire, but these guys were playing for keeps, not for tips. Dirk swished his purple cape and moved RRita to safety behind him, out of the line of the magical fire.

Oorgak dropped the heavy spellbook on the warehouse floor and cracked his knuckles as he strode out of the receiving bay into the open. The horn dogs were still running loose outside, and Alvina chased them around the parking lot.

McGoo stepped up beside me. "Anything we can do here, Shamble? Or are we just bystanders?"

I shrugged. "Is there anything in the police training manual about arresting evil wizards?"

"Could be in the same section about finding dead unicorns," he said.

While we faced the brewing magical storm, Sheyenne used poltergeist powers to release the last horn dogs from their cages. When one latch proved particularly stubborn, she made an exasperated noise and broke the lock with a rattling surge of power. The last captive unidog bounced out, wagging his tail and licking Sheyenne's ectoplasmic palm with enough intrinsic magic to make her giggle.

The black unicorn huffed, annoyed by all these distractions. "Deal with this nuisance, Oorgak, so we can get down to creating a little magic of our own."

Blue lightning crackled between the outstretched fingers of the now-unenlightened wizard. "That prince is an insect!"

I suddenly feared he would transform the handsome prince into a bug instead of a frog, which would be a really bad result.

As Oorgak unleashed his oily power, Prince Dirk swung up his majestic sword. The dark magic reflected off Pointy Thing's polished steel and ricocheted into the cavernous warehouse.

McGoo and I dove out of the way as the magic rumbled, bounced, and careened into Betty Bibbity's product shelves. After an explosive crash, a clatter like a slow-moving avalanche went on and on as boxes of glass slippers cascaded from the high shelves down onto the floor.

"That's going to have dire inventory consequences," I said.

McGoo asked, "Where's a fairy godmother when you need one?"

Oorgak clenched his fists, gathering his power, while Prince Dirk remained unruffled. His hair was perfectly straight and coiffed, and his crown rested neatly on his head. "Do your worst, foul magic user."

"I'll get worse, I promise!" Oorgak growled.

Midnight Pete pawed the cracked asphalt, encouraging the wizard he had duped. Hiding behind the black unicorn's tail, the now-frizzy Gurmin growled.

Oorgak hurled another spell, which Dirk deflected, but this time, he turned his blade to bounce the fetid magic up into the sky, where it scattered a murder of crows who were minding their own business.

"Be careful, Dirk!" RRita cried.

"Everything for you, my love." He swung Pointy Thing, blocking another flurry of spells. The prince took advantage of the evil wizard's growing frustration. "What are you going to do, foul Oorgak? Turn me into a frog again? Ha ha!"

Losing his temper, the wizard strained so hard he seemed to be dealing with severe constipation. His lips twisted in a grimace as he spoke a potent incantation.

Dark magic boiled out, and Dirk incomprehensibly moved his sword at the last minute. I realized what he was doing. He had provoked this attack! Now the transformative spell engulfed him, made his form twist and squirm and reshape.

His black hose melted and retracted into dark spots. His shoulders hunched, his face grew round, and Dirk shrank down until he became a large frog, the same size as the female frog demon. The princely crown now hung around his neck, much too big for his amphibious head. Hunched on his meaty and slimy legs, Dirk belled out his balloon-like throat and made a sound like a burp.

With a squeal of delight, RRita bounded forward. "My prince! My beautiful prince!" She swept him into her squishy arms. "You're back, and you're mine!"

Dirk let out a confused "Ribbit," still trying to find his voice.

Oorgak looked orgasmically pleased with what he had just done. If anything, he seemed even happier than RRita was. "Wow, that felt good," he said to the black unicorn. "I am back in the saddle again."

Pete seemed offended by the very idea of a saddle, but he was focused on his evil plan. "Now we have to round up those unidogs so we can get back to our main spell. You've had enough practice."

Filled with wonder, Oorgak looked down at his hands. "Why did I ever hold back?"

"It wasn't through the lack of us trying," I muttered. But I allowed myself a moment of triumph to realize that we had created another satisfied client with frog-Dirk and RRita.

She put her arm around her prince's purple-caped shoulder, urging him to move. "We've got to get away, Dirk. I won't lose you again."

Drawing my pistol, I ran to join the prince and his frog princess. "We'll get you to safety. That's part of my job as a zombie P.I."

Up in the sky, another majestic fairy-tale creature swooped down toward us in a flash of pinkish feathers—a lavender equine form with pale wings that might have come from an albino eagle. Sunlight flashed on the decorative gold crown wrapped across her forehead.

I waved frantically. "Dava, down here! Dava, we need your help!"

Alvina stared into the sky. "Ooh, pretty!"

The diva Pegasus flapped her wings and landed right in

front of me, RRita, and Dirk. She seemed full of herself, but no different than usual. "Who's making a mess in our warehouse?"

All the barking unidogs ran around in circles, agitated by the arrival of the winged horse.

I quickly explained the situation to Dava. "All those horn dogs were being held in the back of the warehouse, but they've been freed now." I glanced back at the still-fuming evil wizard who reveled in falling back into his addictive cycle. "Right now I have to get my clients to safety." I nudged RRita and Dirk forward. "Can you take them away from here?" This rescue would make great material for Dava and Betty's next HCN spot.

"I will do no such thing," Dava said. "You reached exactly the wrong conclusion. Some zombie detective!"

"Please!" RRita jumped closer to the lavender Pegasus. Dirk, though, was overly enthusiastic when he sprang on his new frog legs. He collided with Dava's head and neck, jostling her ornamental crown. With his squishy finger pads, he tried to grab the mane and succeeded in knocking the gold ornament loose.

Suddenly, I saw that the decorative crown was more than just bling and had been designed to cover up a deformity. In the center of Dava's forehead sprouted a stubby little nub of a horn, an insubstantial and impotent-looking spike no bigger than my thumbnail.

"Wait, you're not a Pegasus," I said.

Alvina gasped beside me. "That's an alicorn! I read all kinds of conspiracy websites about alicorns. They're flying unicorns, and they're normally evil."

Dava flared her wings and made a rude snort. "I am not *normally* evil, child. I am *exceptionally* evil!"

McGoo joined us. "Hey, you don't need to feel

embarrassed about physical inadequacies. It happens to all of us."

"I am not self-conscious about it. I'm proud of who I am," Dava said.

I looked at all her glitzy fabulousness. "But overcompensating …"

"I want to live in a restored, magical, medieval fairy-tale world—with my darling black unicorn!" She shoved the two frogs out of her way as she pushed closer to the warehouse door. "Stinky Pete and I are the perfect couple."

"Don't call me that," the black unicorn grumbled.

"It's a term of endearment, honey."

Pete and the newly revealed alicorn had the upper hand now, or upper hoof, and Oorgak was fully charged and ready to unleash more dark sorcery. Dava pranced about with her chiming glass horse slippers. "I summon my army of defenders to ensure that nothing else interferes!" She let out a shrill whistle, proving that alicorns were even better whistlers than unicorns.

A buzzing sound came from the warehouse, and the swarm of unionized fairies rushed out like angry hornets. They had all been bound together by a loyalty spell, brainwashed and ensnared by some magic that Dava had worked on them.

The angry pixie mob had been annoying before, but after the wizard's blast had smashed shelves of glass slippers, the fairies were now armed with pointed, razor-sharp crystal shards as weapons.

They came directly at us.

CHAPTER 39

The fairies thrummed forward, and the tiny onslaught took even Oorgak by surprise. They loomed just above us, hovering in the air with their crystal daggers.

Midnight Pete rubbed his long bronze horn lovingly against Dava's mane. "I think everything about you is beautiful."

"Don't be a pest. Let me get my crown back on." The alicorn pushed her nose against the asphalt and flipped up the golden headband decoration. She snorted a command, and three fairies broke ranks, darting forward to wrap the fake crown around Dava's forehead. She said, "I'm not vain, I'm just particular about my appearance." Then they fluttered back to regard their mistress, giving a satisfied nod. She turned to Pete. "Now, I'm ready for my closeup."

The black unicorn raised his voice. "Oorgak, are you prepared to make the world a more medieval place?"

The evil wizard's eyes shone with frenetic hunger. "Sure, I'll have another round." With jittering hands, he picked up the waterlogged spellbook on the ground.

Dava flared her wings, regally showing off her gaudy crown. "Then let's get this show on the road. The Middle Ages won't wait all day."

The wickedly armed fairies buzzed around like Tinkerbell stormtroopers, using their broken-glass daggers to herd me,

McGoo, and Alvina together. Sheyenne stayed with us, even though they couldn't harm a ghost.

McGoo and I had our guns, and with so many fairies it would be like a shooting gallery, but the nasty pixies would swarm on us in retaliation. Those glass shards could damage my undead skin and do even worse to McGoo. Most important, we would never let anyone harm our little vampire girl.

We had to bide our time, for now.

Oorgak flipped through his spellbook, trying to find the right page. Flustered, he turned to the index and ran his finger down the tiny, waterlogged writing. "I know it's here somewhere."

Dava flared her wings and snapped at the obedient fairies. "What's taking so long? Round up the unidogs so we can drain their magic!"

Winged pixies chased the loose critters, dive-bombing and jabbing with their glass knives to show they meant business. Urmin stuck close to Alvina, who made rude faces at the fairies. All the corralled horn dogs began yapping and barking, spreading shattered rainbows in the air, but it wasn't enough to mellow the out-of-control evil wizard.

"Found it!" Oorgak held up the spellbook. "Now to wring the magic out of these puppies and make the UQ medieval again!"

I could stop this by shooting Oorgak, but the dark wizard probably had protective spells. Or I could shoot the alicorn or the black unicorn, but even if it was self-defense, I might still be charged with mythicide. "You got a magical plan, McGoo?" I asked.

"Don't look at me, Shamble. I can't even do a card trick."

Then soap bubbles wafted out of the open delivery doors, ethereal spheres that bounced magically about. Soon, larger bubbles boiled out into the parking lot battleground like a magical fanfare.

Drifting along in her lavender skirts and waving her magic wand, Betty Bibbity emerged from the warehouse, and she looked upset. "So many broken glass slippers in there! What happened?" She spotted the crystal-armed fairies in the air and pointed her magic wand at them. "I don't care about union rules. That ruined inventory is going to come out of your wages."

It was the fairy godmother, right when we needed one.

When Betty saw the evil wizard, her expression soured even further. "You again? I thought you'd stopped causing trouble." She looked behind her. "Grbth, maybe you can talk some sense into him?"

The ogre guru emerged from the warehouse in his tie-dyed robes. "I wondered why Walter hasn't come to Wham-Bam services. He needs his maintenance meditation."

Sheyenne glowed beside me. "Miss Bibbity, you can use good magic to save us all."

"Unless she's part of the plot," I whispered. Zombies tend to be cautious.

"I have very little to do with the plot, Mr. Shamble," the fairy godmother said. "I came here to prepare for tomorrow night's big event. It's the first of our monthly magic balls."

McGoo snickered. "She said *magic balls.*"

Two large soap bubbles popped when they bumped against his patrolman's cap.

The fairies buzzed about, uncertain. Their wings sounded like miniature chainsaws.

Dava shouted, "Attack them! Don't let them interfere!"

Betty Bibbity frowned at the tiny pixies. "Oh, posh!" She waved her magic wand at the largest cluster of fairies, and the decorative soap bubbles floated forward with a will of their own. Each bubble engulfed a fairy, trapping them in a spherical prison. The tiny creatures jabbed with their crystal knives, but they couldn't break the membrane.

Betty huffed in disappointment. "Remember your roots! You are loyal to me." She waved the magic wand again, and the soap bubbles popped. The chastised fairies circled around, stunned and docile again, then they came back to hover over the sweet, grandmotherly woman.

The vain alicorn was outraged. "They were mine! Mine!"

"You don't have any hold over these dear creatures, Dava," Betty said in her sweet voice. "I am their godmother, you know."

Now that the fairies had shifted their allegiance, the clustered horn dogs barked with more energy, adding to my rainbow-tinted vision. Urmin faced off against Pete's frizzy black unidog, snarling. The poofy, evil Gurmin snarled back, and they began fighting, clacking their stubby little horns together in a vicious duel.

Dava and Midnight Pete stood together, ready to fight. The black unicorn shouted at the evil wizard. "Now, Oorgak! This is your last chance!"

But the ogre guru stomped forward, resting his big club on his tie-dyed shoulder. "Walter, addiction is not easy to break. You have been strong, and you listened to my counseling. Together we can return you to the path of enlightenment."

Together, the horn dogs wagged their tails and unleashed their sparkly, warm, and fuzzy magic into the air. Even Walter-Oorgak couldn't resist.

"That's cool," McGoo said.

"I'm sorry," Walter moaned and hung his head. "I'm sorry ..." He closed the waterlogged spellbook, and Grbth gently took it out of his hands.

"It's all right. Forgiveness and karma go together. We'll get you into some intensive Zen meditating with extra *Oms*."

"It'll never be enough." The wizard began to sob. "I didn't mean to be evil again. I couldn't help it." He turned to glare at Dava and Midnight Pete. "They tempted me. They dragged me into it!"

The ogre looked stern. "We must not blame others for our weaknesses. Now come with me. I was here to set up for our ashram anniversary reception as part of the magic ball, but that can wait. You are much more important, my apprentice."

A sniffling Walter let the huge ogre engulf him in a massive, colorful sleeve. The wizard mustered his courage. "I'm going to dump that spellbook back into the drainage canal where it belongs."

"Could we just burn it this time?" I suggested.

McGoo withdrew a set of silver cuffs from his belt and looked at the two devious horned masterminds. "I'll call for backup, but in the meantime I'd better put one of these two in hoof cuffs."

Betty Bibbity waved a scolding finger at Dava. "You have broken the law, but far worse than that—you *disappointed me*. Tsk-tsk! I'll cancel your contract with the Home Capitalism Network. You are no longer my business partner."

The alicorn flared her wings. "Then I'll have my own show. My fans will follow me."

"Does HCN broadcast from jail?" I asked.

"We'll destroy you all, even without an evil wizard," Midnight Pete declared. "Unicorns have great power of their own."

Gurmin growled, but it wasn't much of a threat. Urmin pushed him back.

Then the unidogs barked out a rainbow symphony with a clamor as soothing as it was raucous. Peaceful colors brightened in the air, and I realized it wasn't just from the horn dogs. The magic increased all around us.

A herd of majestic horned figures cantered in from the fringes of the Quarter, crossing the warehouse parking lot with pride and confidence: a dappled unicorn, a dirty white unicorn, and two ash-gray beasts—Melissa, Pirouette, Clyde, and Dale. Behind them came even more unicorns, enough to fill an expanded volume of fairy tales. I realized these must be members from other branches of the Secret Society of Horn Brothers and Sisters.

Urmin barked a welcome, and the other horn dogs joined in the chorus, while black Gurmin whimpered and backed away, crouching next to Midnight Pete.

Clyde and Dale, who had been so nervous when I'd met them in the dark alley, now drew confidence. Their horns had strength in numbers. "We know what you were trying to do, Stinky Pete," Clyde said.

"Don't call me that!"

"How about Murderer Pete?" Dale said.

Melissa clomped closer. "We know what you did to Arthur."

While the alicorn was distracted, McGoo clipped his cuffs around her forelegs. Dava reared up in alarm. "That's the wrong color on me! Don't scratch the glass horseshoes."

Betty Bibbity waved her magic wand, and the hoof-shaped crystal slippers shattered. "You are no longer my spokescreature. It goes against my new brand identity."

In dismay, Dava tried to raise her forelegs, but she was hobbled by the cuffs.

The numerous unicorns closed in around Midnight Pete. "He has to pay for what he did to Arthur," Pirouette said.

An old gray unicorn came forward, even more wise and majestic than all the others. He sported a stylish gray goatee on his chin, exuding gravitas in waves. This must be what Sean Connery would have looked like as a unicorn. "Arthur didn't have a chance, and now you don't either."

Now Midnight Pete showed fear. "No, Norman! Not you!"

"I am the president of the Secret Society of Horn Brothers and Sisters," the old unicorn said, "and we are the combined council—unicorns united. We have come to our judgment."

"We want our unidogs back," said Clyde. "And their magic."

The furry critters barked and ran around in circles, bursting with excitement.

The rainbows swelled, growing more and more colorful in the air as all the powerful, incensed unicorns imposed their punishment. The unidogs added their familiar magic, too. Norman raised his horn like a lightning rod to the sky, but the black thunderclouds had dissipated after Grbth led the evil wizard away.

Midnight Pete cringed and closed his eyes, as if he were being blinded. He thrashed and thrust his long bronze horn, but could find no targets. "No! No!"

We watched in horror as his fierce, dominating horn softened, drooped, and finally flopped down limp, like a wilted carrot. The Horn Brothers and Sisters had imposed their terrible punishment.

Chapter 40

McGoo called the paddy wagon for our two large equine prisoners, but the UQPD sent a double horse wagon instead. The black unicorn looked broken, impotent, and dejected as he was booked under the name Stinky Pete.

Though distraught, Dava remained haughty. "I demand a private cell. I need my personal space. You can't make me share lockup with any other lesser alicorns."

"Won't be a problem, ma'am," McGoo assured her as three uniformed police officers herded the mythical suspects aboard the horse trailer.

Meanwhile, the loose horn dogs chased each other's tails, sniffed each other's butts, then bounded about in a rainbow-filled re-unicornification with their stately owners.

Now that they were back with their furry little familiars, Melissa, Pirouette, Clyde, and Dale were swelled with self-confidence and inner horn power. Alvina knelt on the cracked asphalt to pet Urmin, comforting him because his own owner, brave Arthur, had been murdered.

Robin arrived to help us tie up the multiple cases, first meeting with the two traumatized frogs. RRita and Dirk were shuddering with a complicated mix of exhaustion, terror, and joy. The frog prince and his frog maiden wrapped each other in a slimy embrace, locking their amphibious lips in repeated kisses. As their passion increased, they were ready to hop off to some moist, secluded place where they could fertilize another clutch of eggs.

But Robin brought them back to reality. "This isn't over yet, but I will find a satisfactory resolution to bring your tadpoles back." She regarded me with that professional gleam in her eye. "Dan and Sheyenne have already made preliminary overtures to Gil and Finn."

"You're the best, Miss Deyer," RRita said.

Prince Dirk added, "Ribbit."

The fairies buzzed around, looking guilt-ridden. McGoo swatted one away from his face. "And what are we going to do with these things? They threatened a police officer."

"And a zombie detective," I said. "And a little vampire girl." I didn't think Sheyenne, being a poltergeist, had felt threatened.

The fairies flitted in front of us. One buzzed, "We'll never do it again, honest!"

Another managed to whine, "Pleeeeease!" in the same pitch as her whirring dragonfly wings.

Betty Bibbity floated over. "They were just minions, Officer. Fairies don't have large enough brains to be truly evil."

The swarm of little pixies hummed in agreement.

"Let me discipline them. I'll give them the real fairy godmother treatment."

McGoo considered. "They'd probably only get community service anyway. They're all yours, ma'am."

With a heavy sigh, Betty turned toward the open warehouse, dismayed by the tumbled boxes and event-planning supplies strewn about as if a Class 4 indoor hurricane had struck. "So many broken glass slippers," she moaned. "My business is a wreck, and my partner betrayed me. Now how am I going to deliver those crystal footwear orders? We had a big push on HCN this week."

Alvina patted Urmin's head and rubbed his little horn. Cheerful rainbows glimmered out, bringing the smile back to the fairy godmother's face. She brightened as an idea struck her, then she waved her star-tipped wand to marshal the entire fairy workforce.

"Hi-ho! It's off to work you go—every one of you! Clean up that mess, clear all the debris, and make my warehouse spic-and-span! Then inventory the merchandise so we know exactly how much product remains to fill the standing orders."

With military precision, she jabbed the air with her magic wand, dividing the fairies into groups. "You, you're Squadron B. Organize and categorize all the event-planning supplies. I've needed to do that for years."

The fairies darted off to do their work, humming a happy tune.

Next, Robin gathered contact information from the unicorns, on the possibility that they might want to file a class-action suit. Sheyenne drifted over to help her, glad that the Horn Brothers and Sisters were no longer being so secretive. Before long, the herd of unicorns dispersed with their precious horn dogs, leaving us with Urmin.

The ogre guru shuffled up to us, accompanied by the formerly formerly formerly evil wizard. "Betty, if you need to postpone the date for our ashram anniversary reception, I will understand." Grbth nodded his enormous head. "As an enlightened ogre, I try not to be a difficult customer."

"Thank you for understanding," said the grandmotherly godmother. As her fairy army zoomed about doing their chores, Betty's shoulders slumped with the weight of all that had happened. "There's going to be quite a scandal. My audience on HCN tends to be fickle customers, and many of them are actual trolls. I just know they'll start ugly rumors and crazy conspiracy theories about me and Dava."

"I know all about conspiracy theories," Alvina said. "I can show you some of the best ones."

"Sounds like you need a new partner as a distraction," I said to Betty.

Beside me, Sheyenne brightened. "Yes, give it a positive spin. Once the news breaks about Dava's evil schemes, it'll be clear that you're the victim in this scenario."

Walter scratched his unruly, dark beard. "Dava and Pete duped me, too. Tempted me. Tried to make me break my resolve!"

"Now, Walter," Grbth warned, "what did I tell you about blaming others for your failings?"

"Sorry," the no-longer-evil wizard said.

The ogre turned to us. "It's part of our therapy philosophy, a signpost on the road to good karma." He heaved an enormous sigh with his enormous lungs. "But Walter isn't wrong. We had made so much progress, and I'm convinced he never would have slid back into addiction without the meddling of that Pegasus."

"She was an alicorn," I corrected.

Betty Bibbity looked at the wrung-out Walter and pursed her lips, considering. "I do need a new business partner. A fairy godmother and a good wizard might make an interesting magical team. The shopping network would like that."

Walter raised his head with a glimmer of hope. "I could use a job. My business has gone to hell ever since I had my unicorn epiphany. There's not much call for a *kindly* wizard in the Quarter."

"You could carve out a whole new market segment," I said.

"A good wizard is better than an evil fairy godmother," McGoo said.

Betty scolded him with a snap of her magic wand. "Posh!"

"I might have to call myself Oorgak again, though—name recognition," Walter said. "And I've already got the logo registered."

Grbth placed a hand the size of a spare tire on Walter's shoulder. "Let's not get ahead of ourselves. You have much atonement to do before you find and restore your inner self. The Wham-Bam Ashram has special recovery workshop packages for wayward padawans. Start with our workbook and lesson plan, which you can do at home, but you must come to weekly group sessions."

"I will," Walter promised.

The ogre and the recovering wizard walked away from the fairy godmother's warehouse. After Robin finished up with Dirk and RRita, the two frogs hopped up to thank me and McGoo, though we weren't eager to shake their slimy hands.

"I'm optimistic for once," RRita said. It was the first time I had actually heard her happy voice. "Dirk and I are going to insist that my parents accept us. We have to reconcile, because family is stronger than anything."

"Ribbit," said Dirk.

Robin said, "Good. We need to present a united front for our next meeting with the lagoon creatures. I'll set up a conference, so we can resolve this once and for all."

CHAPTER 41

he next time I went to the secret unicorn clubhouse, I didn't need to wear a bag over my head. Clyde and Dale had sent me an actual address, and I used Google Maps for walking directions. Alvina desperately wanted to go along, but I had to say no, because HornPub was a site for adults only.

Even with my GPS, it was still a long and convoluted route to get to the hidden meeting place. I was surprised I'd managed to get there while blindfolded. I went through back alleys and dead ends, into service access doors, and down maintenance tunnels. Finally, I arrived at a dark, wooden door with a red light burning above the lintel, like an illicit speakeasy. There was no sign, no words—only one of those squeeze-bulb bicycle horns was mounted like a doorbell on the wall.

"Ah, a *horn*," I said aloud. "Subtle."

I honked the horn, then saw a shadow cover the peephole. The door opened to a pub full of unicorns along with their horn dogs, who barked a cheerful welcome. The mythical creatures stood around the tables with tin pails full of beer. They all wore funny, spotted lodge caps above their horns. Now it felt like a genuine secret society.

Seeing me, they let out a cheer. "It's Dan Shamble! Hip hip hooray!" The leader was the kingly graybeard unicorn,

Norman, who had handed down Stinky Pete's dysfunctional sentence.

"Come join us," said Pirouette, with a flirtatious whinny. "Handsome guy."

I did not need my arm twisted. "I'll stay for a pint of bitter."

"Tonight we're only serving pints of *cheery*," said Dale, and all the unicorns whickered with laughter.

I went behind the bar and found a pint glass set aside for their non-four-legged guests and pulled on one of the taps. I noticed a deck of cards on the bar, and wondered how unicorns could shuffle with their hooves.

"A toast to Dan Shamble!" Melissa called out. The unicorns dunked their noses into the foamy pails. Not wanting to be left out, I raised my pint, and we all drank to the existence of unicorns.

Norman pounded his hoof on the tabletop for attention. He spoke in a heavy, sage voice as he made a formal announcement. "Tonight, we honor this zombie detective for his service to the Horn Brothers and Sisters. Many of us were uneasy that Arthur had contracted an outside detective service, thereby exposing himself to public notice. But he was proved right in the end. This man—"

"He's a zombie," said Clyde.

"This *zombie* did indeed locate our lost unidogs, restoring our familiar magic."

The furry animals set up a resounding chorus of yips.

"He also solved Arthur's murder," said Dale.

The unicorns stomped their hooves in appreciation, then slurped more from their pails of beer.

Pointing his horn at me, Norman continued, "In recognition of your service to the secret society of unicorns, we hereby name you an honorary Horn Brother."

I was astounded by this, but very proud.

"It comes with a keychain," said Pirouette.

"You are one of us," Norman said.

"One of us!" All the unicorns cheered. "One of us!" The horn dogs yipped and yapped even more rainbows.

"Glad to be part of the club," I said, even if I did have a bullet hole instead of a horn in the middle of my forehead. "If I'm a member in good standing of the club, then I'd like to make a special request."

On Alvina's much-anticipated show-and-tell day at the Nosferatu Academy, Sheyenne, McGoo, and I came as the vampire girl's found family. We even brought Urmin with us, since the school had no written policy against mythical pets. McGoo cradled the horn dog in his arms, just like when he had first apprehended the lost critter running loose in the streets.

In the hour just before lunch recess, we walked down the hall to Miss Nifflesmoth's classroom. The spelling demon stood at the front of the class, holding a ruler, and it was clear she was not afraid to use it (and certainly not for measuring purposes).

Alvina spotted us from her desk in the front row. "Both of my half-daddies!"

She jumped up from her seat, but Miss Nifflesmoth whacked the ruler on her desk. "Sit down, young lady. I will have order in this classroom."

In McGoo's arms, Urmin wagged and wiggled his entire body.

"Excuse me, we're here for show-and-tell," I said.

"Not yet." Miss Nifflesmoth turned her ugly face toward

the clock on the wall and watched the second hand sweep toward the twelve. Finally, she let out a defeated breath. "Very well. It is show-and-tell time."

As we stepped in front of the classroom, I looked out at the rows of desks holding well-dressed and well-behaved young vampires, werewolves, ghosts, trolls, and orcs—the Academy's gifted and talented class, and I knew Alvina fit right in.

The unnatural students said in well-rehearsed unison, "Welcome."

"Alvina, you may make your presentation," the teacher said with an implied "or else" at the end of her sentence.

Alvina popped to her feet and hurried to the front of the class. She stood prim and pretty in her pink sweater and plaid, pleated skirt, grinning to show her tiny, pointed fangs. "Today I have something very special for show-and-tell." She took Urmin from McGoo and cuddled the animal in her arms. "This is a unidog, also known as a canicorn. His name is Urmin."

The horn dog yipped rainbows and wagged his tail. Alvina's classmates let out appreciative sounds.

She continued, "Unidogs are the familiars of unicorns, and they are the source of special magic, even more so than a unicorn's horn is. I wrote about it in my school report." She shot a glance at the dour spelling-demon teacher.

Miss Nifflesmoth rapped her ruler on the desk again. "I'll have no flights of fancy in my class! Unicorns do not exist."

I kept my grin inside. It was exactly what we had expected her to say.

"Our next visitor will be able to shed some light on that," I said, and nodded to Sheyenne, who drifted to the classroom door. She swung it open, and we heard clopping hooves out in the hall. A breathtakingly majestic gray unicorn strode in, holding his pearlescent horn high. His silvery goatee had been brushed to a fine luster.

"This is Norman," Alvina said, "the president of the secret society of unicorns."

The unnatural students gasped and cheered. Miss Nifflesmoth looked as if she had just swallowed a frog whole and it had turned into a prince inside her throat.

Norman entered the classroom, so regal and majestic that I understood how such a sight could have created a do-gooder epiphany in any evil wizard. "As president of the society, I represent unicorns throughout the Quarter, and I am very happy to speak to Alvina's class today."

"But …" Miss Nifflesmoth spluttered, "but unicorns don't exist." Apparently, neither did open-minded teachers.

Norman let out a horsey chuckle. "Until recently, we kept a low profile due to some extremist conservative members of our Horn Brotherhood and Sisterhood. But now there's a new administration, and things will change."

Urmin squirmed in Alvina's arms and jumped down to the floor. He seemed so happy to be prancing in front of the old gray unicorn. Alvina's classmates jumped up from their desks and ran to the front of the classroom to pet the unicorn and the little horn dog. Norman even let them touch his horn.

Even though Miss Nifflesmoth whacked her ruler several more times, the kids remained unruly.

"Way to go, Al," McGoo said, giving the vampire girl a hug. Alvina looked completely vindicated.

Sheyenne addressed the spelling-demon teacher directly. "You're going to adjust Alvina's grade now, aren't you, ma'am?" It didn't sound like a question.

Miss Nifflesmoth wrestled with her own confusion. "Her report relied too much on unverified dark websites, and she didn't cite all her sources."

"But it was still a damn good paper," I said. The teacher knew we had the upper hand.

Miss Nifflesmoth was saved by the bell that announced lunchtime and recess. Since the kids considered recess even more interesting than a unicorn and a unidog, they ran out of the room, but Alvina stayed with us. The teacher shooed us out of the classroom, claiming that she had lots of red marks to make during the lunch break.

As the kids flooded the halls and ran to their lockers, we strolled toward the office to turn in our visitor badges. Urmin trotted along, darting in and out among Norman's hooves, knowing exactly when to dodge.

The Bigfoot custodian was mopping the floor, but the Nosferatu Academy students ran around him without even noticing he was there.

Though the show-and-tell had gone exactly as I had hoped, the old gray unicorn seemed sad. Norman bent down and touched his long white horn against Urmin's stubby one. Suddenly, I realized what I was missing. I had been too distracted to see the obvious question.

"Where's your own horn dog, Norman? I just assumed it was one of those that Dava and Pete had dognapped."

"No." Norman lowered his head. "I had my own unidog named Spot, and he was very special to me. My best friend. But I outlived him."

Urmin nuzzled the gray unicorn's legs.

Alvina sounded sad, too. "And now this unidog doesn't have his Arthur."

"Urmin isn't really ours to keep, honey," Sheyenne said.

I added, "We didn't want to just dump him at the UQ Animal Shelter again. Last time, he was adopted as an emotional-support animal to a dragon."

McGoo stood beside us. "Urmin needs a good home, with someone who knows how to take care of him."

Norman suddenly seemed filled with hope.

Alvina bent down and petted the critter, then she screwed up her courage, and I could tell how much effort it took for her to speak. I was proud of the kid. "A unidog belongs with a special unicorn. I think *you* should have him, Norman."

"Really?" the old unicorn said. I swear, rainbows of delight came right out of his mouth.

We reached the front office, and McGoo ducked in to return our badges to the old werewolf at the front desk. Alvina threw her arms around the fuzzy little pet. "I'll miss you so much, Urmin, but you belong with Norman. That's what Arthur would have wanted."

Urmin licked her cheek.

"You can come visit any time, little girl," the mythical creature said. "I won't be hard to find anymore."

The kingly gray unicorn strolled out of Nosferatu Academy with the eager horn dog trotting along behind him, best friends already. Without a doubt, Norman looked a decade younger.

CHAPTER 42

Though the upcoming negotiations would be grueling, I clung to one bright spot—the frog demon family breach had been healed. Bubo and Lubo accompanied RRita and her frog prince to show their support. The amphibious pool specialists loved their only daughter, and it must have been weighing on them that a feud would keep them from seeing their grandtadpoles.

Lubo had pinned a fresh water-lily corsage to her yellow spring dress, and Bubo wore his best frock coat. "We're still family," he croaked, "and at least Prince Dirk looks more acceptable now."

Dirk, in his frog form, clutched RRita's squishy hand and said, "Ribbit."

"I love you, too," RRita said.

Lubo blinked her large yellow eyes. She had added green eyeshadow for emphasis. "We're going to rename the company Bubo and Lubo and Son-in-Law's Pool Service, aren't we, dear?"

Bubo grumbled as if he, too, had swallowed a frog, but he managed to sound positive. "He still has to learn the business and all the complicated details of water treatment, filtration, pH levels, chlorine systems."

"My Dirk is smart," RRita said, "and we're in this together, forever. Maybe we should call the company Bubo and Lubo and Daughter and Son-in-Law's Pool Service."

"Too long a name," Bubo grumbled.

"There's always the acronym," I said.

"B-L-D-S-L-P-S. Who can pronounce that?" the big frog demon said.

Robin emerged from her office, ready for the negotiations. "Good news on the paperwork front. Now that you're back in your frog form, Prince Dirk, there's no need to refile the bank's change of account forms with your new bodily identity. You'll have access to your royal kingdom treasury."

The frog prince let out a croak of delight, and RRita said, "Then we can live in a castle—or maybe down in the moat."

"Access to the royal treasury?" Bubo raised his warty brows. "I insist that RRita and Dirk get married right away and have joint accounts."

RRita was so thrilled by her father's new attitude that her body slime practically sparkled. "Oh, Daddy, you mean it? You support our marriage?"

Lubo was also pleased. "That'll make our grandtadpoles legitimate."

Prince Dirk let out another ribbit, but this one sounded frustrated.

"Yes, if we ever get them back," RRita said.

Robin ushered us into the conference room. "That's what today's arbitration is for. I am confident we can reach some resolution."

Gil and Finn arrived two minutes late, probably because they didn't want any uncomfortable chitchat with their adversaries. Gil's pointed fins were extended, and Finn's gill slits were wide open. I could see they were incensed and ready to be intractable. Maybe the mutant tadpoles had been particularly troublesome that morning.

The two parties glowered at each other across the long

conference table. Sheyenne entered with a large pitcher of water to refresh all of the aquatic creatures.

Robin took her seat at the head of the table as if she were leading a congressional proceeding. "It is my sincere hope that today we can find an amicable solution to this difficult situation, since all parties here are reasonable adults."

I looked up and down the table, but none of those present looked reasonable to me. "Think of the children," I said.

Gil flexed his webbed, clawed hand. "I can't stop thinking of those monster tadpoles! They're little homewreckers."

"They're our darlings," RRita wailed.

"No telling how many customers those tadpoles would have hurt," Finn said, "if we had any customers come to Bilge Bay."

"We'll take the tadpoles back," RRita said. "We'll get them out of your hair or out of your scales. They'll never cause you any trouble. Please, they're our babies."

Dirk pressed his squishy fingers on the table and said, "Ribbit."

"But who's going to pay for the damages?" Gil demanded. "All we wanted was a nice aquatic park for all ages and species, but now Bilge Bay will never recover."

Robin straightened papers in front of her. "Prince Dirk does have access to his royal treasury now, and we can work out some fair restitution. Let's discuss what it'll take to restore your resort to its pre-tadpole condition, and this young couple can get down to their parenting duties."

Finn placed his forehead in his webbed hands. "What's the use? After all the magical contamination, everyone stays away from Bilge Bay. We're going bankrupt!"

I raised a gray hand. "A powerful wizard owes me a favor. He's the one who dumped the spellbook into the drainage canal. Maybe he could work a spell and clean up the place."

Bubo spoke up in a voice that sounded like a long, gassy burp. "I might sweeten the deal, in order to get the tadpole babies back. Lubo and I are important people in the Quarter. We have a great deal of influence with frog demons in general."

Lubo interrupted, "They all have special home pool needs."

RRita looked hopefully at her father, and the bullfrog continued, "What if we spread the word? Instead of boycotting Bilge Bay, we could encourage every frog demon to take advantage of the fun new water park."

Lubo added, "Give it our squish of approval. That would bring in a bunch of customers—but only if the tadpoles are returned, safe and sound."

The lagoon creatures looked at each other, uncertain. Gil said, "Frog demons were our targeted clientele...."

Robin seized the opportunity. "I believe we have a deal in front of us. Without admitting guilt, RRita and Dirk will pay for actual material damages and arrange to have a magical cleanup of the aquatic park. Bubo and Lubo shall use their influence to endorse Bilge Bay and attract frog-demon clientele. In exchange, Gil and Finn will return custody of the tadpoles to their rightful parents."

Everyone sat in silence for a long, disbelieving moment. We didn't even need unicorns or horn dogs to see sparkles and rainbows in the air.

We met at the humid, mosquito-infested swamp park. Walter-Oorgak, who had decided to hyphenate his name to embrace the yin-yang/Zen duality of his existence, joined us, eager to perform his service. With freshly combed hair and beard and wearing clean robes, he looked as dapper and professional as a rabbi ready to perform a vampire's bat mitzvah ceremony.

The shadowed hollows around his eyes and his pallid skin, though, showed that he still walked the razor's edge. Grbth had been guiding him through intensive meditation and anti-evil-addiction therapy.

We gathered along the lazy river next to the spawning pond—RRita and Dirk, Bubo and Lubo, Sheyenne, Robin, and Alvina. When monstrous torpedo-shaped creatures burst through the duckweed scum and snarled, RRita whimpered and ducked back.

Dirk clutched her hand. "Our babies," he said. I was glad to see that he had finally regained some of his ability to speak.

"Tadpole delinquents," Gil muttered.

Finn turned to the formerly evil wizard. "Can you do anything about them? It was your cursed spellbook that caused the contamination."

"I'm so very sorry," Walter-Oorgak said. "I didn't know the bad magic would leak. I'm very keen to undo the damage I caused."

He muttered the Serenity Prayer for courage and acceptance before getting down to the anti-evil spell. This time, Walter-Oorgak was so centered in his karma that he didn't need a random unicorn appearance to provoke an epiphany. He spoke incantations that sounded like a Pink Floyd album played backwards, then he lit clumps of foul-smelling weeds and waved the acrid smoke around.

The rambunctious tadpoles hurled slimy water in an attempt to distract the wizard, but he completed his spell with a show of strength and defiance. He drew a breath, prolonging the suspense. "Now we shall see the good that is inside those dear little children—just as there was good inside of me."

He snapped his fingers. Magic shimmered throughout Bilge Bay, sweeping the mosquitoes out of the air as if they were unwanted unionized fairies. The monster tadpoles ducked under the water in an attempt to escape the do-gooder spell, but the magic was strong (and apparently water-soluble). The lazy river and the spawning pool bubbled, frothed … and finally settled back into a tranquil, crystal-clear appearance.

RRita and Dirk hopped to the bank and peered down into the water. Suddenly, a flurry of small frog-demon tadpoles swam around in circles, frolicking in the water. They looked as happy as a herd of unidogs.

"Our babies!" RRita said. "They're normal again!"

Bubo and Lubo joined the happy couple and bent down to meet their grandtadpoles. "They take after you, dear," Lubo said to her husband.

"I love a romantic story," Sheyenne said to me, nuzzling close.

"Exactly the way I like to close a legal case," Robin said.

Alvina was grinning from ear to ear. She had brought along her spiral notebook and turned to the page after her written unicorn notes. She rounded out the fairy tale she'd been writing.

"And the prince was turned back into a frog, and Dirk and his beloved amphibious princess lived happily ever after with their numerous tadpole children."

Chapter 43

love to rest in peace between cases, tying up loose ends and replacing the question marks with periods (or in extreme cases, exclamation points). Sheyenne particularly liked sending final bills.

Alvina had settled back into her after-school routine, watching *Escape from the Valley of the Game Show Hosts* each afternoon. Robin had also gotten hooked on the show, and she would sit in the conference room to watch, though she claimed to be reviewing notes for cases.

Our big excitement came the following Saturday, the next big weekend of the Renaissance Faire. The Secret Society of Horn Brothers and Sisters were having a coming-out parade, and we were not going to miss it.

Over-caffeinated with excitement, Alvina jabbered and pointed at countless Renaissance Faire attractions and distractions. I indulged her with vastly expensive and unhealthy treats, from deep-fried hemoglobin nuggets to pickles on a stick. At least she'd had her fill of Mystery Meat corn dogs by now.

Sheyenne, Robin, and I watched two rounds of medieval blob wrestling with the kid, then sat through an authentic historical demonstration of linen wrapping for mummies. We poked our heads through holes in a cartoon mock-up that made us look like fairy-tale lords, ladies, and princesses. (We couldn't take pictures, though, since a vampire girl wouldn't show up on photographs.)

Alice the dragon flew overhead, doing barrel rolls and coughing out entertaining gouts of fire. She received a chorus of cheers, whistles, hoots, grunts, or other species-appropriate noises. I was glad to see the dragon was doing all right, even without her emotional-support unidog.

Alvina grabbed my hand and tugged me to the wide street that had been blocked off for the parade, where we joined the crowd. Working crowd control, McGoo walked up and down the street, blowing his whistle to keep the spectators in line. Spotting Alvina, he blew an especially loud blast that made even the banshee viewers cringe.

From down the street, monster heralds sounded a loud fanfare by tooting on ridiculously long horns. Alvina waved vigorously. "Here they come!"

Emerging from the tent encampment of itinerant Renaissance Faire workers, a front line of ogres stalked forward carrying long lances. The ogres were much too massive to sit on any kind of horse, so their jousting was strictly pedestrian.

The crowd cheered for the hulking lancers, then fell into gasping anticipation as a line of majestic unicorns followed, forming the heart of the parade. Norman led the horned herd with his pearlescent horn held high. Behind the kingly gray unicorn came an entire mythical cavalry—Clyde and Dale, Melissa and Pirouette, and many more from other secret clubhouse branches.

Three of the sturdiest unicorns even had unexpected riders, tall furry Bigfeet whose legs were so long their large feet nearly touched the ground. The Sasquatches waved and tried to draw the attention of the crowd. "We demand recognition for cryptids everywhere!" one bellowed, but the crowd ignored them.

We were distracted by the delightful coterie of unidogs that ran up and down the line, barking and spewing rainbows, darting to the side of the street where they were petted by adoring unnaturals.

"Look, it's Urmin!" Alvina squealed. The brown unidog heard the vampire girl's voice and dashed over to us. She bent down to tousle his fur, scratch under his chin, and flop his ears back and forth. Urmin licked Alvina's cheek, then darted back to prance proudly alongside old Norman.

At the end of the unicorn parade came two more mythical creatures, but this pair elicited boos and catcalls. Stinky Pete plodded next to Dava the alicorn. Both had orange equine convict blankets wrapped around their girths. Heads down, they pushed a pooper-scooper barrow, cleaning up after the parading unicorns, who made a point of giving them something to do.

"That's the tail end of justice right there," I said.

Robin said it was our duty to visit Bilge Bay as customers, and the day was so hot and humid that I decided we could include a bit of splish-splashy fun. Alvina donned a cute pink swimsuit and brought along an inflatable water ring (with a cartoon unicorn, of course). Robin wore shorts and a casual blouse, and I brought along a pair of flip-flops.

McGoo joined us for the family outing, sitting in the back seat of the Pro Bono Mobile with Alvina and Sheyenne's insubstantial form. McGoo made wisecracks about the crummy suspension and the number of potholes I managed to hit; I chided him for having such a delicate butt, considering its size.

The parking lot was mostly full, and we were happy to see that the place was busy and crowded. "That's a good sign," Robin said.

With the beach bag slung over my shoulder, we waited in line to buy our tickets, and inside we saw a crowd of unnaturals in various states of undress. A family of werewolves stood at the towel cabana. Vampires in over-large sunglasses lounged in the shade, their skin slathered with SPF 5000 sunblock. Two trolls on an enormous black inner tube drifted down the lazy river.

I was most gratified to see how many spotted frog demons crowded the park. "This place is hopping," I said.

"Bubo and Lubo made good on their promise," Robin said.

"I want to dive into the ponds and see if there are any leeches left," Alvina said.

Sheyenne led her along. "We'll find a good spot for you, honey."

McGoo headed off to the non-species-specific changing area, and before long he emerged wearing baggy Hawaiian-print swim trunks. I was surprised. "You're actually going swimming, McGoo?"

"I'm not that crazy, Shamble." He gestured toward one of the palm-frond shelters where the tentacled masseuse stood waving his numerous magic finger appendages in a tempting manner. "I'm getting a massage."

At the spawning pool, which had been redesignated a family area, we found RRita and Dirk swimming with their restored tadpole children. Bubo and Lubo lounged on lawn chairs at the edge of the water. The scene warmed my heart.

"You all look very content," I said.

Prince Dirk let out a frog laugh as tadpoles leaped out of the water and jumped over his shoulders. He tried to catch them with his squishy fingers.

"This is all just magical," RRita said. "Thanks to you."

"Cannonball!" Alvina yelled. I looked up just in time to see her running full speed with the blow-up plastic unicorn life ring around her waist. She sprang into the air and landed with a big splash in the weed-covered pool. The water sprayed me and Robin, although the droplets passed right through Sheyenne.

Bubo let out a contented croak. "This is a nice place, considering, but there's room for improvement. I've made suggestions to the proprietors about upgraded pumps and recirculating systems, and I can get them a discount on high-quality effluent."

"I'm glad we could help you make connections," Robin said.

The two lagoon creatures came over, looking harried but happy. "This has been the busiest day I could ever imagine," Gil said.

"We'll have a big fish dinner tonight," Finn added. "We just needed good word of mouth."

Lubo belled out her swollen throat. "And we've got very big mouths."

A group of frog demons had taken over the picnic area. I smelled lighter fluid and saw charcoal briquettes piled under the grill grate.

The two proprietors seemed satisfied, and their slitted eyes were full of gratitude. "Bilge Bay just might make it," Gil said.

Alvina continued to splash in the pond, kicking her little feet and scooting around on her unicorn life ring. She waved at me and then splashed harder to get my attention. "Come on, Half-daddy—join me!"

When have I ever been able to deny Alvina anything?

I sat down on a bench next to Sheyenne and slipped off my shoes. Pulling the flip-flops from our beach bag, I said, "Maybe I'll dip my toes in."

If you want to read news about Dan Shamble and my other projects, please sign up for my newsletter at wordfire.com and receive a free book!

ACK-NOWLEDGMENTS

Maintaining a well-preserved zombie detective, and his entire series, is a lot of work, and I depend on a lot of people. Undead and undying gratitude goes to Marie Whittaker and Tracy Griffiths who keep track of a million moving parts and details for the Kickstarter fulfillment and the book publication and distribution. Hannah Sheldon is a sharp-eyed beta-reader and continuity expert to make sure that Dan Shamble's brains have the right consistency. The Ukrainian art and design team of Miblart gives Dan Shamble just the right look and feel. And Rebecca Moesta gives her support throughout the writing and tells me I'm always in a good mood when I'm writing Dan Shamble.

Special acknowledgments to dedicated Kickstarter backers who keep the undead guy alive and kicking: Erwin Bush, Sean Smith, Stephen Ballentine, Scott M. Sidney, Andrew Bulthaupt, and Gary Randolph Iber.

Shamble on!

ABOUT THE AUTHOR

Kevin J. Anderson has published more than 190 books, 58 of which have been national or international bestsellers. He has 24 million copies in print in 34 languages.

He has written numerous novels in the Star Wars, X-Files, and Dune universes, as well as the unique Clockwork Angels steampunk trilogy with legendary Rush drummer Neil Peart. His original works include the Saga of Seven Suns series, the Wake the Dragon and Terra Incognita fantasy trilogies, the humorous Dan Shamble, Zombie P.I. series and The Dragon Business series.

He has edited numerous anthologies, written comics and games, and the lyrics to two rock CDs as companions to his Terra Incognita trilogy.

Anderson is the director of the graduate program in Publishing at Western Colorado University, and he and his wife Rebecca Moesta are the publishers of WordFire Press.

Read all of the Dan Shamble, Zombie P.I. Adventures!